Two Harbors Public Library
Outreach Collection

DOG CRAZY

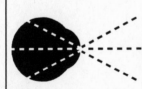

This Large Print Book carries the
Seal of Approval of N.A.V.H.

DOG CRAZY

MEG DONOHUE

THORNDIKE PRESS

A part of Gale, Cengage Learning

GALE
CENGAGE Learning®

Farmington Hills, Mich • San Francisco • New York • Waterville, Maine
Meriden, Conn • Mason, Ohio • Chicago

GALE
CENGAGE Learning®

Copyright © 2015 by Meg Donohue Preuss, trustee of Preuss Family Trust.
Thorndike Press, a part of Gale, Cengage Learning.

ALL RIGHTS RESERVED
This book is a work of fiction. The characters, incidents, and dialogue are drawn from the author's imagination and are not to be construed as real. Any resemblance to actual events, or persons, living or dead, is entirely coincidental.
Thorndike Press® Large Print Women's Fiction.
The text of this Large Print edition is unabridged.
Other aspects of the book may vary from the original edition.
Set in 16 pt. Plantin.

LIBRARY OF CONGRESS CATALOGING-IN-PUBLICATION DATA

Donohue, Meg.
  Dog crazy / by Meg Donohue. — Large print edition.
    pages cm. — (Thorndike Press large print women's fiction)
    ISBN 978-1-4104-8193-1 (hardcover) — ISBN 1-4104-8193-X (hardcover)
  1. Large type books. I. Title.
PS3604.O5656D64 2015b
813'.6—dc23   2015014955

Published in 2015 by arrangement with William Morrow, an imprint of HarperCollins Publishers

Printed in the United States of America
1 2 3 4 5 6 7 19 18 17 16 15

For my family, dogs included,
King Oberon most of all

"Because of the dog's joyfulness,
our own is increased. It is
no small gift."
— Mary Oliver, *Dog Songs*

"If you are reading this book,
there is a high probability that your
heart is broken."
— John W. James and Russell Friedman,
The Grief Recovery Handbook

CHAPTER 1

One.
  Two.
  Three.

Three deep breaths before I open the door to find that Leanne Hadley, my four o'clock, is nearly unrecognizable. Her endearing nest of hair has been tamed into a shiny bob, her mismatched sweatsuit replaced by a turtleneck and tailored slacks. She's wearing makeup, too. My heart sinks.

It's not that I'm surprised by Leanne's transformation, or by what it surely signifies. This is therapy, after all — we're working toward good-bye from the moment we say hello. But Leanne has come to see me every week since I opened my practice three months ago, and though I'm pleased by her evident progress, I'm going to miss her. Even in her grief, she has been excellent company. Her emotions are powerful; she's quick to cry but quicker to laugh, her sweet

9

disposition spiked with wry wit.

Perhaps I look forward to her visits more than I should.

Not "visits," I remind myself. Sessions.

Anyway, it's over now; that much is clear before she even steps inside. She's practically glowing, back in the current of life, bobbing away from me.

"You look well," I say, smiling. I have to push the words out around the lump that has formed in my throat. Beyond Leanne, fast-moving fog rushes through Sutro Tower, the enormous red-and-white transmission antenna that stretches high above the city. To the east, the sky is blue; to the west, it's drained of color, as appealing as dishwater. Keeping track of the San Francisco weather is a battle I can't seem to win, and I'm eager to shut the door.

We follow our usual routine, Leanne taking her spot on the tufted gray couch in my living-room-slash-office while I make her a cup of English breakfast tea. I know just how she likes it — sugary, with a drop of the cream that I started having delivered with my weekly groceries after she asked for it during our first session.

"Did you get a haircut?" I ask, making my way back to the living room. Afternoon light filters through the gauzy white curtains that

I hung when I moved in four months ago and the effect is exactly as I'd hoped: cozy and intimate, peaceful without feeling solemn.

"No, I just blow-dried it," Leanne answers pleasantly. "I forgot how much better I feel when I bother to do it. It lifts my mood."

"There's a joke here somewhere," I say. "Something about the similarities between hot air and therapy."

Leanne has a wonderful laugh, bold and bright. When she tosses back her head, I notice that the dark circles that usually fall like shadows below her blue eyes are gone, faded by sleep and erased by makeup.

"Oh, Maggie," she says. "You've been so good at helping me keep my humor through all of this."

My stomach twists.

Patients are full of flattery right before they say good-bye.

A few nights after euthanizing Sealy, her eleven-year-old Russian toy terrier, Leanne Hadley had done an Internet search using the words "dog" and "death" and "guilt" and eventually clicked her way to my pet bereavement counseling practice's brand-new website. During our first session, she showed me a photograph of Sealy. Russian

11

toy terriers, it turns out, are dainty little animals, shorthaired all over except for the long, crimped hair that trails like streamers from their upright triangle ears. Sealy appeared pert and pretty with a sharp nose and tufts of feathered strawberry-blond hair. *Debbie Gibson,* I'd thought. Identifying dogs' famous doppel-gängers is one of my particular skills. My own dog, Toby, a flat-coated retriever mix, could have been the love child of Elizabeth Taylor (black, old Hollywood waves) and Bruce Willis (thick neck, sparkle in the eye) — though, in his later years, a strong resemblance to Ian McKellan (gray beard) had emerged.

Over the course of our first session I learned that Sealy was an empty-nest consolation present from Leanne's husband, Darren, after their youngest child left for college. Whenever Leanne watched television, Sealy would leap to the top of the couch and curl around the back of her head, as tight and light as a laurel leaf crown, periodically burrowing her cool, wet nose into Leanne's hair for a good snuffle. In the car, Sealy preferred the backseat ("Driving Ms. Sealy," Leanne joked). She performed a winning tap dance complete with a crazed, openmouthed grin whenever a can was opened in the kitchen, and would sulk below the table for a solid hour if the can turned out to contain something other than dog food. She tolerated Leanne carrying her, but no one else ("She had her dignity"). Sealy's tiny toenails clacking against the hardwood floor, close on Leanne's heels, had been the peppy backbeat of Leanne's life for eleven years.

Leanne didn't leave her bedroom for two days after Sealy died. Her cheeks burned with embarrassment when she told me this. I assured her that her reaction was not uncommon; she wasn't alone.

"Love is love," I told her, as I tell all of my patients who are ashamed to find themselves shattered by the death of a dog. "Loss is loss."

She gave me a grateful smile, and I returned it.

Now I open my notebook. "How was your week?"

"Good, thanks," Leanne says. Thirty years have passed since she left South Carolina, but she still has a lovely southern accent, as soft as her round face. "Lots of yard work. I pulled the dried-up geraniums out of our patio boxes and planted some of that snazzy horsetail."

"What inspired the change?"

She takes a sip of tea, considering. "The time of year, I suppose. Spring is on the way, though you sure wouldn't know it from the weather." She looks down into her cup and a crease forms between her brows. "It's hard to believe I've been coming to see you . . . that Sealy's been gone three months. It still feels so . . ." She trails off.

"Three months is like the blink of an eye compared to thirteen" — I shake my head sharply, correcting myself — "*eleven* years of companionship."

Leanne's gaze flits to the rows of framed credentials that hang on the wall behind me — the bachelor-of-arts-in-psychology and master's-of-science-in-clinical-psychology diplomas, both from the University of Pennsylvania, the row of certifications and licenses from the National Board for Certified Counselors, the American Academy of Grief Counseling, and the Pet-Loss Grief Recovery Program. I've noticed the wall is a touchstone for my patients, a reminder of why we're now a part of one another's lives. It's my touchstone, too, though I wait until I'm alone in my apartment to look at it. On the best nights, those diplomas and certifications reassure me that despite recent developments indicating the contrary, I

14

know what I'm doing. I am a skilled professional.

Leanne shifts her gaze back to meet mine. "The other big news from the week is that I was finally able to watch *Titanic.*"

I glance down at my notes.

"Holy smokes!" she says. "I never told you the *Titanic* story?"

"I don't think so."

Leanne brightens. She's an enthusiastic storyteller, a trait she claims was encouraged by her childhood dog, Bert, a Great Dane who had tolerated her elaborate dress-up games and soliloquies with the stoic countenance of a Buckingham Palace guardsman being photographed by a drunken tourist.

"Well, the night Darren brought Sealy home," Leanne says, settling back into the couch, "we watched the movie *Titanic.* And by that I mean *I* watched the movie while Darren sawed his way through a forest's worth of logs. Our new puppy slept through the movie, too, curled up in the tiniest little ball on my lap. I remember petting her soft ears and thinking how crazy it was that I already loved her, how happy I was that there was another life in the house." She shrugs. "Well, *you* know. I missed the kids a lot."

"Yes," I say. "And who wouldn't fall in love with a sleeping puppy?"

"Exactly." She smiles. "So she slept there on my lap through the whole movie until finally the credits rolled and Celine Dion started singing her big 'My Heart Will Go On' song." She pauses. "You know the one, right?"

I begin singing dramatically, terribly, *"Neaaaar . . . Faaaar . . . Whereeeever you are —"*

Leanne laughs, begging me to stop. "I think you've got the right song," she says, "but it's hard to tell."

I grin. "What happened next?"

"Well, the moment she heard Celine's voice, Sealy, who had been sound asleep on my lap, *sprang* onto her tiny paws, pointed her nose at the ceiling, and let loose the sweetest, crooning, elfin puppy howl the world has ever heard."

"So Sealy is short for Celine?" I'd always assumed Sealy's spray of black, seallike whiskers had inspired her name.

Leanne nods. "In her whole life, for the next eleven years, I never heard her howl at anyone or anything else. Only Celine Dion."

"Do you think it was a sign of pleasure or agony?"

Leanne laughs. "Pleasure. Definitely

pleasure. I think she thought Celine Dion had the most beautiful howl she'd ever heard. It moved her."

"Did you ever play her any Whitney Houston? Mariah Carey? Maybe she had a thing for divas."

"No, no, no," Leanne says through her laughter. "It was just Celine."

I nod, allowing a pause to fill the room. "What a gift."

She gives me a questioning look.

"These memories," I say. "They'll always be with you. They're the part of Sealy that has become a part of you."

Leanne's eyes glisten. I can tell she's already thinking of another story and so I lean forward, happy there's more to tell, ready to take it in.

Pet bereavement counselors hear a lot of happy stories. This always seems to surprise people, who assume sessions are soggy, heart-wrenching undertakings. Sure, there are tears, but there are also the stories of the dogs that made people feel less alone, the dogs that taught them about love, that made their hearts feel bigger and stronger. And dog people — the majority of my patients are dog people — have wonderful senses of humor. Some of the funniest, most

17

uplifting stories I've ever heard have come from my patients. They're an eclectic bunch, but the stories they tell have the same simple truth at their core: dogs make us better.

A lot of the counseling I do is as straightforward as honoring these stories — the happy ones and the sad ones. The stories commemorate the life. We laugh; we cry; we get it all out there. Often we discover that there are issues at play beyond the loss of a pet. Emotions can be sly. Years can go by before you discover the pain that lives inside of you, a spiky old barnacle clinging to your heart.

At the close of our session, I'm determined to walk Leanne all the way up the path that leads from my apartment door to the gate at the sidewalk, but with each step a now-familiar sense of dread builds within me. My heart pounds. I hide the tremble in my hands by pressing them into the pockets of my blazer.

In my chest, panic is a small dark bird threatening to spread her wings.

When I open the gate, Leanne walks through it and turns to wrap me in a hug. She's on the sidewalk and I'm on the last stepping-stone of the path, so our hug starts out kind of loose and awkward, but then

18

she shuffles toward me and closes the gap between us.

"Thank you for everything, Maggie," she says near my ear. "Truly, thank you."

I'm afraid she can feel how fast my heart is beating. I try to focus on the palm tree across the street, but suddenly the wind picks up and the tree groans, its dark, misshapen shadows morphing into wounded animals that thrash against the pavement. I close my eyes and suppress an involuntary shudder. Or maybe I don't, because when I open my eyes I see that Leanne is pulling away, a crease denting her brow.

"Are you okay?" she asks, her hands on my shoulders.

"Of course!" My voice comes out breathless. It seems to me that the sky is darkening and I'm not sure how much longer I can stand there at the gate. I take her hands in mine and squeeze them, feeling her newly manicured fingernails press into my palms, and wish her well.

Leanne's face softens into a smile, but I can tell there's still a note of concern there, so I force myself to stay and watch as she searches in her bag for her car keys and then noses her old green Mercedes back and forth what seems like a hundred times, providing plenty of ammunition for my theory that there's an inverse correlation between driving skill and vehicle size. When she finally frees the car from its parking spot, she beeps and gives a jaunty wave. I plaster on a grin and wave both of my trembling hands in the air above my head. It's only when I catch a glimpse of Leanne's face screwing into a puzzled expression that I realize I must look like one of those people who direct planes out of airport gates. Or maybe a Bhangra dancer.

I wait until her car turns out of sight before spinning around and hurrying back down the path to my apartment.

The relief floods through me as soon as I'm inside. I make a beeline for the bathroom and scrub my hands in the sink. Leanne looked like the picture of health, but you never know the truth until it's too late. The water is so hot that my skin turns pink. I persevere, humming the "Happy Birthday" song twice under my breath — a handy little tip I picked up during a recent study of the Centers for Disease Control's website. When I read the CDC's advice, I immediately wondered if my mother knew it. I managed to stop myself from calling her in Philadelphia and asking, but I can't stop myself from thinking of her every time I put my hands below that scalding water and watch my skin change color.

I shut off the water and listen as my shallow, uneven breathing slowly quiets.

Ninety-eight, I think.

I look at my reflection in the mirror above the sink. I'm paler now than I was when I moved here, but my eyebrows are unchanged: amber-colored, well defined, expressive. My best friend, Lourdes, tells me I have trustworthy brows. She calls them my moneymakers. Who knows? She might be right. Even the most reticent patient eventually reveals her secrets to me . . . black pieces of coal held so tight they've turned into sharp, gleaming diamonds.

"Ninety-eight," I say aloud. It's an interesting number, the silky shimmy of ninety, the slammed door of eight. I say the number again. Tomorrow a new one will take its place and it seems important I keep track. "Ninety-eight."

It's been ninety-eight days since I set foot beyond that gate at the sidewalk.

CHAPTER 2

I blame Google.

I'm kidding, of course. I'm a therapist; I know I can't pin this on the Internet. But it *is* true that the logistical difficulties of not being able to leave your home practically disappear when you fall into the welcoming embrace of the World Wide Web. Groceries, books, vitamins and supplements, even alcohol . . . they can all be delivered. The Internet enables me with the faux-casual finesse of a beady-eyed drug dealer. *No need to leave,* Amazon purrs when I run low on antibacterial hand soap. *I'll have a box on your doorstep tomorrow.*

In my friend Lourdes's version of my life story, she is the one who pried me out of Philadelphia four months ago, yanking me from yet another of the sort of dead-end relationships I seem to be particularly skilled at cultivating, and from a job that, while satisfying, never felt like the exact right fit. I let Lourdes believe she was responsible for my move because there's some truth to the claim — I am, after all, now renting the first-floor apartment of her San Francisco home. There's no need to burst her balloon, no need to assert that the real catalyst for the life change was my dog, Toby.

After graduate school, I'd accepted a counseling position in Philadelphia Hospital's grief clinic. I stayed there for seven years, but it wasn't until I began volunteering after work as a pet bereavement counselor at the SPCA that I experienced an "Aha Moment" that would have made Oprah proud. Helping people who'd lost their beloved pets felt like my true calling, the one that aligned my training and experience and personal interests.

By personal interests, I mean dogs. I've always loved dogs. You know how some people can't pass a baby without stopping to coo in his pudgy little face? I'm like that with dogs. And puppies? Forget it. I'm convinced that petting a puppy is good luck. Some people rub Buddha bellies; I pet puppies. I've been known to trail a puppy for blocks just to have the chance. It seems to me that believing in the luck of puppies makes a lot more sense than believing in, say, a lucky number. Can a number remind you of the power of pure, unconditional love? Can a number embody loyalty or joie de vivre or goodness or friendship or . . . Well, you get my drift. I love dogs.

Despite the strong sense that I was meant to be working with other animal lovers, I held on to the hospital job because I felt a responsibility to my patients and it was steady work that paid well and I had a comfortable, if not particularly exciting, routine in place. It's hard for me to accept change (for this, like all good therapists, I blame my parents). Besides, pet bereavement is not exactly a cash cow as far as therapy niches go. The idea remained stuck in pipe-dream territory for a long time.

John, my boyfriend back then, didn't support the career shift either. He'd been cagey regarding his feelings about animals during the early months of our relationship, but I sometimes believed I saw his well-tended hair rise a quarter of an inch when I spoke of my dog, Toby. It was like he was literally bristling — like a dog raising his hackles when he senses danger. John was needy in the way of a lot of well-coiffed, handsome men; I don't think he could handle sharing the limelight, or even just my affection, with a dog. So, in a way, I'd known John and I were ill matched almost from the start, but once I embrace someone, it's hard for me to let go. I began to think of John's forthright self-centeredness as a lovable quirk, not unlike when my paternal grandfather died and at his funeral I found myself speaking fondly of his unapologetically thunderous burps.

Still, everything was relatively fine until what I've come to think of as the Great and Terrible Stir-Fry Incident of 2013.

Five months ago, John started letting himself into my apartment to make dinner for me on the nights I worked late. John, to his credit, was an excellent cook, and the whole dinner thing was a nice idea — in theory. In reality, I came home to a mess in the kitchen and the sound of Toby barking frantically from my bedroom.

"Your dog was giving me the hairy eyeball while I cooked," John told me by way of explaining why he'd shut Toby away in the bedroom. He'd just dumped a pot of spaghetti into a colander and steam rose up behind him from the sink.

I'd never liked how John referred to Toby as "your dog," but I was also aware that not everyone loved dogs the way I did and that dating someone who was not exactly like me was probably a healthy route to take.

Also, I assumed John's hairy-eyeball comment was a joke. I mean, Toby had the standard canine, hair-*around*-the-eyeballs thing going on, but his expression rarely strayed from one of trusting good cheer.

The second time I came home to Toby barking from the bedroom, I understood that John had not been joking. Or at least that I no longer found him funny. John pretended to be baffled by my anger, but I could see something callous and hard lurking behind his innocent expression. His actions were a power play, I realized — an ultimatum. John wanted me to choose his side, to pick him over Toby, to prove that I loved him more than I loved my dog. His lack of self-esteem was sad, and as a mental health professional my heart went out to him, but as his girlfriend it was becoming increasingly clear to me that I was dating an asshole.

Still, I kept my cool. I tried to explain Toby's state of mind to John. "Toby is lonely and confused," I said. Except for the high school girl who stopped by to walk him in the afternoon, he was on his own all day. "He's probably underfoot when you get here because he's hoping for a quick walk . . . or at the very least, a little attention."

It broke my heart to think of the disappointment and maybe even dread that my dog might have felt when the front door opened to reveal John instead of me walking in at the end of the day. Toby was fourteen years old — he didn't deserve that sort of treatment.

I'd had two dogs before Toby — a beautiful, high-energy spaniel named Bella followed by a dignified white shepherd named Star. I'd loved those dogs, really loved them, but Toby was different. I picked him out from the shelter when I was nineteen years old. According to the information sheet attached to his kennel, he was a flat-coated retriever mix, weighed sixty-four pounds, and was about one year old. I liked the idea of adopting a dog that was beyond the puppy stage, a dog with an unknown span of life under his belt. It seemed only fair; he didn't know what he was getting into with me either. Toby looked solid and strong, his black wavy hair spilling over his paws like bell-bottoms, and the clever, playful spark in his chocolate-brown eyes caught mine immediately. When I opened his kennel gate, he ran to me, and a wonderful lightness expanded in my chest. I remember that I laughed out loud, the sound mixing in with the din of barking dogs. The only thing missing from the scene was orchestral music soaring to a grand, heart-swelling crescendo. That's how big that moment felt to me, and still feels years later, looking back on the memory: the moment I chose Toby and he chose me.

And so Toby became my constant companion throughout that strange terrain of my twenties when I was trying to get my bearings in the new world of adulthood, no longer living at home, wading through boyfriends and college and graduate school and then my rewarding but draining work as a grief therapist. Toby was there through all of it, a goofy, loving friend who kept my spirits up. Boyfriends had come and gone, but Toby had remained.

I have a theory that you get the right dog, the dog you need, for a particular stage of your life. Bella and Star were the dogs I needed in my childhood — comforting, undemanding, and sweet. Toby was the dog I needed to help me break out of my shell as I became an adult. He provided humor and heart and unwavering friendship, never letting me retreat too far into myself. We understood each other, Toby and I. In many ways, I thought of him as my dog soul mate.

I'd never explained to John exactly what Toby meant to me, but really, did I have to?

It was my apartment, my rules, my dog. I told John in no uncertain terms not to lock up Toby again.

So when I returned home a third time to the smell of stir-fry in the kitchen and the sound of Toby barking in the bedroom, my frustration boiled over into rage. I raced down the hall, glaring at John as I passed the kitchen.

Toby stopped barking the moment I opened the bedroom door. It may seem strange to describe a dog as charismatic, but that was Toby — high-spirited, gregarious, brimming with good-humored mischief. How could anyone not love him? He had a wide, handsome head, bright, intelligent eyes unclouded by age, and soft black fur that was lately streaked with gray. Now his lip was caught on his gum, exposing a couple of teeth, giving him a funny, disheveled look that made me laugh despite the fact that a moment earlier I'd been fuming. Toby seemed a bit offended by my laughter, or more likely at having been shut in the bedroom, and shook out his fur with a proud little swagger. I grabbed his leash and headed for the door without a single word to John. No amount of perfectly stir-fried, teriyaki-coated baby corn was worth this bullshit.

29

We were a block away from my apartment when my cell phone rang.

"We're done!" Lourdes said by way of greeting. She and her husband, Leo, had finally finished construction on the rental unit below their house and were about to post the listing on craigslist. She'd been trying for months to convince me to embrace the idea of starting my own practice, but to do it in San Francisco, where, in her words, "the hippie-dippy Bay Area animal lovers would flock to pet bereavement counseling like hipsters to hand-brewed coffee shops." She'd never been much of a fan of John's, and ever since she and Leo had entered the home stretch of renovating their rental unit, her effort to get me to move had reached a fever pitch.

As I listened to my friend launch into one final push to convince me to take the apartment, I glanced down at Toby. His hips seemed a bit stiff, but his gait, if slower, was as happy as ever. When we reached the corner, he looked up over his shoulder at me. *Where to next?* his eyes, alight with enthusiasm, seemed to ask. *Let's go!* Already, he'd forgotten his confinement in the bedroom and was eager to move on. That's the wonderful thing about dogs — they're always looking forward.

What am I doing with John? I asked myself. *Why am I still working at the hospital?* At thirty-two years old, I'd never lived anywhere but Philadelphia. I'd been in the same apartment, blocks from my parents' house, for ten years. I'd been treading water, embedded in routine, for so long — waiting, but for what, exactly?

On the phone, Lourdes had reached her final and most desperate apartment-selling point — the energy-efficient toilet. "There are two levels of flush," she was saying. "One is for pee, and the other —"

"Lourdes," I interrupted, laughing, "I'll take it."

"What? You're not dying to know about the second level of flush? This kind of information isn't going to make or break your decision?" She paused. "*Shut the fucking front door.* Did you just say that you'll take it?"

Lourdes's excited squeal was so loud that Toby froze, cocked one silky salt-and-pepper ear toward the sky, and barked.

Four months later, here I am, knocking on Lourdes's door. If you must come down with a touch of agoraphobia, I highly recommend doing it in an apartment where your best friend from college lives upstairs, safely

31

within the confines of a fence that separates the property from the city sidewalk.

The moment Lourdes opens the door, her poodle, Giselle, races forward and wedges herself between my legs. I steady myself on the doorframe and laugh.

"Well, it's happened," Lourdes says, staring at her dog. "The girls have finally convinced her that she's a pony."

I kneel down to Giselle's level and smooth back the funny bouffant of ginger hair between her ears. It springs right back into place. Giselle is gangly and cheerful and smart and I imagine that if she spoke she would sound just like Julia Child, whose television show my mother watched in reruns throughout my childhood. Her tongue shoots out and I turn my head, laughing, so it lands on my cheek.

Lourdes takes in our little exchange, amused. "Wine?"

"I thought you'd never ask."

At the kitchen table, Lourdes's daughters, Portia and Gabby, are drawing on a long sheet of white butcher paper that is anchored by two plastic bins of crayons and two glass-sphere terrariums filled with dirt and succulent plants. The succulents are cuttings from the rows of raised beds that Lourdes herself built in the backyard.

If I love my downstairs apartment for its tidy quiet, I love Lourdes and Leo's house for its energy, the jazz rhythms of family life. It's a pale slip of a home that all winter long seemed in danger of having its edges erased by fog and rain. There one moment, gone the next. It looks like a modest Victorian from the front, but they gutted the inside a couple of years ago and now there is an open floor plan with concrete floors and an entire wall of glass that can be folded like an accordion when the weather allows. The glass wall is closed today. In the distance, fog clings to the steep, dark tilt of Sutro Forest, a hint of sunset searing its edges. I feel a twinge of vertigo and look away.

"Hi, girls," I say, heading toward the table.

"Mags!" Gabby squeals. She's three and recently had her first haircut; her round, angelic face is newly framed by the jet-black bowl cut favored by serial killers.

"Hi, Maggie!" says Portia, who is seven.

Lourdes opens a bottle of wine and fills two glasses. In the decade since college — despite marriage and children and years of running her own landscape design business — it seems to me that Lourdes hasn't changed a bit. Her wardrobe is still a study of efficiency — a rotation of button-down shirts, usually in a bright check print, and dark jeans that now have knees rubbed threadbare from gardening. She still wears her shiny black hair tucked behind her ears and puts on thick black glasses every day because she can't be bothered with contacts. On someone else, those glasses might seem severe, but Lourdes has one of those faces that can never appear anything but affable. Even when she's unleashing a torrent of sarcasm, cursing up a blue streak, my friend's dark eyes never lose their velvety warmth.

She finishes pouring the wine and holds out one of the glasses. "Good day at work?"

I nod, taking a long sip of wine. "I just had the final session with one of the first patients I saw when I moved here."

"Therapy," Lourdes responds, shaking her head. She's flicking through the pages of one of the supermarket coupon books she loves, stopping occasionally to rip something out or circle a deal with a green crayon. "It's a horrible business model. If you're good at what you do, you lose clients."

"Patients," I correct.

"Is a virtue I don't have." She looks up and releases a catlike grin.

"Add it to the list," I say. "How's the garden project?"

Lourdes had put her landscape design business on hold after Gabby was born, but she recently became involved with Portia's elementary school's efforts to plant a vegetable garden in a corner of the school yard. Accustomed to designing elaborate gardens with only a homeowner as a guide, she's grown increasingly frustrated by the slow decision-making pace of the large committee of parents assigned to the project.

By way of answer, she lofts her eyebrows and takes a gulp of wine. We sometimes communicate in sips of alcohol, a little trick we established in college.

Gabby runs belly-first over to me and clambers onto my lap. She's not, generally speaking, a calm child — I once caught her crouching beside Giselle's bowl, squirreling dog food in her cheeks with a sheen of manic glee in her eyes — but she seems to enjoy sitting on my lap and staring at my face. Her whole body stills as she studies me. The experience is both comforting and unnerving. She is so full of trust, so fearless. It makes my throat tighten.

"Hello, Gabby," I say.

"Hi, Mags," she lisps. And then, with a casual motion that reminds me of the time a guy on a bus in Philadelphia opened his blazer to show me rows of stolen iPhones,

Gabby lifts her shirt to reveal that her entire belly is covered with Trader Joe's stickers. She pulls one off and hands it to me. She doesn't even wince when she rips that sticker off her skin, that's what a wonderful little bruiser she is.

"Oh, thank you. I've always felt I was missing something riiiight" — I press the sticker to the tip of my nose — "here."

Gabby laughs. Lourdes watches as her daughter lowers herself off my lap and begins dancing around the table. There's classical music playing, something so mild and soothing I'd hardly noticed it before, but Gabby is jerking her shoulders and shaking her hips.

"She dances like her father," Lourdes says ruefully, causing me to snort into my wineglass. "All right, *chiquitas.* Time for pajamas." Portia and Gabby groan, but scamper out of sight. We hear their feet stomping up the staircase and then the sound of drawers opening and shutting.

Giselle trots over and sets her head on my lap. She's an affectionate dog, easy to love. When Toby and I first arrived at Lourdes's house after three days of cross-country driving in a cramped rental car, Toby and Giselle had immediately begun racing around the small yard together. Well, "rac-

36

ing" is a bit of a stretch — Toby wasn't doing much racing by then. But the dogs had bowed to each other and wagged their tails and batted each other with their paws, teeth merrily exposed. I've always believed there is something infectious about dogs at play, and, sure enough, Toby and Giselle's happy energy cast a spell over our arrival. By the time Lourdes led me down the stepping-stone path to the bright blue apartment door tucked away at the back of their lovely home, the seeds of doubt that had sprouted in my mind as I'd driven across the country were gone.

I'm still petting Giselle, but I must lose track of where I am for a moment because next thing I know I'm reaching into my pocket and scooping out a handful of my evening vitamins. I toss them into my mouth and wash them down with a gulp of wine.

"What was that?" Lourdes asks.

"What?"

"Nobody told me we'd reached the pill-popping portion of the evening."

"Sometimes a girl needs a little pick-me-up."

"Maggie."

My laugh has a tinny ring. "It's just vitamin C."

"That's a lot of vitamin C."

Upstairs, someone shrieks. I watch Lourdes as she holds her breath, head tilted, debating if she has to go up and intervene. When the sound doesn't escalate, she sighs audibly and sinks deeper into her seat. We clink our glasses together and I think maybe she's forgotten about the vitamins but then she says:

"When Leo gets home we should take this party on the road. Head down to Kezar's for a dirty martini."

I sip my wine, hoping it will do for an answer. She raises an eyebrow.

"Moment of truth," she says. "What's the tally?"

I take a deep breath. "In today's performance of *The Agoraphobic Therapist*," I say, "the title role will be played by Maggie Brennan." Then, to the tune of "Seasons of Love" from the musical *Rent,* I begin to sing. *"How do you measure / three months at home? In Netflix — In Amazon / In Google — In cups of coffee . . ."*

Lourdes laughs. "Really, Maggie. How many days?"

"Ninety-eight."

She's my best friend, and I've told her everything. Well, not everything. I haven't told her that I'm worried about my practice, that if there isn't a serious uptick in the number of patients I see, I'll need to dip into my savings to pay rent. Worse, that I'm afraid I might be a fraud — after all, a therapist who doesn't have her shit together is like a hairstylist with a bad perm. Or that I seem to be having trouble saying good-bye to my patients, even the ones that I know I've helped, and it's not just that I'm concerned about the loss of income. Some things are too hard to say out loud, even to Lourdes. It would be all too easy for the stickiness of our dual relationship — landlady/renter and best friends — to become like tacky floor between us; I fear that we would eventually keep our distance from each other, not wanting to get stuck.

But she does know that I haven't left the property in months, and she knows about my family history. She knows that I've recently graduated from neat freak to germaphobe, that I worry about the illnesses my patients might introduce into my little haven, that I've been steadily working my way through a stockpile of vitamins and medicinal teas and antibacterial soap. Really, what choice do I have but to be vigilant? What would I do if I caught something? Even my good friend Google would have trouble locating a doctor willing to make a house call for less than a small fortune. Still, I normally remember to keep my vitamin intake to a minimum around Lourdes; I try to exercise restraint.

"Ninety-eight days," Lourdes says. Despite her casual tone, I can tell she is troubled. "That's too long."

I know that it's not fair that Lourdes and Leo are the only ones who know that I haven't left the property in three months. Every once in a while she threatens to call my parents and fill them in, but she won't follow through. She feels responsible — she thinks she's the one who convinced me to move across the country, to leave my job and my old life behind. She worries that the stress of so many changes at once hit me hard, and she's not wrong. Her guilt works to my advantage. I hate that she feels accountable, but my parents can't know what is going on. The news would crush my father — my mother, maybe worse.

I lift the wine bottle and pretend to read the description on the label. "Have you ever noticed that they never describe wine as tasting like grapes? Leather . . . nutmeg . . . but grapes? Never." I turn the bottle in my hand and address it sternly. "What, you're too good for the fruit that made you?"

Lourdes holds up her hands. "Fine, fine, I

get it. We can change the subject right after you tell me you'll try to go outside. I'll go with you. Let me help you. Please, Maggie."

Even though we joke easily about it, I don't want Lourdes to see me in the grip of a panic attack. It's too embarrassing. As a mental health professional, I know mental illness is nothing to be ashamed of; as a woman, I have my pride.

Ninety-eight days ago, just a week before opening my practice, I sat in a veterinarian's office and watched my beloved Toby die. Afterward, I walked home through Golden Gate Park, heartbroken. It was dusk, the park a web of unfamiliar, darkening paths. The panic didn't descend gradually. I felt the very moment it took hold of me, plunging me into an icy black sea that I'd heard patients describe, but into which I myself had never dipped more than a toe. My heart felt grotesquely swollen, shuddering and pounding in the space of my suddenly too-tight chest. Inky holes, opaque as oil slicks, traveled across my vision. I gasped for breath, and when I swallowed, my saliva tasted sour, toxic. All around me, the trees moved, bending toward me, shadows closing in on me, and then I was running, stumbling, terrified, desperate to be safely home. I felt as though I were running for my life.

It was only much later, after hours of sobbing in my horribly empty, Toby-less apartment, that my breathing slowly returned to normal and I was able to put on my Mental Health Professional cap. I knew that what I'd experienced in the park was not a heart attack, but a panic attack; despite how it had felt, my life — even my sanity — had never been in true danger. And then, the next day, when I finally tried to push open the sidewalk gate and walk to the market for coffee, I realized how little my years of education and training and counseling helped. Being armed with knowledge was like bringing a knife to a gunfight. Immediately, my heart began to pound. My throat tightened and then I was shaking, crumpling in half, gasping for air. My fear morphed into an enormous, hungry beast that gripped my chest in its claws, stealing my oxygen, blocking the sun.

And so even though I know better — even though everything I have ever studied has stated otherwise — I'm convinced the panic is not something that can be controlled, only avoided. This is what I had never fully comprehended when I heard my patients describe the panic they felt, what I am not sure is possible to understand unless you experience it firsthand: the panic is so terrifying that the decision to change your entire life so that you might avoid feeling it again seems reasonable, even rational.

But I can't go on like this. I know I can't. I can't let my life crumble because I'm unable to follow the very advice I've doled out to my patients for years. And chatting comfortably with my best friend here in her home, it's easy to pretend I'm the same person I've always been; someone with a few quirks, perhaps — a bit of an allergy to change, a slight fear of heights, something of a neat freak — but nothing that can't be controlled with a good tug on my own bootstraps. It's easy to sit here and analyze and dissect the enormous panic I have recently felt and, in so doing, contain it. After all, I know it's just a big physiological misunderstanding; my anxiety makes my heart race, which makes my brain think I'm in physical danger, under attack, and it kicks my body into fight-or-flight mode, pumping out adrenaline, making my pulse soar, my hands shake, my vision narrow. It's a chain reaction of misguided and misinterpreted signals. Nerve cells. Chemicals. From a distance, it all fits into a neat equation. And for the moment, rational thought and the warm buzz of wine and friendship and the sweet sound of Giselle's sleepy breathing below the table all join forces to quiet the hulking beast that is my fear.

"Okay," I promise Lourdes. "I'll try." I take a sip of wine, my throat excruciatingly dry all of a sudden.

Lourdes beams, clearly relieved.

I'm eager to change the subject — I've always felt more comfortable listening to others' problems than discussing my own — so I ask Lourdes again about the vegetable garden project at Portia's school. Now that the wine has loosened her up a bit, I know she won't be able to resist airing her grievances.

"Oh, Maggie, these parents." She groans. "They can't seem to wrap their minds around the fact that the vegetables will *grow*. They want to pack the veggies in an inch apart, and mix them all up without any plan. They think it will provide teachable moments about *diversity*. Those plants are going to choke the life out of each other. It will be gruesome. Little kids watering dying plants day after day. It will be a teachable moment, all right. A teachable moment about death. A teachable moment about assholes."

"Mama."

We both jump in our seats. Gabby stands nearby in her pajamas, a naked baby doll dangling from one of her hands. She'd somehow come back downstairs without us hearing her.

"Did you brush your teeth, pumpkin?" Lourdes asks. Gabby shakes her head. "Go back upstairs and ask your sister to help you. I'll be up for books in a minute." As Gabby pads silently away, Lourdes turns to me and whispers, "How is there not a horror movie about toddlers in footed pajamas? They're so fucking stealthy!"

I must be drunk by the time I leave Lourdes's because I find myself standing at the bottom of her front steps, swaying slightly as I stare at the line of fence in front of me. The pretty, arched gate at its center is one of the quaint touches that had so charmed me when I first pulled up in front of the house. In a flash of memory, I see Toby lumbering out of the rental car and trotting toward it. In that intuitive way of dogs, he'd somehow known exactly where we were going and decided to lead the way.

I turn away from the gate and instantly feel better. Just looking in the direction of my apartment makes something dark and heavy evaporate from my chest, freeing

45

space for air. I practically float down the path to my apartment, my feet barely connecting with the stones that hug the side of Lourdes's house and mark my way home. By the time I feel the cool metal of the doorknob turn in my hand, I'm smiling. When I shut the door behind me, the breath I exhale sounds like a laugh. It's a sort of mild euphoria, returning home, a delicious loosening in all of my joints. I sink into the couch, feeling dull and mellow until I remember the promise I made to Lourdes.

I'll try, I'd said.

As if it were simple.

CHAPTER 3

The next morning when I embark on my usual scroll through my in-box, I find an e-mail from Sybil Gainsbury, the executive director of SuperMutt Rescue.

During my first month in San Francisco, I'd busied myself with the logistics of setting up my practice, sending introductory e-mails to dog-related organizations and veterinary clinics all over the Bay Area. Sybil Gainsbury in particular seemed to have her finger on the pulse of the local dog-lover community; a few of my first patients found their way to me after Sybil forwarded my contact information to her vast network. It was out of both gratitude and sincere interest that I began volunteering for her dog rescue organization.

Over the past few months I suppose I've become SuperMutt's unofficial Webmaster. Foster families e-mail me descriptions of the dogs they are hosting and I post them, along with photos of the dogs, to the organization's website. It's work I can do from home and it keeps me busy during the hours of the day that I'm not seeing patients. If I can't be out there gathering abandoned dogs from the street myself, this feels like the next best thing.

Lately I've also been helping Sybil organize SuperMutt's annual fund-raiser, a cocktail party and auction that will be held at the home of a wealthy dog lover and patron in San Francisco's tony Sea Cliff neighborhood. A few of the dogs in foster care will be auctioned off (to suitable, vetted families), as will a long list of items and services that I'm in charge of convincing local businesses to donate.

As usual, Sybil's e-mail is full of exclamation points. Great work getting that sunset cruise donated, Maggie! she writes. I have a feeling we're going to raise more money than ever before and it's all thanks to you! Can't wait to finally meet you in person at the party!

I have never said that I will attend the fund-raiser, but it's only natural that Sybil assumes I'll be there. Even though we haven't met in person, we e-mail several times each week and have formed a fast friendship. Somewhere along the way I started imagining her as a cross between a relentlessly chipper version of Joan Didion and a female Saint Francis of Assisi, the patron saint of animals. In other words, I picture Sybil birdlike and earthy, with graying hair, long skirts in shades of granola, eyes blinking behind oversized glasses, surrounded by a pack of mutts representing every dog breed under the sun.

My plan is to e-mail an apology on the afternoon of the event, explaining that I'm not feeling well. It won't be a lie; just thinking of attending makes my heart race. This reaction isn't new; I've always felt vaguely uncomfortable at parties — the press of people, the noise. In the past, my uneasiness at parties, like my fear of heights, never overwhelmed my life, but now I worry that any emotional discomfort might trigger a panic attack.

I e-mail Sybil to let her know about a couple of the other donations that I'm working on securing: free grooming for a year from a dog spa in Russian Hill called The Pampered Pup and a wine class with a well-known local sommelier who adopted a dog through SuperMutt a few years ago.

I don't say anything about the party.

I have a new patient that afternoon. In theory, this is a relief; I'm glad to fill one of the many holes in my appointment book. In actuality, it turns out to be something else entirely because she shows up filthy and pissed off, her eyes flashing like those of a feral cat about to be dropped into a hot bath.

"You must be Anya," I say. "I'm Maggie Brennan." Her eyes slide away from mine, one bony finger shooting out from the cuff of her enormous coat to swipe violently at the bottom of her nose. There isn't enough antibacterial soap in the world to make me comfortable with the idea of shaking her hand, so I just wave her through the doorway and hope the gesture seems welcoming. "Please come in."

She skulks by without a word, the arm of her coat brushing my blazer. A musky, sour scent follows in her wake. Before I know it, I'm coughing into the crook of my elbow. *One Echinacea, one probiotic, two vitamin C, peppermint tea with honey, saline nose spray (two per nostril).* The prescription practically writes itself — a modern spell to ward off the germs carried on bone-chilling blasts of wind and the unclean hands of visiting patients.

The only thing I know about this woman — girl, really, she can't be more than twenty years old — is that her brother is worried about her. He's the one who found my website and reached out to me via e-mail to schedule the appointment. It's a curious arrangement, but after years of counseling patients through various forms of grief at the hospital, it would take more than an e-mail from a concerned family member to surprise me.

My sister might be difficult, Henry Ravenhurst had warned in his e-mail. But she really needs to speak with someone.

Anya stands a few feet inside the door now, her molten gaze moving slowly over the living room and kitchen, the potted jade plant in the corner (a housewarming gift from Lourdes), the fireplace with its bare mantel, the pair of yellow armchairs across the coffee table from the dove-gray couch, the framed diplomas and licenses and certifications on the wall. As she studies my apartment, I study her. Her long hair, which might be auburn but is too dirty to tell for sure, hangs in front of her shoulders like a damp dish towel slung around the neck of a faucet. Scuffed leather combat boots poke out from the bottom of the bulky army-green jacket that swallows most of her body. Those boots look as though they weigh as much as she does, and are clearly cleaned with even less frequency than her hair.

51

"Can I take your coat?" I ask, though really what I'd like to do is ask her to remove her shoes.

"I'm not staying long." Anya hefts her bag — a big black canvas thing covered with pockets — higher on her shoulder and crosses her arms in front of her chest.

"Well," I say. "Please sit anywhere you like. How about something to drink? Water or tea?"

She shakes her head and drops onto the couch. Something in the middle of her face catches the overhead light and glitters — a tiny green nose piercing, I realize, a pinprick of color on her sallow face, like the distant beam of a lighthouse in a sea of fog. Underneath her hard expression, sadness looms, irrepressible.

"My dog is gone," she says, staring at the floor. Her voice is flat, affectless.

My heart contracts. It's a knee-jerk reaction. All of my patients have lost their dogs; that's why they come to me. Still, every time I hear the words, the hard thorn of loss draws blood.

I sit down across the coffee table from her and tell her how sorry I am. She's boring holes into the carpet with her eyes, so I direct my words to the milky, jagged line of skin exposed by the part in her hair. "Would

52

you like to tell me about him?" I ask. "What kind of dog was he?"

"No." Anya's lips clip the word but she still doesn't look up. She begins unzipping and zipping her jacket, the motion electric with a fierce sort of frustration.

Already, I can see how a dog must have been good for someone with her uneven swings of energy, how the schedule and activity of the care and feeding and walking of a dog might have helped to balance her. Even petting a dog can lower your heart rate, producing endorphins that mirror the effects of antidepressants and pain medication. It's just one of many reasons why some people take the death of a pet so hard. Another of my patients recently compared the experience to being cut off from Prozac.

The word "no" still hangs in the air.

"We don't have to talk about your dog," I say. Some patients can't contain their emotions — anger and anguish and even laughter bubble up and out of them as urgently as water gushing from a broken hydrant. Others need time, encouragement, or sometimes silence before they can begin. "We could start by talking about something else."

At this, she finally looks up. Her eyes are a murky shade of green, the color of plant

53

life at the bottom of a lake. "No," she says
again. "Billy isn't dead. He's just . . . gone.
I'm only here because my brother Henry
blackmailed me into coming."

I glance down at the open notebook on
my lap. At the top of the page I'd written
Anya's name. Below this I'd written: *Brother
— Henry.* Now I add: *Dog — Billy.*

I've never had a patient with a missing
dog, let alone one who claimed to have been
blackmailed into seeing me. The relationship between each patient and his or her
dog is unique and the symptoms of grief
vary, but the fact that the dog is dead has
always been the same.

"How long has Billy been gone?" I ask.

"Twenty-four days."

I write this down. "How awful. Can I ask
what happened?"

When Anya begins moving the zipper of
her coat up and down again, I notice that
the outline of an old-fashioned camera is
tattooed on the top of her right hand.
Inwardly, I wince; it strikes me as a
particularly painful place to pierce repeat-
edly with a needle.

"What good is talking about it going to
do?" she asks. Her voice is losing its flat af-
fect now, splintering into hard, jagged
pieces. "I just want to find him." Then,

before I have a chance to respond, she leans toward me, eyes darkening. "Let me ask you something, Doctor —"

"Oh, please call me Maggie. I'm not —"

Anya interrupts before I can remind her that I'm a bereavement counselor, not a doctor.

"Maggie." She says my name the way I imagine she would say the words "day spa" or "decaf." "Do you have a dog?"

I only hesitate for a moment, but in that moment I see her eyes flick back and forth between mine, a spark of interest briefly lit.

"No," I say. "But I love dogs."

"You love dogs. Okay. So let's say one of these dogs you *love* disappears. He's just . . . *gone.* Would you want to come to some lady's office and drink tea and chat about how he disappeared? Or would you want to be out *there*" — she jabs her thumb toward the door, her words rushing out in a frustrated hiss — "where you had at least a fucking chance in hell of finding him?"

"I'd want to be out there," I say immediately. And I'd like to think it's true. I'd like to believe that if I thought I could find Toby somewhere in the city, I wouldn't hesitate. I'd grit my teeth through the galloping heart, the breathlessness, the fear. I'd walk the streets until I found him.

Anya must have thought I was going to say something else because now she sits back, studying me through narrowed eyes. After a beat of time she stands and slings her large bag onto her shoulder.

"If Henry gets in touch with you again," she says, "just let him know I was here. I told him I'd come; I didn't tell him I'd stay."

"Sure."

I know how to keep my expression calm even as my mind races. My boss at Philadelphia Hospital was always eager to tell me that it can be dangerous to become too invested in your patients. *There's something to be said for emotional distance,* he warned me over and over again. *Distance is necessary for the process.* I was never very good at heeding his advice, which was undoubtedly why he spent all that time repeating himself. I can't afford to lose patients, but more importantly, everything about Anya — her anger, the hollow, haunted look of her face, the sadness that lurks below, not to mention her blatant disregard for basic hygiene — worries me. I want to help her. I *have* to help her. I can't let her leave.

"Before you go," I say, "do you have a picture of Billy? I could send it to the animal rescue organizations that I'm connected with and check if anyone has seen him." I say this casually, like it's just an idea.

Anya hesitates. Then she shifts her bag and begins rifling through it. "Here." She thrusts a photocopied flyer toward me. I'm hoping she'll sit again, but she just stands there watching me as I study the piece of paper.

The words BILLY RAVENHURST IS MISSING blare from the top of the flyer in big block letters. And then: $100 REWARD FOR ANY INFORMATION. Below this line is a photograph of a dog leaping through the air, his face turned so that he looks head-on at the camera. The wind is caught in one of his cheeks, endowing him with an elastic, cockeyed grin. I'd been envisioning Billy as a stoic shepherd or a rough-and-tumble pit-bull mix — something to match Anya's hard-as-nails exterior — but it turns out he is small and scrappy with bristly white hair, mischievous black eyes, and — even when flying through the air — more than a passing resemblance to Albert Einstein.

I look up from the flyer and smile at Anya. "Are you a photographer?"

"No. I used to take some photos, but not anymore." She crosses her arms. "Whatever. They're just pictures."

I set the flyer with Billy's photograph on

57

the table and tap it with my finger. Anya's eyes move over it.

"This doesn't seem like 'just a picture' to me," I say. "I feel like I know Billy, just from looking at it. It's wonderful. I'd do anything to have a photo like that of my dog, Toby."

Anya looks at me.

"He died," I say. "Ninety-nine days ago." I feel something unspool within me, bouncing out of reach. I haven't told any of my patients about Toby, and I don't know why I'm telling Anya. The words just come out.

When I force myself to look up, Anya's expression wavers and straightens itself so quickly that I wonder if I imagined the change. But then she's walking back toward the couch. When she sits down, I'm relieved.

"My brother Clive thinks I'm dog crazy," she says.

"In this office," I respond, deadpan, "we call it 'dog normal.' "

Anya's lip twitches. *Is that the beginning of a smile?* I sense something shifting between us. The line was a joke, but I was also serious. It's important that my patients know they aren't alone in caring deeply for an animal companion. Our dogs see us at our best and at our worst, and love us with unparalleled devotion through it all. We share our lives with them. They know our deepest, darkest secrets, things that sometimes our closest human confidants don't even know. No one should feel ashamed for caring for another being, for feeling heartbroken when a friend is gone. What is more "normal" than love?

I add Clive's name to my notebook and ask Anya if people have responded to the flyer.

"Yeah," she says, "but nothing pans out. Henry thinks the reward is too high — it's pulling liars out of the woodwork."

"Why do you think your brother suggested you see me?"

Anya rolls her eyes. "Suggested? *Forced.* He said if I didn't come talk to you he'd tell my grandmother that he's worried about me — about my *mental health.* My grandmother is old and sick and the last thing she needs is to get worked up over me. Anyway, I think Henry just feels guilty. He's moving to Los Angeles next month and he's trying to tie up all the loose ends before he leaves. If he makes me come see you he can tell himself that he *tried* to help me."

I jot down a note about her grandmother, and another about her brother moving away. "Are you close with Henry?" I ask.

She shrugs. "I guess."

"Why do you think he's concerned about you?"

Anya begins biting the nail of her pointer finger, which is when I notice that all of her nails are bitten down to the quick. Some are bloody, others just ragged.

I ask her if she's having trouble sleeping and her eyes shoot to mine.

"Would *you* be sleeping if your dog went missing?" she asks. "If you just came home from work one day and he wasn't there?"

That explains the dark circles. I don't blame her; sleep hasn't come easily to me lately either. When I finally drift off in the early hours of the morning, I always hope I'll see Toby in my dreams. I never do, waking only with an empty feeling, his absence highlighted.

From the look of Anya's scarecrow limbs and the hollows below her cheekbones, I'm guessing she isn't eating much either.

Instead of answering, I ask, "Is that what happened? You came home and Billy was gone?"

"Yeah, but he didn't run away. He would never do that. I walk him without a leash all the time and he never goes more than a few steps away from me." She starts playing with her coat zipper again.

"If he didn't run away, what do you think

happened to him?"

"Someone stole him." She juts out her chin, challenging me to argue.

"That's terrible! Did someone break in? Was there . . . was anything else taken?"

"No, no." She looks away, her shoulders slumping. She takes a deep breath, and when she speaks again she sounds exhausted. "I know what you're thinking. Who would steal an old mutt? Believe me, my brothers have all been sure to tell me how nuts I sound. But nothing else makes sense. Billy wouldn't run away, so someone must have stolen him. He's somewhere in the city and I'm going to find him." She tells me that she's been walking through the city, looking for her dog, every morning of the last twenty-four days.

I can't help but agree with her brothers; who would bother breaking into a house and stealing a dog and nothing else? It doesn't make any sense. I decide to put this part of her story aside for the moment.

"Does anyone go with you on these walks?" I ask. It seems like a lonely endeavor. I wonder if she really thinks there's a chance she'll find her dog, or if searching for him is a way to stay busy, to keep her mind off the reality that she'll likely never see him again. People do all

61

sorts of things when they're grieving — just when I think I've heard every coping mechanism in the book, a new one comes to light.

"Henry came a few times at the beginning, but lately he's been refusing. My brother Terrence says he's too busy. And Clive thinks it's a waste of time. He doesn't even like dogs."

"There's no accounting for taste."

Anya's lip twitches into that tight, surprised smile again. "Everyone thinks I need to stop looking and accept Billy is gone," she says. "Like I can just decide to forget about him." She shrugs. "I don't care. If I need to do it alone, I'll do it alone. I'm going to find him."

I realize now that Henry Ravenhurst set up this appointment with the hope that I would convince his sister that her dog is dead. He wants me to help Anya move on. But who am I to say Anya won't find Billy? Years ago, at a veterinarian's recommendation, I had a microchip placed under Toby's skin so that he could be identified if I ever lost him. The microchip company *still* sends me e-mails full of stories of families who have been reunited with their microchipped dogs years after the dogs had run away. In fact, I received one of those e-mails just this morning. These things — these improbable, Disney-esque reunions — actually happen.

"You're not alone," I tell Anya. "I'd like to help you."

She looks at me through her curtain of dark, oily hair, and for the first time since she walked through my door I think she might be on the verge of tears. "Yeah?" she asks. Her voice emerges thin and tough, sinewy, threaded with the smallest shimmer of hope.

My heart aches for her. "Of course. Send me that photo of him and I'll e-mail it around to all of the rescue organizations I work with."

Anya looks so fragile then, twisting one thin leg around the other, one boot knocking against the other, picking at her nails. I realize that she hasn't mentioned her parents, and I wonder where they are.

"But I mean, out there, too," she mumbles, waving one pale hand toward the door without looking up. "Will you help me look for Billy *out there*?"

"Oh." My throat tightens, the beat of panic quickening in my chest. "I . . . I don't think I can do that. But let's set up another time for you to come see me. How about next week? Will you come back so we can talk again?"

Anya's face darkens, the smudges below her eyes somehow lengthening. She yanks her bag onto her lap and begins digging through it.

An anxious feeling curdles inside of me when I realize she's leaving. In all my years of counseling, I've never had a patient walk out before the end of a session. My mind races. Despite Anya's dirty, bloody, surely bacteria-ridden nails, I have to fight the urge to lean forward and take her hand in mine. If I can't help someone like Anya — someone clearly devastated by the loss of her dog — what right do I have to pretend any of those diplomas or certificates that hang on my wall mean anything?

"I can't do that *exactly*," I tell her quickly. "But I really would like to keep talking with you about Billy. I hope you'll come back to see me again. Or today . . ." I glance at the small clock on the table. "We still have more time. You don't have to leave."

Anya ignores me. She stands and drops a crumpled check onto the table. "Just make sure to tell my brother that I came so he gets off my case."

She has already opened the door and is headed up the path by the time I catch up with her. Before I can stop myself, I reach for her arm. The filthy material of her jacket

64

folds between my fingers, Anya's actual elbow lost somewhere within the large sleeve. She turns. My stomach lurches and I release the cloth, knowing that the warm, slick feel of it will leave a specter of dirt on my fingers long after I've scrubbed them clean. I flick out my fingers, frantically rubbing them against my pants and then immediately regretting the instinct — I'll have to wash them, too, now.

Anya stares at me with a look of such intense curiosity that I feel my cheeks burn.

"Please stay —" I begin, but her expression rearranges itself instantly.

"If you really wanted to help," she says, swiping angrily at the tears that have risen at last to her eyes, "you'd help me find Billy. I'm not wasting any more time here."

And then she's striding up the stone path toward the gate.

Oh, for Chrissakes. Maybe I should let her go, but I can't. I follow her. Those spindly legs of hers have a motor on them, and by the time I reach the gate, it's swinging shut again. I yank it open and step through.

Panic sinks into my chest like a hook. The black ribbon of road in front of me wavers; the sidewalk tilts. *You're fine,* I tell myself. *You're fine. You're fine.* But I'm not. I lurch back and feel my spine smack against the gatepost. I start to count my breath; it's one of my mother's old tricks, a calming technique, and now it's mine, too.

In, out: *one.*

In, out: *two.*

In, out: *three.*

"Wait!" I call to Anya. My voice is husky and raw and the gust of wind that rushes up the hill toward me swallows it easily. My heart is pounding — not just from fear, but from frustration, anger, and shame, too.

Anya is far down the slant of sidewalk now, her edges softening as she recedes into the dingy swirl of fog. If she hears me, she makes no sign of it, and there is nothing I can do but watch her go.

CHAPTER 4

"The positive effect of dogs on people afflicted with agoraphobia never ceases to impress me," says Dr. Kirin Himura. He goes on to explain that a dog eases the transition between inside and outside for people prone to panic in public or crowded places; the dog remains familiar in every environment, a reassuring presence, a constant companion, a buoy in a sea of unknown. Some dogs, Dr. Himura notes, are even attuned to the earliest swells of panic in their human charge, sensing the nonverbal distress cues such as increased heart rate or trembling hands that often precede an episode. When these dogs sense an attack building there are little tricks they might do — either through training or simply nature — to defuse the situation. Sometimes the dog will swiftly guide his human companion away from whatever is triggering the symptoms of panic. Other times, a dog need only press his nose into the hand of the person who has suddenly found herself on the edge of panic's chasm, and it's enough to calm her.

I find the article in an online journal called *Alternative Therapy*. After Anya Ravenhurst left, I'd scrubbed my hands under hot water and swallowed a fistful of vitamins and pro-biotics, all the while a single refrain running on loop through my thoughts:

If I can't help my patients, who am I?

I knew I was being too hard on myself — what therapist can be expected to chase after an unwilling patient, or help her search for her missing dog? — but I couldn't shake the feeling of having failed Anya. I kept thinking of the sad, exhausted air of desperation that she tried so hard to mask with a stony expression and flat voice. It must have been nearly impossible for her to ask me to help her, but she'd done it, and I'd said no. Perhaps more than any other patient I'd ever seen, Anya needed me, and I'd turned her away. My anxiety wasn't just affecting my own life now, it was affecting my patients' lives, too. I couldn't bear the person I was becoming. What I needed was a plan, a course of attack. I'd crawled into bed with my laptop and a pile of books and manuals from my graduate school days, and now, hours later, I'm still researching treatment options.

I know that exposure therapy, or desensitization, is the recommended course of treatment for panic disorders, but until I came across the *Alternative Therapy* article, I'd never studied the use of dogs for this type of therapy. I do a few more Internet searches, and what I find — article after article about dogs that help people with mental health issues — fascinates me. The twenty-three-year-old soldier returning from Iraq with post-traumatic stress disorder who stopped self-medicating with alcohol thanks to the companionship of a terrier mutt named Abe. The yellow Labrador who helped the teenage girl reestablish a sense of security and overcome the debilitating anxiety she experienced after her uncle sexually abused her. The trained and untrained dogs of all shapes and sizes that have helped agoraphobics leave their homes for the first time in months, years, sometimes decades. The articles are heartwarming and beautiful and inspiring, and every so often something gets caught in my eye and I have to stop reading.

I wonder if my mother knows about the positive benefits of dogs for people dealing with agoraphobia. She has always encouraged my love of dogs, and I remember her often talking about how good dogs were for children, how they instilled a sense of responsibility and routine and provided love and companionship. I'm an only child and I always thought she considered a dog an easy substitute for a sibling, but now I wonder if there was more to it than that.

Because, as far as I know, my mother has not left home without the aid of heavy-duty antianxiety medication in twenty-five years. Even with an artillery of pills, she rarely ventures outside. I don't know when her panic attacks began, but I suspect some of her more compulsive behaviors — her extreme concern with cleanliness, for one, and her connected fear of germs — were around long before the panic swelled to the point where she couldn't bring herself to leave home. She hardly talks about her childhood, but when she does her stories have an edge of darkness; the only thing she ever told me about my maternal grandmother, who died before I was born, is that she had cheap taste in liquor and men.

If my mother's biggest fear was stepping outside, her second biggest fear seemed to be that she would pass her fears on to me. I remember from a young age the feeling of my mother watching me, searching for signs that I'd inherited her anxiety. Even so, most days she was a lot of fun to be around. At home, where she was comfortable, she was full of life, smart and funny, a quick-witted observation about the FedEx man or the Chinese-food delivery guy or her therapist — "the Holy Trinity," as she called these frequent visitors — always on the tip of her tongue. I loved listening to her, and I became quite good at it, unconsciously learning how to interpret conversational pauses, fleeting facial expressions, and even body language, and how to use this knowledge to encourage her to continue (in graduate school, I would learn that I'd been engaged in an intuitive version of "active listening" for most of my life).

Somewhere along the way, my mom seemed to decide that creating a nonstop schedule for me was the best way to ward off any inclination I might have had to spend too much time at home, to ensure that I never sensed the shadows that she saw beyond our door, and, I realize now, to keep herself from putting an undue burden on me for companionship. A babysitter or a classmate's parent or sometimes my father shuttled me around to all of the activities my mother lined up for me — dance classes and piano lessons and tutoring and even a volunteer gig walking dogs for a local organization that supported pet owners living with HIV. I think my mom thought that if she created a solid routine for me, if I always knew what to expect on any given day of the week, I would feel confident and safe. She wanted the act of walking out of our home to come to me as easily, as inconsequentially, as breathing.

As a result, I grew to love and thrive on routine. Even when I went to college, I enjoyed living close to my parents, walking the city blocks I knew so well, shopping in the same stores I'd frequented for years. In my twenties, I think my mother saw her mistake and started telling me I should move away, see the world, or at least the country. I'll never forget the look of relief on her face when I told her that I was moving to San Francisco. She would be devastated to learn how I've been living for the last three months, and I'm determined she'll never know.

I try to envision walking beyond the sidewalk gate with a dog at my side and feel the cool beat of panic, low and steady, pulse in my ear. Still, I'd rather attempt to overcome my fear with the aid of a dog than with medication. Even if it were an easy endeavor to get a prescription for an anti-anxiety drug, it's a route I'd prefer to avoid. I never liked how my mother acted when she took the pills that she relied on to leave the house — they made her a quieter, less interesting version of herself, dampening her humor. At home she had an elastic face, full of life and love, but her range of expressions narrowed when she was medicated.

She mostly left the house for me — to attend school plays, swim meets, an annual back-to-school shopping trip. She was never herself on these outings, always heavily medicated, always moving her lips, counting her breath in an effort to remain calm. I longed to tell her not to bother, but I never did — not even when I was my most petulant teenage self. I was afraid she would think I was embarrassed of her. I was afraid I *was* embarrassed of her.

Lourdes keeps offering to help me, but even though she is my dearest, closest friend, I don't want her to see me the way I saw my mother whenever we stepped outside and she struggled to ward off a panic attack. Maybe I'm too proud, but I know that it changes the way you feel about someone when you witness her shaking, struggling to keep her feet, in the hard wind of terror. I don't want to do that to Lourdes, to myself, to our friendship.

This dog thing, I decide, might be worth a shot.

I'm finally peeling myself out of bed to make dinner when my dad calls.

"How's Toby?" he asks. It's always his first question.

"Oh, you know," I say. "Toby is Toby." I haven't told my parents that Toby died a month after I arrived in San Francisco. I'm afraid they'll somehow sense the specific ways his death has affected me, and I don't want them to worry.

My dad, as usual, breezes by my answer on his way to his inevitable follow-up question. "And how's work?" He owns his own business, too, a real estate development company. I know he's proud of me for taking the risk of opening my own practice, and he's warned me that the early months, and even years, can be difficult.

Without giving her name or going into specifics — not that I have many to share — I tell him about Anya Ravenhurst, how she doesn't believe her dog is dead and won't return to see me again.

"It sounds like you did everything you possibly could for her," my dad says.

I find myself blinking back tears. My dad's kind voice often has the power to do this to me, tapping some vulnerable vein that pulses back to a time when it seemed he could solve all of my problems. I swallow. "No, I didn't. I don't think I helped her at all."

"Maggie, you don't know that. Maybe you nudged her closer to accepting that her dog is gone."

"Oh, she's not ready for that. She's still really upset." I try to think of how I can make my dad understand Anya's state of mind. "Imagine how you would feel if something you really loved just disappeared one day," I tell him. "Imagine if someone stole your golf clubs."

"WHAT KIND OF MONSTER WOULD STEAL A MAN'S GOLF CLUBS?"

I laugh. My dad loves golf, and since my mom isn't exactly the golfing type, I was often his companion for his Sunday round. I loved sitting beside him, zipping along in the cart, watching the leaves change color in autumn and the little tree buds burst into pink flowers in spring. I was a city kid, so going to the golf course with my dad was like taking a trip to the countryside. I became a pretty good golfer myself, but the truth is, I enjoyed the activity more for my father's cheerful company and the fresh air than for the sport itself.

I tell my dad that the only way for me to keep seeing Anya is to help her look for her dog.

My dad is quiet for a moment and then, softly, he says, "You can't help everyone, sweetheart." I hear years of sadness and defeat in his voice, the hardship of loving a woman he can't seem to help, and I feel guilty our conversation has brought us here.

My mother's voice is in the background. I can see them perfectly: my dad poking around the fruit bin in the fridge; my mom giving the counters one final scrub for the night.

"Hang on," my dad says. "Here's your mother."

"Maggie?"

"Hi, Mom."

"What's all this?"

So I tell her about Anya, too, everything I've just told my dad. She's quiet, listening, until I get to the part about Anya wanting me to search for Billy with her.

"Well, you have to help her find her dog," my mom interrupts. "It sounds black and white to me."

"No, no," I say. "Billy isn't a Dalmatian.

He's a mutt."

My mom laughs and then abruptly stops, so it's clear she's only humoring me. She knows that jokes are my go-to diversion tactic; I learned the trick from her. A nice thick blanket of humor gives all sorts of unpleasant emotions a safe place to take cover and hide.

"Really," she says, "what's the difference if you talk to her in your office or out on a walk? If you think she should be talking to someone, go help her look for her dog, and talk to her while you do it."

"But what if the best thing for her would be to accept that her dog is gone?" I ask. "I don't want to enable unhealthy behavior."

"This patient of yours is looking for something," my mom says, her tone decisive. "And she's made it clear that she's not going to find it in your office."

After I hang up with my parents, I call Lourdes. I can hear her phone ringing upstairs, her footsteps against the floor as she moves to answer it.

"Howdy, stranger," she says.

I take a deep breath.

"Lourdes," I say. "I'm going to need your dog."

CHAPTER 5

Giselle is practically apoplectic with excitement when Lourdes brings her down the next morning. She springs from paw to paw, tail furiously whipping the air. Even her fur seems more tightly wound than usual, her ginger curls reverberating with each step. I don't think that she's feeding off my nervous energy, just happy to be out of the house, but who knows? In my experience, all rumors of poodles' impressive, and sometimes troublesome, intelligence are well founded.

Lourdes hands me a grocery bag filled with dog food and bowls and toys and a leash. When I told her my plan, she decided she and Leo and the kids would take the dog-free weekend as an opportunity to go up to Napa for the night.

"Don't forget," Lourdes says, "she's a toilet drinker."

"Noted."

"And she'll hop up on the furniture the minute you walk out the door."

"Lourdes. Don't worry about us. Go have fun."

"Okay. I'll bring you back a bottle of something. It might or might not be empty, depending on how many times Gabby asks if we're there yet on the drive home." She frowns. "Are you sure it wouldn't be better if I stayed? Isn't there anything I can do to help?"

I nod toward Giselle. "You *are* helping."

Lourdes glances doubtfully at her dog. Then she breaks out her jazz hands and begins singing, to the tune of "Master of the House" from *Les Misérables, "Never leaves the house, never through the gate, orders so much from Amazon that she gets a special rate!"* She mimics the sound of a crowd cheering. "And the audience goes wild following Maggie Brennan's final performance in the *The Agoraphobic Therapist,* this year's Tony winner for Weirdest New Musical." Lourdes throws her jazz hands around me, squeezing me within one of her signature robust hugs.

"Good luck," she whispers. "I love you."

After she leaves, I pour water into Giselle's bowl. It's the first time I've had a dog in the apartment since Toby died. She laps up water in a different way than he did; her sounds are softer, daintier.

"Exposure therapy," I say aloud. "Systematic desensitization."

When the house is silent and I know Lourdes and her family have left, I clip Giselle's leash to her collar.

As we near the sidewalk gate, I do all the things I know I should do — the very things I tell my patients to practice when they are overcome by anxiety. I concentrate on my breathing, drawing air in through my nose and expelling it through my mouth. I visualize our walk — a quick, uneventful trip to the corner. I reach down and run my hand along the length of Giselle's back. As if on command, she sits. Her gaze is nailed to the gate, her body shivering with anticipation. I wrap the leash around my hand until it's so short that I can touch the ends of Giselle's curls with my fingers.

I open the gate.

Something black and cold courses through me.

I breathe and count, count and breathe.

One.

Two.

I force myself to picture Anya's pained face, to consider the possibility of not helping her, and in the same moment, Giselle tugs me forward onto the sidewalk. In a blur, I reach out and shut the gate behind me. I put my hand on top of Giselle's head, steadying myself, warding off the panic with my breath. I'm not quite leaning on her, but I get the sense that I could if I needed to, that she would not let me fall.

I squeeze the leash in my hand and begin to walk. I try to imagine that I'm breathing out the negative thoughts, that my chest is expanding instead of constricting, but mostly I focus on Giselle, her warm, solid presence at my side, the softness of her strawberry-blond fur against my taut knuckles. She's cheerful and confident, completely unfazed by how short I've made the leash. I pretend I have blinders on, that I couldn't look around even if I wanted to, that I'm only able to see Giselle, but with each step, my skin tightens, my muscles tensing. Bile rises into the back of my throat. Panic buzzes in my ears, swarming through me, filling my chest, and I can barely breathe. The sound of Giselle's nails clicking against the pavement cuts through my haze. The tags on her collar chime together. Her collar and leash are pale brown leather, good, sturdy tethers that will not fail. I slip my shaking fingers into her soft neck and begin again.

One.

Two.

When I spot the curb ahead, I realize I've made it to the corner, about half a block away from Lourdes's house. I immediately turn around and hurry back toward the gate. Giselle lopes along at my side.

When the gate latch falls into place behind me, I double over, pressing my hands against my knees, and inhale deeply. After a couple of minutes, my head begins to clear, and I straighten. *It actually worked!* I hadn't gone far, but for the first time in one hundred days I'd made it beyond the gate. It was a start.

"Well," I say to Giselle once we're in my apartment. I'm scrubbing my hands under hot water and she's standing in the doorway of the bathroom, watching me. "That was some adventure, kid."

Giselle is too polite to argue.

"Baby steps," I say. Then I try to translate: "Puppy steps." But the translation doesn't really work — a puppy would have bounded joyfully down that street instead of hobbling along like someone recently released from a full-body cast. A puppy would have kept going beyond the curb.

There's still a box of dog biscuits in a kitchen cabinet. I hold a treat out to Giselle, smoothing back her soft bouffant with my other hand, and she takes it delicately, her muzzle brushing my fingers like a light kiss. She trots over to the rug and bites the biscuit into pieces, letting chunks of it fall out of her mouth and onto the rug, and then licks up the pieces one at a time. Afterward, she snorts into the rug a few times, hunting for crumbs, and then looks up at me expectantly. When I don't make a move toward the cabinet that holds the biscuit box, she stretches out her long legs in front of her, separating all of her claws, and yawns.

"I'm sorry," I say. "Am I boring you already?" I feel punch-drunk, so adrenaline-addled that I'm almost giddy. I'd only been beyond the gate for a couple of minutes, but the length of time is beside the point. I'd done it. I'd felt anxious and breathless and my heart had raced, but the mushroom cloud of panic had never darkened the sky — or at least I'd never looked up to see it. That was important. I can't push myself too far, too quickly. A full-blown panic attack would only make things worse. What I need is a series of short walks that go well enough to work as positive reinforcement — a foundation upon which I can build when I'm ready.

Giselle rolls over on her side and looks up at me, thumping her feather duster of a tail against the rug.

Two more walks, I decide. I'll force myself to take two more walks today, each one longer than the last.

It would be easier if I didn't live in a city of hills.

Even as a kid, I wasn't a fan of heights, a fear that I now see as a precursor to my current phobias. I was eight years old when I first realized that I couldn't remember the last time I'd seen my mother leave our house; I realize now it's surely no coincidence that it was also the year I felt my first spell of vertigo. That year, my mother signed me up for a ballet class that took place in a fifth-floor studio just high enough to overlook the tops of three streets of row houses and the flat expanse of the Delaware River in the distance. During the first class, I ran with all the other girls to the window to take in the view, but as I stood there touching the cool glass with my fingertips I felt my mouth go dry. I turned away, worried I was going to be sick, and spent the rest of class wondering why the floor kept wobbling. After watching me stumble around for a couple of sessions, my teacher decided I was unfocused and clumsy and stuck me, to my relief, in the back row of class, where I learned to keep my eyes trained on my classmates' bright hair bows rather than the view that was multiplied in the studio's many mirrors. I never told my parents how I felt about that view, how I didn't like seeing my world look so large, how it made me feel lost and alone. I must have sensed that the news would worry them.

Lourdes's house is tucked into one of the steep hills that rise out of Cole Valley, a neighborhood in the geographic center of San Francisco, and an expansive view of the city threatens me from every direction. I didn't mind this so much when I first moved in and my fear of heights was relatively easy to ignore, but now I can't help feeling that living here, of all places, is akin to someone deathly allergic to bee stings setting up a picnic under a swarming hive.

Nonetheless, I force myself through the gate and down the street, past the curb that ended my first walk of the day. The steep hill makes me feel woozy. When I catch sight of a nearby café, its sidewalk tables filled with people, my heart races into overdrive, each beat a painful squeeze. If I must deal with the humiliating symptoms of panic, I'd rather face them alone on a quiet street than on a bustling city block. I try to focus my attention on Giselle, but I'm distracted by the sounds of the café and my imaginary blinders aren't working anymore. I slow my pace, debating whether I can continue in this direction. Giselle stops short and I nearly fall over her. Her nose is buried in a food-stained paper bag on the sidewalk.

"No," I say, my voice barely a whisper. "Leave it." I give a little tug on the leash and we keep walking . . . haltingly, because within a few steps she finds a gum wrapper and then a soiled napkin, and I have to keep a close eye on her and repeat myself. When she spots a plastic coffee lid on the ground, I swear she looks up at me and winks before scooping it into her mouth. I grab the lid from her and she releases it easily, tail wagging, her nonchalant strut like a shrug.

Can't blame a girl for trying! her expression says.

Giselle finally stops scouring the sidewalk long enough for me to look up and get my bearings, and I realize we've passed the café without my even noticing. I turn the corner and we're on our way home.

When Lourdes's fence comes into view again, relief cracks open inside of me, and I allow myself to jog toward the gate. My legs are creaky, sand-filled, after so many inactive months, but it's good to move, to feel my body working with me instead of against me. I push myself into a sprint. Giselle bounds beside me, her funny bouffant bouncing on top of her head.

Back in my apartment, I scrub my hands and gulp down water. I give Giselle another biscuit and make myself a sandwich for lunch. When she finishes the biscuit, Giselle curls into a ball on the rug and within moments she's snoring.

There's another e-mail from Sybil Gainsbury of SuperMutt Rescue at the top of my in-box. This time, she's writing to tell me that we need to find a new foster-care family for a dog named Seymour. I sigh. It's not the first time Seymour has needed to be moved.

I thought he only had that troublesome leash issue, Sybil writes, but it seems he has problems with trains, too! His current foster family lives on the N-Judah line and apparently he wedges himself behind the couch and pees a little each time a train passes the building — every fifteen minutes or so. Poor guy!

She has attached a photograph. Of all the dogs that have moved in and out of Super-Mutt since I began volunteering with the organization, Seymour is the one who gets to me the most. He's one of those dogs that are so clearly forged from two vastly different breeds that the result is comical; he has the dense, creamy-yellow coat of a golden retriever but his thick torso is stretched improbably long and balanced — barely, it seems — on the stubby legs of a basset hound. His face, too, is a distinct mix; he has the wide muzzle and blocky forehead of a golden and the large, drooping ears of a basset.

A dog as adorably funny-looking as Seymour should have been in and out of SuperMutt in a week; he should already be living happily-ever-after with his bighearted forever family. He isn't even one of those dogs that are so ugly that they're cute — a specific aesthetic that I've learned appeals tremendously to the dog rescue community. Seymour isn't ugly-cute; he's *cute* cute. And no wonder! He's a mix of two of the country's most popular breeds. He should be a slam dunk; an easy case; an adoption success story. Instead, he's been lingering in the SuperMutt system for months, bouncing from foster family to foster family.

The problem is that he is always pulling out of his collar on walks and darting away into traffic. Not a smart move for a city dog.

And now this train issue. As I study his photograph, I realize that it all shows in his expression. Seymour's eyes, while soft brown and shaped like a golden retriever's, hold neither a golden's friendly confidence nor a basset's droll charm. The look in his eyes, unfortunately, is straight-up neurotic. And whoever took that photo snapped it at a moment when Seymour's eyes were so wide open that you could see crescents of white around his golden brown irises, lending him a particularly nutty look. Everyone can see his vibrating nerves right there in his expression before they even hear the stories from the various foster families between which he's been shuttled.

But he is *lovably* neurotic! Can't they see this, too? Neurotic, but *sweet.* The sweetness in his eyes is obvious. An eagerness and an ache.

Owen Wilson, I think.

I'd take him myself if I could. Of course I would. I'm a dog person and I know that eventually I'll get another one, but I don't want to rush it. And even if I believed there was room in my heart for a new dog right now — which I don't — I'd still know that I'm the wrong companion for a dog like Seymour. How could a person in my state teach him to let go of his anxiety? How could I assure him he was safe, his future secure? We'd probably end up hiding behind the couch together.

I briefly consider asking Lourdes if she'd take him in. They have plenty of room for another dog, and Giselle, with her buoyant good cheer, would surely be a good influence on a timid dog like Seymour. But if I speak to Lourdes, I know she'll just try to convince me to adopt him myself.

I write back to Sybil, letting her know that I'll update Seymour's status to "urgent," bump him to the top of the "adoptable" list, and add "no trains" to his description.

As I'm clicking through the SuperMutt website, I remember an article I read recently about a rescue organization that increased interest in its animals by naming them after celebrities. Figuring it can't hurt, I decide to go through all of the SuperMutt dogs' pages and add celebrity doppelgängers to their descriptions.

I study a photograph of a tawny pug-beagle mix with toothpick legs and a long pink tongue hanging out of the side of her mouth. *Aka: Miley Cyrus,* I write at the top of her description.

A pale brown American pit-bull terrier–Labrador with hazel eyes, a strong jaw, and a chiseled physique: *Channing Tatum.*

A glossy-coated shar-pei–shepherd leveling a flat, unamused gaze at something just beyond the camera: *Silver Medal Gymnast McKayla Maroney.*

And sweet, fretful Seymour: *Owen Wilson.* What else can I do?

Several naps later, Giselle snores so loudly that she wakes herself up. She stands and stretches her front legs in front of her, butt in the air, tail wagging. I'm sprawled on the couch, reading a book. She ambles over to me and unceremoniously shoves her long snout under my hand.

"Time to go out?" I ask, dreading the thought. The sun is low now, the sky darkening. I consider just letting Giselle relieve herself in the yard, but at the sound of my voice, she starts hopping around as though the floor has turned into a pit of hot coals. When she does a full-body, loosey-goosey shimmy, I can't help but smile. I clip on her leash, wrap it around my hand, and we head up the path. I count out long steady breaths, willing the pre-panic bird that flutters uncomfortably in my chest to stay small. The little bird I can handle — the beast, I'd rather not have to find out.

This time, I make an effort to lift my eyes from Giselle's back every few feet. Even though I feel more confident, I keep the leash short. My heartbeat is a loud, staccato thud in my ears, but it's not racing. I feel clear-eyed, determined. Giselle doesn't call too much attention to herself as she trots along at my side, barely glancing at the people we pass on the sidewalk as we near the shops on Cole Street. She has a self-contained, focused air that, happily, doesn't invite the fawning intrusion of strangers.

Toby would not have been so stately. He was more social butterfly than dog on our walks, always prancing up to people, grinning and mugging for a bit of attention. His eyes were joyful, sparkling below his sprocket of bangs, and his furry black bell-bottoms were, in all seriousness, hilarious. I'm not bragging when I say he really was a head turner. Even the most hardened, late-for-work Philadelphian seemed susceptible to Toby's goofy charms, stopping to pet his silky coat, or tell him what a ray of sunshine he was in the neighborhood, or ask me what kind of dog he was. Even with all of the extracurricular activities my mother enrolled me in, I'd been a reserved kid, a reader and an observer, more inclined to sit on the side and watch than jump in. Toby changed that — he changed *me.* He taught me that I really could talk to anyone; in fact, it was with Toby by my side that I discovered how comfortable people felt opening up to me, telling me stories of their own dogs, and in so doing, their lives. With Toby by my side, I blossomed from a self-conscious teen to a more confident adult. Some of that was just growing up, but some of it, I really believe, was Toby.

I'm not saying Toby was perfect. For reasons I can't begin to understand, his usually melodious bark turned high-pitched and annoying when he was around water. He seemed physically incapable of pooping in an easy-to-pick-up pile; instead he walked in circles as he went, resulting in a chain of poops that looked not unlike a miniature Stonehenge. He was a clown who liked to be the center of attention, trotting around constantly when I had company over, to the point where even *I* sometimes wished he would just lie down. And when he sat beside me, he always liked to put his paw on top of my arm. I'd read somewhere that this was a sign of dominance and shouldn't be allowed, but I didn't mind. I let him think he was in charge, and I suspect he let me think the same.

Giselle and I cross Cole Street and head down Stanyan Street toward Golden Gate Park. There are some scruffy-looking people with big backpacks milling around the entrance to the park at Stanyan and Haight Streets. Some are sprawled out on a patchy stretch of grass. Quite a few of them have dogs — playful, bounding puppies and older, thicker mutts adorned with bandannas. I don't begrudge those drifters the warm comfort and affection of a dog, but I can't help worrying about the level of care their dogs receive. Sybil Gainsbury has told me that injured, sick, often simply flea-ridden dogs are sometimes abandoned in the area. Every couple of weeks, she walks through the park handing out travel containers of dog food, flea powder, and flyers for inexpensive vaccination clinics. She has invited me to join her on those walks, but I've always told her that I'm too busy with work.

I'd like to continue to the park entrance now to check if the dogs look healthy, but something stops me. It's the crowd, I realize. What if the panic hits me when I'm in the middle of it? Just the thought of falling to pieces in front of so many people makes my skin prick with dread. Better to stick to quieter areas where I have a chance of keeping my anxiety under wraps.

Baby steps, I remind myself, and turn down a path that hugs the southern edge of the park. The path rises and falls, offering glimpses of the city on one side, the park on the other. There is beauty in every direction, and I try to look up every so often before dropping my eyes back to the path ahead.

When I finally allow myself to turn toward home, I immediately search the sky for a glimpse of Sutro Tower, the huge red-and-white transmission tower that looms atop Mount Sutro. There it is, high above Cole Valley, looking like an upside-down claw from one of those arcade games, poised to snag the clouds. Lourdes once told me that San Francisco needs the three-pronged tower because the city's many hills block reception, and I remember from my early weeks here that from just about anywhere in the city's maze of streets you can still see that tower. It's comforting to know that no matter how far I walk, I can look for it and it will show me the way home.

Back in my apartment, Giselle laps up the water and then, panting, wanders into my bedroom. I stand at the kitchen counter, chewing vitamin C and listening to the sounds of her poking around in the other room. When she doesn't come back, I follow her.

I find her standing in front of my bedside table, sniffing the box that holds Toby's ashes.

Yes, I keep Toby's ashes next to my bed. Where else should I put them? In a drawer? On the mantel? There's really no right place to put a dog's ashes, is there? Anyway, I live alone; I'm the only person who has been in my bedroom since I moved here.

During our third week in San Francisco, I borrowed Lourdes's car and drove up the coast with Toby. Those first few weeks in San Francisco had been wonderful. There's something to be said for starting over in a new city after a breakup. I was happy. The weeks had passed in a whir of activity — tackling the logistics of setting up a private practice, decorating the apartment, catching up with Lourdes and Leo, and finally getting to know their children better. I was looking forward to a spell of quiet that afternoon with Toby, just the two of us.

A couple of hours north of the city, I pulled the car into the parking lot of a small beach. I pushed my vertigo aside as Toby and I made our way slowly along a narrow trail that zigzagged down a steep hill and deposited us on a crescent of sand tucked against the cliffs. The ocean roared with waves far bigger than the little East Coast swells we were used to, and the sky was bright turquoise. We were the only ones on the beach. Toby was usually wild in open spaces like beaches, racing around and doing his irritating barking-at-water thing, sending sand flying out from below his paws. But that day, when I sat in the sand and took off his leash, he just trotted a few feet ahead of me and lay down and gazed out at the waves. I was surprised, and amused, and I let him be. His body was still but his neck was long, his ears perked and alert as he looked out at the sea. It was as though he was mesmerized. We both sat like that for a stretch of time, separate but not alone, taking in the enormous beauty of this place we found ourselves in.

I realize now that his regal calm that day might have been an indication of the illness rapidly spreading through him. But at the time it just seemed to me that he was awestruck, and grateful, and experiencing one of those fleeting moments of true peace that are available to each of us if we are wise enough to sense their presence, step into them, and breathe.

I plan to bring Toby's ashes to that beach. Someday. But at the moment, even with three trips beyond the gate under my belt, even if I were to bring Giselle with me, it seems an impossible feat.

That night, sleepless as ever, I pull my laptop into bed and open a new e-mail. Giselle, who is curled up with her head on the pillow beside mine, opens her eyes and looks at me but doesn't move. I might be a little nuts with all my hand washing and vitamins, but I have no problem with a dog sleeping on my bed. Mental illness. Go figure.

I start typing, feeling Giselle's gaze on me the whole time.

Dear Anya,
I hope that Billy has returned. If he hasn't, I'd like to help you look for him.
Maggie Brennan

I insert the e-mail address from the flyer that Anya had left with me, take a breath, and press send.

Moments later, Anya's name appears in my in-box. Meet me tomorrow at nine a.m., she writes, followed by an address.

Tomorrow is Sunday and I don't have any patient sessions scheduled. I Google the address Anya sent and see that she lives within walking distance of Cole Valley in a neighborhood called Ashbury Heights.

I look at Giselle, silently asking her if she's up for it. She rolls onto her side, groans, and then the smell hits me. It seems that the poodle's delicate system is no match for Toby's old biscuits.

"Giselle!" I moan. I yank the covers up over my head, sealing myself away. My computer glows in the darkness of the cave I've created.

I'll be there, I respond, and send the e-mail before I can change my mind.

CHAPTER 6

The winding streets of Ashbury Heights have an eccentric, storybook feel. Unlike Philadelphia, where the rows of homes have an elegant, colonial monotony, the houses in San Francisco are all different — a Victorian flanked by a Craftsman flanked by a midcentury modern. It's architectural mayhem; trying to guess what one house will look like based on the neighboring house is like trying to forecast tomorrow's weather based on today's — in this city, you just never know. I'd forgotten this in my months in the apartment.

I keep Giselle close and search for Sutro Tower after each turn, breathing through waves of dizziness and dread. Anya's flyers — the ones with the photograph of Billy — are taped to every telephone pole and street sign I pass along the way. Those wildly leaping and grinning Billys keep me going. The woman who took that photo loves her dog and is lost without him, and maybe I can help her.

When I reach the address Anya gave me, I double-check her e-mail. *This can't be right,* I think, looking up at the house from across the street. But it is.

The house is set on a double-wide lot and is twice the size of the neighboring houses, each of which make Lourdes's perfectly lovely Victorian seem about the size of a Pomeranian's doghouse. I stand rooted to the sidewalk for a moment, surprised not only by the sheer size of the house but also by the fact that it is, quite literally, falling apart. Every inch of the painted white trim appears to be peeling. Rotted shingles cling so tenuously to the roof they seem in imminent danger of dropping to the ground, like browned petals from a dying bloom. A driveway of crumbling concrete runs beside the house, barred at the sidewalk by a gate covered in shiny, poisonous-looking vines and cinched tight by a rusted padlock.

I wonder which floor Anya's apartment is on, and hope, for both of our sakes, that it isn't the top story — two of the three windows up there, tucked into a row of eaves, are boarded over.

Giselle, naturally, isn't bothered. She looks up at me and slowly wags her tail. *What's the holdup?* she seems to be asking. I take a deep breath and cross the street.

A rustling sound stops me in my tracks. When a man emerges from the shadows in front of the house, I jump, gripping Giselle's leash tight in my hand, and stumble backward, heart pounding.

"Sorry! I'm sorry. I didn't mean to scare you." The man holds up his hands apologetically. "I'm Henry. Anya's brother."

I stare at him. "Why are you hiding in the bushes?"

"No, I'm not . . . I'm not hiding. I was waiting for you." He glances curiously at Giselle and then up at me. He seems to be in his midthirties, and though his skin has more of an olive cast than Anya's, his eyes are the same brownish-green color as hers. He has high cheekbones like his sister, too, though his don't jut out in the same unnerving way.

"*You're* Maggie Brennan?" he asks. His brow creases as he studies me, color rising in his cheeks. He seems flustered, rattled, though I can't imagine why — after all, *he's* the one who just jumped out of the bushes.

I nod. "Nice to meet you." I hold out my hand. Unlike Anya, Henry is pleasantly tidy; the cuffs of his button-down shirt are rolled into crisp folds on his forearms, his thick brown hair is neatly cut, and his jaw is clean-shaven. He looks like the kind of guy who washes his hands with some frequency, who makes a concerted effort not to contract or spread illness. In fact, *he's* the one who pulls curtly away from our handshake, shifting his gaze toward the house and then back to me again.

"What are you doing here?" he asks in a low voice.

"I'm — well, I'm supposed to be meeting Anya." I swallow, confused by his accusatory tone. "Is she here?"

"Don't you usually meet your patients in your office?"

"Yes, but your sister —"

Henry interrupts. "My sister is in need of professional help, not a walking buddy."

I take a deep breath. "Oh. I see. I understand your concern —"

"I don't think you do," he says sharply, interrupting again. I can see he is attempting to contain his anger, struggling to keep his voice low. "I don't think you understand just how detrimental your actions could be to my sister's mental health. Why on earth would you promise to help look for her dog?"

I gesture toward the front door and try to make my voice sound smooth and professional despite a growing uncertainty about my decision to come here. "The situation is complicated. Why don't we go inside and include Anya in this conversation?"

"No." Henry's expression is pained. "I . . . she doesn't want me to be involved."

"Ah." I lower my voice to match his. "And you're trying to find a way to help without her knowing that's what you're doing?"

He gives a small, tight nod.

"Sounds like we're in the same boat. Anya doesn't want me to be her therapist. She made it very clear during our appointment, which she left early, that she would not be returning to my office. But I think you were right to reach out to me; she needs to talk to someone about losing Billy. If the only way for me to keep seeing her is to help look for him, then that's what I'll do. But I won't be counseling her in the conventional sense." I remember that the crumpled check Anya gave me was signed by her brother, so I add, "And I won't send a bill."

I can tell that Henry is listening to me now, really listening, but he's not quite ready to relent. "You know," he says, "I called your boss, Dr. Elliott, at the grief clinic at Philadelphia Hospital. And I spoke with Cheryl somebody at the Philadelphia SPCA, too. I didn't want to send my sister to some quack. They both assured me that you are one of the best grief counselors they've ever employed. They told me there wasn't a doubt in their minds that you would be able to help Anya."

I feel my face flush. I'm pleased to hear the votes of confidence from Greg and Cheryl, but I'm embarrassed, too, as though just thinking of them might allow them to see how I've changed since I left Philadelphia. If they knew how I'd allowed panic and grief to rule my life for the last three months, I doubt they'd recommend my counseling services so readily. I straighten, pulling Giselle closer. *All the more reason to prove that I can help Anya. I'll get both of our lives back on track at the same time.*

"I thought I'd covered my bases," Henry continues. "I really thought I was doing the right thing setting up an appointment with you. But if you help Anya look for her dog, you're only going to be encouraging her to believe she might actually find him. It's been a month. A *month.* Billy is not coming back and my sister needs to accept that. I know how much she loved him, but love can't bring him back. She needs to . . . *grieve.*"

"I don't necessarily disagree with you," I

tell him. "The problem is that Anya is going to keep looking for Billy whether I help her or not. And I don't think she should look for him on her own. It worries me when someone dealing with loss isolates herself."

Henry rakes a hand through his hair, the gesture full of frustration. "But how long is this going to go on?" he asks. "How long can she keep looking for him? Isn't the definition of insanity doing the same thing over and over, expecting a different result?"

"I might argue that you've just defined hope."

He sighs. "You don't know Anya. She could hunt for that dog for years, and in the meantime her whole life will have fallen apart. She's only nineteen. She had a hard childhood. She's not as tough as she looks."

In our session, Anya had accused her brother of simply wanting to "tie up loose ends" before he moved to Los Angeles, but I don't get that sense. He's clearly protective of her, racked with worry — and perhaps guilt, too. The heat in his voice has dampened; now he just sounds sad.

"But you can't force her to do — or stop doing — anything, can you?" I ask. "She strikes me as the sort of person who needs to draw her own conclusions, follow her own path. I hope you'll trust me, Henry.

I'm trying to help." I glance down at the clock on my phone. "I don't want to be late. I'd like Anya to know she can depend on me."

Henry nods slowly. He seems resigned, and, perhaps, slightly less suspicious of me than he'd been ten minutes earlier. "You go ahead. I'll come in soon."

I nod. "Is there an apartment number?"

"An apartment . . . ? No. This is our grandmother's house. Anya has lived with her since our parents died when she was seven years old. She didn't tell you?"

Henry is studying me skeptically now, and I feel whatever headway I made toward earning his confidence slipping away. "No," I answer, stretching out my fingers to pet Giselle. "She didn't tell me, yet."

When Anya opens the door, she doesn't look like she has slept or bathed since I saw her last, but now a tangle of crisscrossing bobby pins holds her greasy hair off her forehead. I immediately foresee plenty of hand sanitizer, hot-water hand scrubs, and vitamin C in my near future. She's changed her clothes at least, and wears a loose black sweatshirt with a trail of holes near the neck and a pair of faded black jeans. She still has on the huge boots she wore to my office.

They don't strike me as the best choice for walking shoes.

"Who's Fancy Pants?" she asks, looking down at Giselle. Her green nose ring, I notice, has been replaced by a tiny silver spike that looks sharp enough to draw blood.

"Giselle. She belongs to a friend of mine. I hope you don't mind that I brought her along."

Anya holds out her hand matter-of-factly, palm up. Giselle instantly places her paw on it as though she walks up to strangers' homes and shakes their hands all the time.

"Hello, Giselle. You're a good dog, aren't you?" Anya's relaxed, almost tender tone is new. "We'll have to swap modeling stories later." She steps back and opens the door wider so we can pass through.

The inside of the house is in as bad a state as the outside. Overhead, a huge brass-and-crystal chandelier shakes when Anya shuts the door. Small Oriental rugs with frayed edges are scattered haphazardly on the warped wood floors. I wonder if they're hiding holes. A long wall leading toward the back of the house has been repaired at some point but not repainted; the patches of dry wall are a dingy white color that makes the wall look like it's oozing curdled cream.

To the left, dark molding frames the entry to a large room that must have once been used as a living room. Now there's a tightly made hospital bed — the grandmother's, I suppose — blocking a faded brocade couch. Rows of amber prescription bottles litter the fireplace mantel.

Behind me, Anya is turning locks. There are three of them, shiny silver dead bolts that look out of place on the thick old door with its lead-plated, stained-glass windowpane.

All those locks, I think, *and yet she believes someone stole her dog.*

I pull Henry's check from my back pocket. "I'd like to give this back to you. You didn't even stay for the whole session, so it doesn't feel right to keep it."

Anya looks at the check for a moment before shrugging and sliding it into the pocket of her jeans. "He's coming, by the way. My brother Henry."

"Oh?"

She nods. "Clive's here already. Terrence will be here eventually. They all come for breakfast every couple of weeks. We're just about to eat."

I'm surprised, but before I can suggest that perhaps I should come back later, Anya points at Giselle.

"You can take her leash off."

"It's better if I don't," I say simply. Giselle seems quite happy to be pressed against my leg, and when she looks up at me with anticipation in her eyes, I imagine this is a bit of an adventure for her — after all, she's used to long days spent lounging on her dog bed in Lourdes's kitchen. But then I smell it — the vaguely unpleasant food scent wafting down the hall toward us — and realize she's just angling for something to eat.

Anya seems to take in the scent at the same time. "Shit. The eggs." She doesn't sound particularly concerned. "Follow me."

When we walk through the swinging door at the end of the hall, I'm so startled by the view that for a brief moment I forget to look away. Beyond a trio of windows, the entire western half of San Francisco fans out like a sequin-strewn, patchwork gypsy skirt in shades of pearl and mauve and moss. The city is bathed in the golden glow of morning sun; the wild band of frothy sea sparkles in the distance. To the north, the bright orange crown of the Golden Gate Bridge spans the bay, majestic in the honeyed light.

The view from Lourdes's kitchen is tempered by the roofs of the houses below hers on the hill — this view, on the other hand, makes me feel like I'm suspended in the sky, untouched by neighbors. It's impossibly gorgeous, and I enjoy it for a knife-sharp sliver of time before the vertigo hits. My stomach lurches and the floor shifts below my feet. I sink to my knees and close my eyes and begin to count my breath. I'm up to three when I feel Giselle's wet nose on my cheek and I open my eyes.

Anya is at the stove, stirring a pan of scrambled eggs, her back to me. She shows no sign that she has witnessed any of this. I cling to Giselle for another few seconds, trying to catch my breath. The vertigo has never hit me so hard before, and I feel unnerved. When my heart no longer races, I straighten, angling myself away from the windows.

"This house is amazing," I say. To my own ears, my voice sounds thin. I clear my throat, pressing my hand against my chest. Giselle shakes out her fur and the tags on her collar jingle.

Anya looks over her shoulder at me. In the light, her skin is so pale it appears nearly translucent; the circles below her eyes make her look as though she's been punched. Her gaze moves around the kitchen and I have the sense she hasn't noticed the state of the house in a long time. She gives a half grimace, half shrug and resumes scraping the spatula along the bottom of the pan.

The kitchen itself, admittedly, is not amazing. Cupboards hang from broken hinges and spidery cracks litter the ancient tiled counter. The grout between the tiles is speckled with what might be black mold, but is certainly ripe breeding ground for bacteria. I'm beginning to question whether anyone should eat anything that emerges from the room. Still, falling apart or not, a property like this — the double lot, the view — must be worth millions of dollars.

I notice that there are several paintings on the wall, beautiful, unframed cityscapes in vibrant colors. One of them depicts the view from the kitchen window — in it, a thick blue bank of fog hangs over the ocean, looking every bit as solid and unchangeable as a distant mountain range.

"Did you paint these?" I ask.

Anya glances over her shoulder. "No, Rosie, my grandmother, did. She only stopped recently. Arthritis. But she says she's still painting in her mind, and that's where she's always done her best work anyway. She calls those poor translations." Anya points the spatula in her hand at the painting with the fogbank. "That's *Poor Translation Number Two Hundred and Four*." She turns back to the stove and gives the eggs one last, half-

hearted poke. "These are . . . whatever."
She turns off the burner. "Let me introduce
you to everyone."

I follow her through another swinging
door into a dining room, relieved to put
distance between that view and myself. At
the end of a long table, an elderly woman
sits in a wheelchair, her white hair loose
around her shoulders. She is frail-looking
but beautiful, emitting a sort of Earth
Mother elegance in an ankle-length batik
tunic. Her dark eyes dart right to mine as I
step into the room. She is flanked on one
side by a stout, middle-aged woman with a
bored expression and on the other by a
sandy-haired, broad-shouldered man who is
handsome in a self-aware, movie-star way.

"Everyone," Anya announces, "this is
Maggie Brennan."

"Hello," I say.

The blond man arches an eyebrow. "What
is *that*?" he asks, looking at Giselle.

"Clive," says Anya. "It's just a poodle."

"Her name is Giselle. I'm exercising her
for a friend." Giselle looks up at me as if to
say, *You call this exercise?* I rest my hand
on her head.

"That's my brother Clive," Anya tells me.
Clive nods at me without rising out of his
chair, the look in his eyes one of cool

amusement. "And that's my grandmother, Rosie, and her nurse, June."

"Nice to meet you," I say, holding out my hand first to Rosie. "Thank you for having me." I expect her hand to feel fragile, but instead it is plump and warm in a way that makes me think of Lourdes's daughter Gabby.

"Pleasure," she says. Her voice is clear and strong, but her hand falls to her lap when I release it as though she'd drained her small reserve of energy lifting it to meet mine.

As I'm shaking hands with June, Rosie begins to cough, a wet, rumbling sound that rolls through the room. When the cough clears, she gives me a droll smile. "I'm fine in *here*," she says, raising one trembling hand to tap her forehead. Again, her hand falls back to her lap like a stone. June murmurs something in her ear. Rosie nods and rests her head against the pillow behind her. She closes her eyes, and I wonder if she has fallen asleep.

Henry appears at another door at the far end of the room. "Good morning," he says, striding toward us. When he bends to kiss his grandmother's cheek, she smiles, but doesn't open her eyes.

"Henry, this is Maggie Brennan," Anya

says. "But I guess you two have already met."

Henry turns toward us. "Have we?" he asks quickly. "No. I don't think so . . ."

"Maggie Brennan," Anya repeats. "She's the therapist you made me see. You e-mailed her."

"Oh, right. Of course. We met over e-mail. Hello." He shakes my hand, holding the grip only slightly longer than he had outside.

Clive sets his coffee mug down on the table with a thud. "Where the hell is the Prince?"

"He means our other brother Terrence," Henry tells me. "He's always late. I vote we start without him."

Anya clomps toward the kitchen door.

"Can I help you?" I call after her.

"Yeah," she says without turning. "You can help me find Billy."

I can't tell if she is giving me a hard time or if it's just her blunt way of answering my question. I feel my cheeks flush. "I meant in the kitchen," I say, but she's already gone.

I catch Rosie's nurse, June, looking at me with what appears to be pity in her eyes. She stands and brushes her hands down the side of her navy-blue nurse's top. "I'm going for my walk," she says, glancing at Rosie, who appears to be asleep. "I'll have my cell phone if anyone needs me."

"I'm sure we'll be fine," Henry tells her. "Thanks, June."

Henry pulls out a chair for me and then seats himself between Rosie and me. After a few beats of silence that no one seems in any hurry to fill, Anya pushes back through the swinging door, carrying a tray of toast surrounded by containers of jam and a butter dish. She sets the tray beside me and then clomps into the kitchen again without a word.

Rosie's eyes pop open as the door swings shut. "You'll want to fill up on the toast, dear," she says to me, her dark eyes glinting with mischief.

Clive glances sideways at his grandmother and laughs.

After I place a piece of toast and some jam on my plate, I hand the platter to Henry, and then reach down to stroke Giselle's head. She's lying at my feet, but her head is up and her ears are alert as though she, too, is trying to sort out the tangle of tension in the room. I tuck her leash under my thigh.

"You seem young to be a doctor," Clive says. He is meticulously spreading jam over his toast and doesn't look up as he speaks.

"I'm not a doctor. I trained as a therapist

and now I run a pet bereavement counseling practice."

Clive's smirk communicates that as far as he's concerned I might as well have said I make balloon animals for a living.

"But I'm not here in any professional capacity," I add. "I'm just a friend."

The kitchen door swings open again and Anya comes in with another platter, this one holding the mound of eggs, now speckled with herbs. She holds out the platter so I can serve myself.

Clive glances at me, one eyebrow raised. Henry, too, is watching me. Even Rosie is leaning slightly forward in her wheelchair.

When I scoop a modest spoonful of eggs onto my plate, I realize the little black specks aren't herbs. I wonder if they're bits of burned egg or if that ancient nonstick pan shed its toxic lining into the scramble.

"Do you always cook for these breakfasts?" I ask Anya.

Across the table, Clive does an exaggerated shudder. "God, no!"

Anya drops the platter down next to him. "They hate my cooking."

"Your cooking is fine," Henry says. "Clive is just being . . . Clive."

I lift a forkful. "I think it looks delicious."

When Anya shrugs and looks away, I set

the fork down, eggs untouched. Giselle lifts her nose and sniffs the air and then turns her head away, not meeting my eye. Anya yanks out the chair beside mine and sits. The room fills with the scraping sound of jam being spread over toast.

"Maggie is going to help me find Billy," Anya announces.

I hurry to swallow a bite of toast. "Well," I say, "we're going to look."

"Who the hell is Billy?" Clive asks. His knife hovers in midair above his plate, jelly oozing off its sides.

Anya doesn't answer. I notice her plate is empty.

"Clive," Henry says. "That isn't funny."

"Billy?" Rosie asks. "Where is he?"

Henry turns to his grandmother. "You remember, don't you? He ran away last month. He's gone."

"He didn't run away," Anya mutters.

Henry looks at his sister. "He's been gone a month," he says again, his voice both gentle and emphatic.

"Oh," Rosie says. She presses her head back into the pillow and studies her granddaughter. "Well, it proves what I've always suspected: Billy is the smartest member of this family. When the wanderlust bug buzzes in your ear, you don't swat it away."

118

Anya looks like she is about to respond, but voices drift in from the kitchen and two men push through the swinging door. Giselle jumps to her feet and I catch her leash before she can spring toward the newcomers.

"I'm late, I'm late, for a very important date!" the older of the two men sings. He is tall and sandy-haired like Clive, but where Clive appears to be made of stone, this man is made of soft clay. His face is pudgy and defined mostly by a big, bristly blond mustache. "I ran right into Huan . . ." he says cheerfully, clapping the other, smaller man on the shoulder. His face freezes and his voice trails off as he catches sight of me.

"Terrence and Huan," Anya says, hardly looking at them, "this is Maggie Brennan."

"Brennan," Terrence repeats. He looks questioningly at Henry. "The dog whisperer?"

I laugh. "Bereavement counselor. All of my patients are two-legged." As if to prove me wrong, Giselle's wagging tail sends my fork sailing off the table. It lands on the floor with a sharp clatter.

Terrence stares at Giselle, a perplexed smile on his face. Huan picks up the fork and hands it back to me, grinning. He has shaggy black hair and a sweet, youthful face.

He's probably a decade younger than I am, closer to Anya's age than my own.

"I'm the neighbor," he says. "Nice to meet you." It's the first genuine welcome I've received all morning and I like him instantly.

Terrence seems to recover from his surprise at seeing me and shakes my hand heartily. "Please excuse me for being late," he says.

Clive tells me that Terrence owns a chain of stores called Mattress Kingdom, adding drily, "So he's a very busy man — far too busy to consult a clock."

Terrence doesn't seem to register Clive's sarcasm. "You've heard of us?" he asks me eagerly. "You've probably seen our TV commercial."

"Well, of course she has!" Clive says.

"It rings a bell," I venture, though it doesn't.

Terrence's smile fades. He looks crestfallen. " 'Sleep like Royalty'?"

"Terrence," Clive says, "give our guest a moment before you proposition her, won't you?"

Terrence flushes, barely glancing in his brother's direction. "It's our slogan," he explains. " 'Sleep like Royalty'!"

"Oh, well . . . I've only been in the area a

few months," I say. "I'm from the East Coast."

Terrence brightens. "New to San Francisco! If you're in need of a mattress . . ." He pulls a business card from his pocket and hands it to me. "We have one store in the city and last year we opened two more in —"

"Terrence," Clive interrupts. "Let it go. You're being as dogged as the merciless march of time." He looks at me and smiles a smile that stops on his lips. "That was for you, Maggie. A little pet bereavement humor."

"Hilarious," Anya says.

"Right, well," Terrence murmurs to me. "Call the number and ask for me. I'll make sure you get a good deal. A good night's sleep is so important."

"Thank you," I say. These days, I think I'd do almost anything for a good night's sleep, so I tuck his card into my pocket.

Clive's humor, such as it is, seems to have run its course. His voice turns clipped. "If you two latecomers would deign to join us, I might have time to do something other than eat breakfast during this century."

"Is there enough?" Huan asks. "I don't want to impose."

"Anya cooked!" Rosie says, masterfully

arching an eyebrow.

"In other words," says Clive, "there's plenty."

Anya crosses her arms in front of her. "Oh, just sit down."

Huan, blushing, pulls out the chair on the other side of Anya. Terrence sits down heavily between Clive and Huan.

"Terrence," Rosie calls from the other end of the table, "that's my seat!"

Terrence struggles to his feet, his face red, and Rosie begins to laugh.

"I'm only teasing. When's the last time you saw me sit anywhere but this damn wheelchair?" She cranes her head and searches the table until she catches my eye. She winks. "Terrence takes everything very seriously," she says, as though we're the only two people in the room. I smile.

"It's a good thing he does," Clive mutters. "For your sake." Rosie is still looking at me and I'm not sure she hears him.

Sitting in the midst of this uneasy breakfast, I can't help but wonder why Anya told me to come today, at this particular time. She must have had a reason. I decide to do what I do best: listen.

"Where are Laura and the kids this morning?" Henry asks Terrence.

"The mall." Terrence crunches loudly into

a piece of toast and his mustache immediately grows shiny with butter. He reminds me of a cartoon walrus. As far as Ravenhurst brothers go, I decide he might be the best of the bunch; I'd take his earnestness over Henry's distrust and Clive's derision any day.

Clive holds up a forkful of eggs and peers at it, turning the fork in his hand so it catches the light. A speckled piece of egg falls to his plate. "Say, Anya, what kind of fancy tricks are they teaching you at that culinary arts class at City College?"

"It's a *photography* class," Anya says. "And I'm not going."

"You're not?" Henry asks. "Since when?"

Anya is staring at the camera that is tattooed on the back of her hand and doesn't answer. I remember her telling me that she doesn't take photographs anymore. What would it be like to abandon something you love, only to have to look at a reminder of what you've given up every day for the rest of your life?

Rosie taps a pale finger against her temple. "As long as you're still shooting in here," she tells Anya.

Anya gives her grandmother a shimmer of a smile, and her tense shoulders seem to drop an inch.

Terrence turns to me. "Are you helping Anya look for Billy?"

Before I can answer, Clive cuts in. "Anya, I thought you said someone *stole* Billy," he says. "One of those dastardly thieves that rove the city looking for smelly old mutts to nab. I hear it's practically an epidemic. Front page of the *Chronicle* week after week. 'Flea-bitten Mutts Targeted by Crime Ring! Humane Society Paralyzed with Terror!' "

I can feel the anger radiating off Anya. "Someone *did* steal him, Clive!" Her bony fingers with their blood-rimmed nails fan out on the table in front of her and I have the sense that she's about to launch herself across the table at her brother. "Some fucking *prick* stole my dog. And when I find out who did it, I'm going to rip out his rotten heart and *crush* it." She swings one of her legs up so that her huge black boot lands on the table. A crust of mud falls off the bottom and lands an inch from my plate.

Everyone is silent.

I don't have siblings, so I never experienced the sort of fiery, combative banter that seems to be status quo for Anya and Clive, but I know every family has its own idiosyncrasies. I look around the table, trying to get a read on where Anya's outburst falls on the range of normal for this family. Clive is biting blithely into a piece of toast. Henry is glaring at him. Terrence is keeping a close eye on his grandmother, who, in turn, watches Anya, her brow knotted. Huan appears to be frozen in the act of staring at his own plate.

"Anya," Terrence pleads, "your behavior . . . You have to get ahold of yourself."

"It would be easier for her to do that," Henry says, "if Clive stopped taunting her."

Clive snorts. "She knows I'm only joking!" He looks at Anya. "Since when are you so sensitive?"

Anya slides her boot off the table. "Wow, Clive," she says. "What a touching apology." The flush has cleared from her face and her voice even has a hint of warmth in it. I'm amazed at how quickly she is able to shift from rage to sarcasm.

If I'm not careful, I think, *I'm going to walk out of this breakfast with food poisoning* and *whiplash.*

"Hey, Huan," Clive says. He slides the platter of eggs down the table. "Have some eggs."

Huan stares at the cold, black-flecked mound of eggs. Slowly, carefully, he puts a spoonful on his plate. He takes a bite, looks stricken, and turns to Anya.

"They're really good," he says in a solemn voice.

Clive and Rosie both laugh. Even Henry is struggling to keep a straight face. With his serious expression finally lifted, I realize he is actually quite handsome — not a showy, manicured handsome like my ex-boyfriend John, but a subtler, more thoughtful version. He catches me looking at him and I quickly glance away.

"Thank you, *Huan,*" Anya says, shoving her empty plate to the center of the table. "The rest of you can go to hell." She stands and gestures for me to follow her. "Let's go find Billy."

CHAPTER 7

I follow Anya out of the dining room, feeling oddly invigorated. All of that verbal sparring, those undercurrents of anger and love bubbling up to the surface in ever-so-brief bursts — it's a therapist's dream, really, and it's more real-life action than I've seen in months. My enthusiasm quickly fades, however, when we step outside and head off in the direction, Anya tells me, of Buena Vista Park. Before we're even a block away, I look for Sutro Tower, and I feel better when I see it.

Anya charges down the sidewalk, her eyes darting back and forth as she searches each driveway we pass. For such a wiry little person, she makes an awful lot of noise, her boots crunching loudly against the sidewalk with each step. When the leaves of a hedge rustle, she whips her head toward the sound, but it's just a bird hopping out onto the sidewalk in front of us. Giselle bounds forward gleefully and the bird is gone.

"How have you been these last couple of days?" I ask.

She shrugs. "My boss told me not to come in to work anymore." She barely glances at me as she speaks, her eyes still pegged to the driveways we pass.

"You lost your job?"

"I told a customer that he had shitty taste. He *did* have shitty taste — you should have seen the frame he picked out — but I get that that isn't the point. I work in the store that sells that crappy frame, so who am I to yell at a guy for picking out something I sell? It wasn't my finest moment. It also wasn't my *worst* moment. It was just the final straw. That's what Ray, my boss, said. Ray's not a total shit. He's holding the job for me, but I'm sort of on probation."

Here's what I've learned this morning: Anya's parents died when she was seven years old and she's lived with her grandmother ever since, she is nineteen years old, she's *not* working at a frame shop, and she's *not* attending a photography class at City College. I wonder if she is taking other classes. Something tells me she's not. Does she have any friends? It's difficult to imagine her relaxing, laughing. I wonder what she was like before she lost Billy. How different is the person I'm meeting now from the person she was a month ago?

We stop at an intersection while a car passes. Giselle sits back on her haunches, her head cocked. All those obedience classes Lourdes took Giselle to when she was a puppy have certainly paid off.

"I bet she's photogenic," Anya says, looking down at her. "Dark dogs are tough. They can end up looking like blobs. But she has good coloring for photos. Her fur has nice texture, too."

It seems to me that Giselle adds some spring to her step as we cross the intersection. Her poufy ears bounce luxuriously along with her gait; she looks like she's auditioning for a shampoo commercial. "Maybe you could photograph her sometime," I suggest.

Anya shrugs. I decide not to push the idea.

"I think she looks like Julia Child," I say.

She looks down at Giselle and Giselle looks up at her. "You're right," she says, and her lip does that little half-smile thing. I feel like I just won the lottery.

We turn into Buena Vista Park, and to keep my mind off the fact that we are walking up a path in a park that has "vista" in its name and are therefore surely headed toward the sort of expansive view that turns

129

me into a pile of jelly, I ask Anya if she photographs people, too, or just dogs.

"I photograph everything," she answers. "But I prefer dogs."

We cut up the hillside through a cypress grove. The air has a damp, pleasant, earthy smell. Every so often I glance up from Giselle's back and catch a glimpse of the spires of a peach-colored church in the northern distance, the bay and green mountains of Marin beyond. Each time, my pulse spikes uncomfortably and I drop my eyes back to Giselle.

I have so many questions I'd like to ask Anya — about her parents' death, her relationship with her grandmother and each of her brothers, Billy's disappearance. But I remind myself to take things slowly and allow Anya to steer the course of our conversation. I don't want to push too hard and risk being shut out before I've even had a chance to help.

When we're halfway up the hill, Anya suddenly cuts to the edge of the path and peers down into the wooded hillside.

"Billllyyyyy!" she screams. Her voice is piercing, an ice pick of anguish and grief and fear.

I race to her side, my heartbeat thunderous. I expect to see a dog — or, given the tone of Anya's voice, maybe the lifeless body of a dog — somewhere in the wooded hill below. But I don't. The park is still and silent, crisscrossed by empty paths. I can't shake the sound of Anya's terrible scream from my ears.

When she finally looks at me, her face is impossibly composed. "It's something I do," she says. "It's primal. Cathartic. Keeps me off the drugs." Before I can respond, she turns and stomps up the hill. I hurry after her, still rattled by her scream.

On the path, dappled sunlight glows between blotches of dark shade, little negative-image Rorschach tests everywhere. As we near the top of the park, I ask Anya how she feels about her boss asking her not to come in to work.

She shrugs. "It's fine. I can't focus on anything but Billy and it was driving me crazy to be there. I felt like I was going to explode. I guess I did explode. Anyway, I live for free at my grandmother's, so I'll be okay without a paycheck for a little while. I guess that's the upside of not having your life all figured out. It's cheap. Especially," she adds, "if your shrink is free."

"Well, remember," I say, "I'm not your shrink."

"Then what's with the interrogation?"

"We're just talking. Like friends." I smile at her, but she looks down at Giselle.

"Are you going to let her off that leash?"

"She's a therapy dog," I say quickly. "Well, she's going to be. I'm training her." Lies have always left a metallic taste in my mouth.

Anya looks at me. "I thought you were just taking her out for exercise."

"I am." The metallic taste spreads from my tongue to the roof of my mouth. "Exercise is part of her training. It helps her focus."

Anya squints at me, cocking her head. "You're strange," she says, deciding. Maybe I should be disturbed by this pronouncement, but there's a note of surprise in Anya's voice and new warmth in her eyes, and so, instead, I find myself smiling.

"Aren't we all?"

"I don't know." Anya shrugs. "But I'm fine with strange."

A few minutes later we reach the top of the park — a small, flat circle of lawn. Even without looking, I sense that we're high above the city now. *Don't look don't look don't look,* I chant to myself. I'm doing a solid job of keeping my eyes on the ground until Anya strides to the edge of the lawn and releases another one of her bloodcurdling

"Billy!" screams. I immediately look in her direction. Beyond the canopy of cypress trees, I can see much of downtown San Francisco, the steely line of the Bay Bridge above the glimmering water, the hazy curves of the Oakland hills in the distance. I'm practically blinded by the sparkle and grit of it all, the teeming mix of nature and city, the wild and the concrete pushing right up against each other.

The panic knocks me to my knees. My heart is a twisting, painful mass within my chest. My throat constricts; my breath has to find its way through the eye of a needle. I reach blindly for Giselle, gripping her fur in my hand, and take long, reedy breaths.

One.

Two.

Three.

"Are you okay?" Anya stands above me. I nod, but I can't seem to speak. Even through my panic, I'm humiliated, burning with shame. What has happened to me? Why can't I control this? I'm afraid of everything and nothing at once; rational thought darts away from me before I can pin it down.

I'm supposed to be the stable one here and I can't even stand on my own two feet.

Anya sits down beside me. She pulls a

bottle from her bag and hands it to me. "It's water."

My hands are shaking and I can't get the top off the bottle. Anya takes it back from me, unscrews the top, and then hands it to me again. I take a drink. I close my eyes and think about the path we just walked up. I try to make a map in my head — an imaginary line that links me from that bright, exposed spot on top of the city to my small, contained apartment. The panic ebbs from my chest, a full balloon that a moment ago had been on the cusp of bursting is now slowly releasing air.

"Every time I hike up that hill I have this feeling in my gut that Billy is going to be here," Anya says gloomily. "Every single time, I'm sure of it." I look over at her, waiting for her to say something about the fact that I'm shaking and mute and breathing quickly, but she only says, "He loves this park."

After another few moments, I feel well enough to speak again. "My dog, Toby . . ." I clear my throat. "He would have loved this park, too."

She glances at me. "What happened to him?"

"Cancer."

"I'm sorry."

I nod.

Anya stands. She kicks at the ground with one of her heavy boots. "Should we head back?"

I stand, feeling shaky but mostly just embarrassed now. I can barely bring myself to look at Anya. We begin walking back down the hill, listening to our footsteps and the soft, happy, hop step of Giselle's paws against the path. I keep waiting for Anya to bring up what happened to me at the top of the park, but she's quiet at my side.

As we leave Buena Vista, I take in a reassuring glimpse of Sutro Tower. "Why did you want me to meet your family this morning?" I ask Anya.

She shrugs. "I guess I just wanted you to see what I'm up against. They treat me like I'm nuts. Well, not Rosie. But my brothers all say I'm crazy for thinking someone stole Billy."

"*I* don't think you're crazy," I say carefully, thinking of the violent rage she'd flown into at breakfast, "but I am curious why you think someone stole him."

"I told you, even if someone left a door open, he wouldn't run away. No one has come up with any other explanation."

I'm wary of pushing her, so I just nod.

After a few moments of silence, she says,

"I didn't have a lot of friends in high school. I spent a lot of time in the art room. There was a darkroom there, and I'd taken photography as a freshman and was hooked. Mr. Lane, the art teacher, let me use the darkroom whenever I wanted. If the weather was nice, I'd walk home after school and get Billy, and then I'd take him back to school and tie his leash to a tree outside the art room window where I could keep an eye on him. He loved sitting there in the shade, trying to catch flies, or napping in the grass, or chewing on a bone I'd brought for him.

"When I was a sophomore, I was in the darkroom for a bit, maybe twenty minutes, and when I came out I looked out the window and Billy was gone. I ran outside and saw these three guys leaning against the wall of the school. They were all smirking and jostling each other and watching me. One of them was this dick senior who was always making comments to his friends when I walked by in the hall — he was one of those guys you just know, just by looking at them, is thinking all sorts of fucked-up thoughts.

"So I asked him if he'd seen my dog. He asked me how he could possibly have seen my dog when dogs weren't allowed on school property. I looked at him and that smirk on his face and knew he'd done something to Billy. So I started running. I ran all the way around the school and I finally found Billy tied up to a fence in the school parking lot, right in the bright sun where the pavement was black and practically boiling."

She takes an angry, ragged breath. "He was fine. But, you know, the moral of the story is that people are pricks."

"Not all of them," I say. "But, yeah, they're out there." No wonder she thinks someone stole Billy — it has happened before.

"Anyway, I walked back around the school and punched that kid in the face. I broke his nose. Broke two of my fingers, too, and I was suspended for a week and had to see the school counselor for the rest of the year, but breaking his nose was worth all of it." Her eyes have a sly glint. "He told everyone he didn't hit back because he doesn't hit girls, but the truth is he didn't hit back because he was writhing around on the ground, blubbering like a baby."

Grief, I know, is a shapeshifter. Sometimes the form it takes is a fog so thick and gray that you find yourself forgetting the places where you once saw color. Other times, it's floodwater, dark and toxic and rising quickly within you. I think of Anya losing her parents at a young age. I think of the sadness and loneliness and anger that lives within her, waiting to be released.

In seventh grade, a boy in my math class used to tease me for having a crazy mother. Gossip about my mother's agoraphobia was rampant by then, the cat was out of the bag, and I often felt my classmates watching me, wondering if my bookishness was something more, whether I was crazy, too.

"Did it feel good?" I ask Anya. "Hitting that guy?"

She looks at me, surprised. "It felt awesome," she says. *Awesome.*

Then she breaks into a grin — a real grin — and I find myself grinning right back at her.

Ten minutes later, we stand in front of Anya's house. "I usually head out to look for Billy around nine in the morning," she tells me. "If you ever want to come again."

I check the calendar on my phone. "I have an appointment at nine tomorrow, but I could be here by ten thirty if you don't mind waiting for me."

I can tell Anya is happy even if she seems reluctant to show it. "Sure. I can wait." She leans down until her nose is inches from

Giselle's. "If you come tomorrow, I'll make you bacon." Anya straightens abruptly. "I mean," she says, her voice falling flat, "if Billy's not home by then."

Lourdes is eager to hear everything when she gets back from Napa that night. I assure her that I did, in fact, manage to leave the property. She lets out an exaggerated sigh of relief.

"Oh, thank God! Does this mean you're back to normal? I mean, not *normal* normal. We couldn't be friends if you were *normal* normal. But, you know, your version of normal. Weird normal."

"I wouldn't say I'm quite back to weird normal. But I do think *The Agoraphobic Therapist* has reached the end of its run. Maybe it's just the *The* Anxious *Therapist* now. Or *The* Cautiously Optimistic *Therapist.*"

"Doesn't sound nearly as catchy as the original, but I guess that's a good thing." Lourdes looks down and rubs Giselle's head. "And this one? How did she behave?"

"Like a very frisky angel," I answer. "How was your trip?"

"Gabby put a Skittle in her ear."

"A what?"

"You heard me. A Skittle. Why would she

139

do that?"

"To see if it would fit?"

"Well," she says, "it did. It fit so perfectly that it took an ER doctor twenty minutes to remove it."

"No!"

"Oh, she's fine. Hopped up on ice cream now." Lourdes studies me. "You got some sun. You look good, Mags." Her eyes narrow. "Wait, can vitamin C turn your skin orange? Tell the truth: How many vitamins did you take today?"

"None!" I say, startled. I laugh. I'd completely forgotten to take my usual bucket of pills. "I guess it's just sun and fresh air." I tell Lourdes a little about Anya, and how I've agreed to help her look for her missing dog. I ask if I can take Giselle with me on morning walks for a while.

"She helps me," I admit. "I'm not sure I'm ready to go out without her."

"Sure. It'll be a relief, actually, having one of her walks off my plate." Lourdes looks down at her dog. "And it's about time you pulled your weight around here, old girl."

That night, I fall asleep halfway through the movie I'm watching in bed. I wake up when the credits are running and stare blearily at the clock, surprised to see that it's only

140

midnight. I can't remember the last time I fell asleep so early. *All that walking,* I think, closing my laptop. The steep hill of Buena Vista Park must have worn me out. I barely form the thought before I'm drifting off again, this time into a deep sleep that lasts straight through to morning.

CHAPTER 8

Over the next five days, I learn a lot about Anya. Walk an hour a day for nearly a week with someone and it turns out that's what happens. Maybe it's the physical act of walking side by side instead of facing each other, static, in chairs. Sometimes it's easier to tell someone something if you don't have to look her right in the eye while you speak.

When Anya's parents died in a car accident when she was seven, her brothers were all in their twenties and living away from home. Anya went to live with her grandmother Rosie. She tells me it's not as traumatic as it sounds — since she was so much younger than her siblings, she was already used to a quieter, single-child upbringing, and she'd always had a strong bond with her grandmother. But, of course, it must have been incredibly hard. She lost her parents. Grief, I believe, is cumulative — each experience of loss shaping the size and scope of the next, each loss holding reverberations of the losses a person has experienced over a lifetime. The pain of grief is real, but it's also an echo and an aftershock, the spirits of past emotions rising up to grip your hand again. Examine one loss and you're likely to find another inside of it, and then another inside of that one, all that grief repeating like a set of Russian nesting dolls.

So, really, it's no wonder she refuses to stop looking for Billy.

Each morning when I leave my apartment to meet Anya, I ask myself if I'm ready to go beyond the gate without Giselle at my side. But when I put my hand on the gate to open it, I lose my breath, that crushing sensation crackling through my chest. And so I turn around, knock on Lourdes's door, and collect Giselle.

We walk the streets around Anya's house, setting off on a slightly different route each day. Anya tapes her "Billy Ravenhurst Is Missing!" posters to every pole and mailbox we pass. I'm better on the streets than I was in Buena Vista Park, especially the streets that are cut off from views by houses or hills. It's a sly city, I'm learning, with its hills and valleys breeding long shadows, its whispering fog, its sudden, heart-quickening, coastal views, its unstable earth below. The streets can't be trusted; glimpses of wide-open vistas suddenly appear when I'm least expecting them, so I'm careful about where I look.

Occasionally, when we pass one of these views, I notice Anya reach into her bag, a look of confusion darkening her face, and I realize she's searching for her camera. She probably used to take it everywhere, and now she doesn't take it anywhere. Sometimes grief cuts us off from the people and activities we love for the simple reason that we don't want to feel happy, which feels too much like moving on.

She tells me that although Henry signed her up for a photography class at City College, she hasn't been to school in weeks. Anya shrugs. "I'm responsible for Billy," she tells me. "He depends on me. I have to find him. Everything else can wait."

I nod, listening to her tell me again how she had come home from work to find Billy, simply, gone. When she tells me that each one of her brothers stopped by that day to check on Rosie, I feel sure that one of them let him out by accident, and doesn't want to admit the mistake to her. What other explanation could there be? Anya is certain Billy wouldn't run away, but even the most unadventurous dog would feel the tug of an open door, wouldn't he? And if Billy wandered out into the city streets, a car might have hit him. I'm sorry to even think the thought, but *something* happened to Billy. Dogs don't vanish. He hadn't turned up at the San Francisco SPCA, and none of the other rescue organizations I contacted had seen him. So either he was picked up by a family that was kind enough to keep him, but not kind enough to contact his rightful owner (assuming his collar with Anya's contact information hadn't fallen off), or he is dead.

I glance over at Anya, knowing that despite her determination to find Billy, she has run through these scenarios, too. She just won't admit it. She stops then, as she does every once in a while on these walks, and screams out Billy's name, cupping her hands around her mouth. She lets her hands fall and keeps walking.

I smile apologetically at an approaching teenage girl who promptly cuts across the street, glancing nervously over her shoulder at Anya.

It's hard not to wonder, just as Henry had, how long this will go on.

After my last session of the day, I call home.

145

"How's Toby?" my dad asks.

I sink down into the armchair, and run my hand over my face, exhausted. "Toby is Toby."

"And work?"

"Slow," I admit. I'd like to maintain the upbeat tone I usually strike in these calls home, but I'm feeling deflated tonight. I'm less discouraged by Anya's lack of progress than my own. It's hard to believe that only four months ago I drove all the way across the country. Now it feels like an enormous act of courage just to open a gate.

"You're just starting out," my dad says. "A practice like yours is going to take some time to establish. You're resourceful. You'll figure it out."

"Where's Mom?"

"Well, let me think. It's Friday, so I guess she's out at her rock-climbing class." In the background, I hear my mom's peal of laughter. A punch of homesickness lands in my gut.

"Hi, honey!" my mom says, coming onto the line. "Did you find that girl's dog yet?"

"No. I'm not sure we're going to find him. He's been gone awhile."

My mom clucks her tongue. "What a shame. You would have been heartbroken if one of your dogs had run away. Remember

Star? What a good dog."

I murmur my agreement, but my mind is elsewhere.

"What are you afraid of, Mom?" I ask suddenly. "When you try to go outside?" I've never asked her this exact question before, but I'm feeling very low and I wonder if understanding my mom's mental state will give me some key to understanding my own.

My mom is silent for a moment. "Why do you ask?"

"Maybe I can help. What's the point of having a master's in psychology if you can't give your mom a little free therapy every once in a while?"

"Maggie. You didn't become a therapist to try to save me, did you?" I know she has wondered this for a long time. Of course she has; we all have.

"No," I say. "Yes? Absolutely, definitely maybe."

She laughs sadly. "Honey, I have a therapist. The only thing I want you to be is my daughter. My happy daughter."

I sigh.

"Anyway," she says, "I don't want to talk about it with you. What I feel when I try to go outside — I don't want you to even have a glimpse of it."

It's a dark bird, I think, feeling it beat

inside of me, threatening to grow. *A beast.*

Later that night, I get an e-mail from Sybil.

The Seymour situation is now even more urgent! she writes. His foster family is getting restless. I'm not sure how much more peeing behind the couch they can take before they give up on him entirely! Have any other volunteers expressed interest? I'd take him myself but I'm fostering that aggressive akita, Zack, right now and I'm afraid that even if I kept them separate, his barking and pacing would give poor Seymour a heart attack!

Once again, as if I might have forgotten which dog she's referring to, Sybil has attached Seymour's photograph. I wonder if there's something calculated about the act — I'm sure she's surprised I haven't volunteered to foster him myself. In truth, I hate myself for not offering. My apartment is quiet and blocks from a train line — perfect for an anxious dog like Seymour. But I'm not ready to let another dog into my life. A new dog's scent would overwhelm the distinctly Toby smell that still lingers in parts of my apartment. A new dog would surely win my heart, and that would be a wonderful, healing thing. But I'm not ready.

Besides, I tell myself, Seymour has already been through a lot in his life, and he

148

deserves more than I can offer him right now.

Still, I'm not prepared to see him wind up in a shelter either, and I'll have to come up with some sort of plan for him to avert that from happening.

I click on his picture and study it. Again, his eyes strike me as brimming with quivering nerves — that bright, unmistakable flash of anxiety. I'd bet anything that he leaped toward the person behind the camera a split second after the photograph was taken. He probably licked him all over, starting under his chin the way submissive wolves greet their pack leader. He might even have nipped a bit at the photographer as he licked him, his whole body trembling with a nervous abundance of affection and need. Then again, he might have just raced away and wedged himself behind a couch.

As I study his photograph, an idea forms.

Maybe it's the photo, I write to Sybil. He looks a little . . . nuts. I just met a photographer who might be willing take another photo for free. Maybe if she captures Seymour in a calmer light we'll get some new interest from SuperMutt website surfers or the foster volunteer pool. Worth a try?

I'm not surprised to learn that Sybil is willing to try anything at this point. Go for it! she writes. And put him in a tuxedo if you need to! Make him look dapper and suave!

Bond, I write. Seymour Bond. We'll photograph him with a martini shaker. Who wouldn't want a dog that makes cocktails?

I have a few ulterior motives in suggesting that Anya Ravenhurst might be just the photographer to capture Seymour's more adoptable side. I've had a feeling since our first meeting that photography might be a way for Anya to work through her grief, and it saddens me that she stopped taking photos when Billy disappeared. And then there's Anya's house — huge and quiet with, I imagine, a yard out back that is probably perfect for a dog. I think of the gentle tone Anya uses to address Giselle during our walks. She doesn't love just Billy; she loves *dogs*.

The devotion of someone like Anya might be just what Seymour needs, and vice versa.

CHAPTER 9

The next morning, Saturday, Leo opens the door in flannel pajama pants and a T-shirt with the words NERD ALERT in an old-school computer font across the chest. Leo works at an IT consulting firm, and I'm sure the T-shirt was a gift from Lourdes. He's bleary-eyed, lifting his glasses to rub his hand over his face, and the house smells of coffee. I hear Gabby wailing in the kitchen.

Giselle flies at me, wedging her body between my legs. Her leash trails from her collar and writhes on the floor behind her, smacking against Leo's bare feet. He looks down and blinks slowly.

"Please don't report me to the Humane Society," he says. "I swear I haven't given her a drop of coffee."

I reach for Giselle's collar and she immediately sits on her haunches in front of me, trembling with excitement. "If only we could bottle her energy."

"Or just *be* her. Just for a day."

I smile. "Is it Lourdes's morning to sleep in?"

Leo nods. He glances over his shoulder toward the kitchen, where Gabby is still wailing. "We're out of frozen waffles," he murmurs. He looks shell-shocked.

"Ah." I think for a moment. "Do you have cinnamon?"

He frowns, considering. I'm sure they have cinnamon, but I also suspect Leo is capable of staring at their well-organized spice rack for five full minutes without finding it. All men, in my experience, have this problem, which I've diagnosed as Male-Pattern Blindness. I send Lourdes a telepathic apology for the fact that her husband is probably about to wake her up to ask if they have cinnamon.

"I think so," he answers finally.

"Butter? Sugar? Bread?"

He nods, this time with more confidence.

I wrap Giselle's leash around my hand. "Cinnamon toast. My mom used to make it for me when I was upset. It's like kiddie crack. Beats waffles any day."

"Cinnamon toast," Leo repeats. I think he might kiss me. "Cinnamon. Toast." He straightens his shoulders resolutely, looking a degree or two more awake than he did a moment ago. I have the sense there's something else he'd like to say. He scratches at the scruff of dark hair along his jaw, adjusts his glasses, then reaches down to pet Giselle a few times. Finally, he says, "I'm really glad you're getting back out there, Maggie. I know you know that Lourdes is here for you, but I hope you know that I'm here for you, too, if you ever need anything. I'm cheering you on."

I'm touched. Leo and Lourdes began dating in college, so I've known him nearly as long as I've known her. If Lourdes is like the sister I never had, then I suppose Leo is like the brother I never had. "Thanks, Leo. That means a lot to me."

He scratches at his jaw again. "I've been thinking. Is there an agoraphobia spectrum, like an autism spectrum? If so, I think a lot more of us fall somewhere on it than we'd like to admit. I don't mean to make light of the people who really suffer from the, um, illness," he says quickly. "But there's so much social interaction and consumption we can do from our homes these days. I think we're *all* losing some of our practice with negotiating the real world outside our doors and face-to-face relationships. And the less you practice, the harder something becomes."

"Why, Leo. If I didn't know you were a tech guy," I tell him, smiling, "I'd say you're starting to sound like a Luddite."

He shrugs. "You should see some of these guys who work for me. Their skin gets all lobster red and blotchy when they're faced with the daunting task of saying 'good morning' to me in the hall. Honestly, it's a miracle they make it out of their bedrooms in the morning, let alone their apartments."

"Hmm," I say. "Maybe I need to find myself a nice, awkward tech guy. We could share the cost of a Netflix subscription. Solid relationships have been built on less."

Leo laughs. "Please don't do that. For Giselle's sake, at least. She's growing quite fond of your city explorations — I don't know how she'd handle it if you went back into hiding." In the kitchen, Gabby seems to be attempting to break the sound barrier. Leo winces. The fact that Lourdes is sleeping through the noise is a truly impressive testament of her willpower.

"Soooo, is there anything else we can talk about?" Leo asks, deadpan. "Let's see, we've covered cinnamon toast, the agoraphobia spectrum . . . Oh, fine. I guess my time is up. Thanks, Maggie." He glances wistfully beyond me, toward the front yard. It's a sunny, clear-skied morning, a hint of the sea in the air. "Enjoy your walk —"

At the sound of her favorite word, Giselle leaps to her feet, races past me, and springs off the top step. Barely hanging on to the other end of the leash, I spin around and stumble down the stairs after her, yelling good-bye to Leo as I do.

When Giselle and I turn onto Anya's block, I see Henry waiting for me in front of the house.

"Morning," I say, walking up to him. "We really should stop meeting like this."

He's clearly in no mood for jokes. "I wanted to catch you before you went inside," he says straightaway. "Anya told me you'd be here. She said you've been coming all week."

I shade my eyes, squinting up at him. Now that I've decided he's handsome, it's hard to notice anything else. *You need to get out more,* I tell myself. *Obviously.*

"Is something wrong?" I ask.

"Terrence had dinner with Anya and my grandmother last night and apparently Anya blew up again, ranting about Billy. Terrence said Rosie was completely shaken up by the whole thing. June had to take her to bed early." Henry crosses his arms. "Anya isn't getting any better. I don't think your plan

— going on all these walks with her — is working."

"Well, it's barely been a week." I think for a moment. "And you may not see it yet, but I actually do think we're making a little progress. I think she's relieved to have someone to talk to."

Henry winces. "She knows she can talk to me. We've always been close. I'm the one who brought Billy home for her in the first place. I thought having a dog would help her. Growing up in this big old house with my grandmother . . . I didn't want her to be lonely."

I smile at him. "She didn't tell me. That was nice of you."

"Well, now I'm not so sure. If I'd known this was going to happen —"

"Trust me," I interrupt, perhaps a bit too sharply. "Billy was good for Anya. I'm sure she wouldn't trade one moment of the time she had with him even if it meant feeling less heartache now."

He looks at me and nods.

"Listen," I say. "I know you want Anya to let go of Billy, to accept that he's gone, but she's not ready. That's not something you can force. These things take time. *She* needs time."

"I get that, I do, but I'm not sure you

understand how critical it is that she snaps out of it." He gestures toward the house. "Don't be fooled by this place. There's *no* money. Clive and Terrence and I — we're the ones who support my grandmother and Anya. And Anya lost her job. Did she tell you that?"

"Yes, she did."

"Well, she needs to work. She needs the paycheck, and she needs the stability of a schedule. I enrolled her in a photography class at City College with the hope that it would inspire her to take more classes, maybe even pick a major, but apparently she stopped going as soon as Billy ran away. She needs to find her way back to some sort of emotional equilibrium. Billy isn't the only loss she's going to have to deal with in the near future. Rosie is very sick. She's probably not going to be around much longer." He swallows. "Yet another thing that Anya refuses to acknowledge."

My heart sinks. "I'm so sorry, Henry. I knew your grandmother was ailing, but I didn't realize how serious it was."

"Anya won't discuss it with anyone. After I move, she's going to be on her own dealing with all of this. Clive, as I'm sure you gathered, isn't exactly the nurturing type, and Terrence has a lot on his plate right now

157

with young kids at home and a business to run."

I nod. "And you're sure moving is the right thing to do at this point? Have you considered staying closer to home until Anya finds her way through this period? I think she might rely on you — emotionally, I mean — more than she lets on."

Henry's expression changes, darkening, and I immediately sense my mistake. "I hate that I have to move right now. But this is my career we're talking about . . . the career that helps to support my grandmother and Anya. Who will pay Rosie's medical bills if I don't go?"

Henry looks so tormented that I have to fight the impulse to reach out and touch his hand. "I'm sorry. I don't know all of the details of your situation, or Anya's, and I shouldn't have said anything."

"I *have* to go," he says again. "And I thought that if I knew Anya was at least seeing a therapist . . ." His voice trails off. "But this isn't how it was supposed to go. This was a mistake. You're only confusing her, giving her hope. You're going to make things worse, which means *I've* made things worse."

Before I know it, I'm inviting him to join us on our walk. "You'll see that you didn't make a mistake. All I'm doing is listening to Anya, talking with her. I like her." Even as I say it, I realize how sincere I am. I think of my old boss arguing for professional distance. But Anya isn't a patient — if she were, I never would have seen her again. "When she's ready to mourn for Billy, I'll be here. That's what you really want, isn't it? To know someone will be here for her after you leave? Come with us," I say. "You'll see."

Henry listens closely, his expression thoughtful. "Fine," he says when I'm finished. He sounds less convinced than defeated.

"Good," I say brightly, but I'm already regretting my suggestion. I'm trying to convince Henry that he hasn't introduced a negative presence into his unstable sister's life, but what if I have one of my panic attacks while he's watching? Anya may not have been flustered when I fell to the ground and hugged a dog for dear life during our first walk, but I don't think Henry would view such an episode so lightly. I haven't had another incident like that one all week, but my anxiety flares at the thought of Henry observing my every move. *What was I thinking?*

Henry gestures for me to lead the way. I

159

head toward the front of the house and Giselle falls into step beside me, tail wagging, the only one of the three of us who seems unfazed by what is about to happen.

"What are you doing here?" Anya asks Henry when she sees him standing behind me at the door.

"I want to come with you and Maggie this morning," he answers. "On your walk."

Anya releases a hard laugh. "It's not for fun. We're not a couple of ladies going for a power walk. We're looking for Billy."

"Yes, I know."

"But you think Billy is dead."

"No, I just . . . Anya, you know I don't sugarcoat things for you. You're not a child. I have no way of knowing whether or not Billy is dead, but to be honest, either way, I don't think he's coming back."

Anya crosses her arms and scowls. She looks like she's about to rip into her brother, so I speak up before she can, turning to Henry.

"If you don't think he's coming back," I say, "what *do* you think happened to Billy?"

"I think someone let him out by accident. Clive or Terrence, most likely, and they don't want to admit it either because they feel bad about it or they don't even realize

160

they did it."

I nod. It's my best guess, too. But Anya lets out a frustrated huff and shakes her head.

"That doesn't make sense. Billy wouldn't run away. He's never run away before. Not once. Why would he start now, when he's old and clearly prefers being home to being anywhere else?"

Henry sighs. "You have to admit it makes a lot more sense than jumping to the conclusion that someone stole him."

Anya purses her lips, and the angular lines of her cheekbones rise from below her pallid skin. "Why are you *really* here, Henry?"

"Please don't be like this. Let me come with you. I just want to spend time with you." He sounds sad and I'm relieved to believe him — to know that he's not joining us for the sole purpose of evaluating my relationship with his sister.

Anya looks at me. "What do you think?"

The way she asks this — as though she wants to make sure it is okay with me — makes me feel both touched and uneasy. I have the distinct sense that she's been questioning my state of mind as much I've been worrying about hers.

I give a blithe shrug. "Why not?"

"I was going to head toward Kite Hill

today," she says, holding my gaze. "It's sort of an upward climb."

I look away, pretending to busy myself with Giselle's leash. "Sounds great!" *Just great.*

"Okay. Whatever. Fine."

Anya clomps between us, heading toward the sidewalk at her usual brisk pace, leaving us in her wake. I can practically feel Henry's skepticism growing as we travel block after block in silence. I'm not going to force Anya into conversation just to prove to Henry that we're becoming friends. Sometimes the best thing you can do for a person is to simply walk with them in silence, letting them be alone with their thoughts even as you remain a physical presence at their side. Dogs are experts at this, letting us be alone without being lonely. Letting us find a way to be content with ourselves.

The streets rise and fall, twisting and hooking back on themselves. Aside from one or two more trafficked corridors, the areas we walk though all seem remarkably quiet. Within half a mile, I have no idea where I am. I look toward Sutro Tower to orient myself, relieved both for its presence as a marker and for the fact that, if necessary, it would provide the reception that I would need to pull up a map on my phone and find my way out of this tangle of streets.

The whole time we're walking, I sense Henry's frustration mounting. "How's Rosie doing?" he finally calls out to Anya. I'm sure the note of reproach in his voice is meant for me.

"She's fine. I don't know. She might have a cold. She sounded a little groggy this morning."

"She did?" Henry asks.

"June's keeping a close eye on her. I think they were going to sit on the back deck for a bit. Get some sun." She says this as though she really believes that a little fresh air will solve Rosie's health problems.

"Has she been in the wheelchair a long time?" I ask.

"Oh, that," Anya says, finally slowing down. "She fell and broke her leg about a year and a half ago and she never gave up the chair, even once her leg healed. I think she just likes it; she says she's always wanted her own chariot. She keeps asking June to take her out on the hills and see how much speed they can get. She's fine."

"She's not fine," says Henry. He's walking beside his sister now, and Giselle and I are a step behind.

"Well, she's old! *Obviously.* But her mind is fine."

"Rosie's mind is fine," he concedes. "But her health is not. She has a serious chronic respiratory condition. You understand that, don't you, Anya?"

"Of course I do. I just don't see how talking about it is going to help. Why aren't you ever positive? Rosie would want — Rosie *wants* us to be positive. That's what she's always said. You and Clive are always so determined to focus on what's wrong."

"That's not —"

"Terrence stopped by for dinner last night," Anya interrupts. She's addressing me.

"Oh?"

"He said he understands why I need to keep looking for Billy. He said he supports me and that I shouldn't let anyone tell me what to believe. So at least someone in the family understands."

"That was nice of him," I say, wondering what sent her spiraling into the meltdown that Terrence reported back to his brother.

"He said if I believe in my gut that Billy is alive, I should do everything I can to find him."

I shoot Henry what I hope is a meaningful look. It seems to me that he should be happy that his brother is reaching out to offer support. If Terrence expressed more interest in Anya, wouldn't Henry feel less worried about leaving?

"He said," Anya continues, "that I remind him of Mom." She glances at her brother, and then away.

Henry squints, appraising her. "You look like her," he agrees. "Not today, though. Only when you bathe — what is that, every third Tuesday? Every third Tuesday is the day you look the most like Mom."

Anya pushes him, biting her lip to keep from smiling. "I think Terrence was referring to my optimism."

Henry grins. "Mom *was* stubbornly, sort of insanely, upbeat. She used to let us go to school in short-sleeved shirts, even on foggy days. As long as we brought a sweater in our backpack, she was fine with us wearing whatever we wanted. 'Hope for sun,' she'd say."

" 'Hope for sun,' " Anya murmurs. I have the sense that she's concentrating, trying to remember her mother saying these words.

Henry slings his arm around his sister's thin shoulders. "It's not fair that I had so much more time with Mom and Dad than you did," he tells her. "I'd give you some of my memories of them if I could. You know that, don't you?"

Anya's eyes are pinned to the sidewalk.

165

"Yeah," she says. "I know."

The sentiment is so touching that I feel tears prick my eyes. I hang back, giving them a little space. Henry's love for his sister, his devotion to her, is incredibly moving.

After walking in silence for a minute or two, Anya shakes his arm from her shoulder, shoving him, playfully, away. "God, Henry. I know you're old, but I can't carry you all the way up there. Next time, bring a walker."

Kite Hill turns out to be a half-acre expanse of scruffy grass in the middle of a quiet neighborhood. It has a hidden-in-plain-sight feel; there's no visible sign or official entrance. We troop up the hill single file, following a narrow dirt path that traverses the grass and weeds. It strikes me as a strange place to look for a dog — if Billy were here, we'd have seen him immediately. There's really nowhere to hide.

"Hey, Maggie," Henry calls from behind me on the trail. "We're the only ones here. Do you want to let Giselle off her leash so she can stretch her legs?"

Anya stops abruptly and wheels around to address her brother. "Maggie is training her to be a therapy dog. Giselle needs to learn to stay close."

I smile at Anya, but her rush to defend my actions rattles me. Just how much has she guessed about what is going on with me? I realize that while I think I'm helping her, she might think she's doing the same thing for me.

We're at the top of the hill now. The city falls and rises and falls again, leading out to the bay in the east. In the distance, the hills of Oakland are a dull green. The view — the water, the hills, the high-rises and low-rises and bridges and pocket parks — is unlike anything you'd see even from the top of the highest building in Philadelphia. I wish I could enjoy it, but I'm thinking about what Anya knows, and feeling the pressure of Henry's presence, and the glare of the sun is too bright in my eyes and something is squeezing my chest and the ground is tilting and suddenly I'm bent over, breathing hard, steadying myself by burying my hands into Giselle's fur.

"*Billlyyyy!*" Anya does one of her primal screams, her voice ripping through the park. Out of the corner of my eye I see Henry racing toward her. She yells Billy's name again. By now I'm as used to this as I'll ever be — she's done it on every walk — but it seems to be the first time Henry has experienced it.

"Do you see him? Why are you screaming like that?" I hear her give him the same explanation she gave me: yelling makes her feel better. Their conversation gives me time to hang on to Giselle for a few beats, count my breath, and then straighten. By the time they walk over to me, the panic has subsided. I can feel Anya watching me.

"I still don't understand the yelling," Henry is saying.

"I told you, it clears my head. It calms me. It's better than taking prescription drugs, isn't it?"

Henry doesn't respond.

Anya turns to me. "My brother wants me to be normal. I'm a constant disappointment. He'd rather see me sedated on medication than yelling in public."

"That's not true," Henry says. "I love you just the way you are. I just don't always believe that you feel the same way about yourself."

Anya kicks her boots against the ground. I feel badly for Henry. There is nothing he can say that will make Anya forgive him for not believing that Billy might still return. I suspect that she is also deeply hurt by the fact that her brother is moving away; all of her barbed digs are a way to protect herself from the pain of losing him.

"Actually, Anya," I say, "in giving you Billy, Henry might have circumvented the need for medication. Studies have shown that playing with a dog can increase levels of serotonin and dopamine in humans, making us calmer, happier, *without* the use of drugs."

Henry smiles at me and my stomach does a little flip that has nothing at all to do with the view from the hill.

"Great," Anya says. "So the one thing that might make me feel better about losing Billy, is finding Billy."

"No, that's not what I meant," I say. "But it is true that one of the hardest things about losing someone that you love is that you have to allow yourself to seek and accept comfort in other areas of your life."

Anya hunches her shoulders and marches away, heading down the hill. Giselle has become fascinated by some sort of animal hole in the dirt, and I hang back to allow her a moment to investigate it. Henry waits with us. A warm breeze carries the scent of wildflowers across the hill and Giselle lifts her head, twitches her nose, and sneezes.

Henry grins, stroking her back. "Thank you for saying that," he says.

"What did she say?"

He looks up at me and laughs. "I meant *you*. The thing about dogs making us calmer and happier."

I smile. "Let's catch up with Anya. I think I might have one more trick up my sleeve today."

Henry gestures with a small, gallant flourish for me to lead the way.

"Anya," I call as we near her, "I wonder if I could ask you for a favor. There's this dog, Seymour, at the rescue organization I volunteer for. He has some issues — I mean, who doesn't, right?" I laugh. "Anyway, he's been bouncing between foster families for months and just can't seem to get himself adopted —"

"I don't want a new dog," Anya interrupts.

"Oh, no. I know you don't. That's not what I'm asking. It's just that we have photos of all of the adoptable dogs on our website and Seymour's photo isn't great. He looks like a bundle of nerves. The poor guy hasn't had any interest in weeks."

Anya slows her pace slightly, and I quicken mine so that we're walking side by side.

"I can't stop thinking about that photo you took of Billy. You're clearly great at capturing dogs in their best light, and I'm hoping I can convince you to work your magic with Seymour. It's not a paid gig, but if you're willing to donate your time . . ."

I trail off when Anya finally glances over at me. Something akin to excitement burns in her green-brown eyes.

"Is his fur black?" she asks.

"Nope. It's yellow — gold, really." I remember how she mentioned that it's hard to photograph dogs with black fur.

"Oh." She thinks for a moment. "Okay."

"Really? That's great, Anya! Thank you so much. I think this is going to make such a difference for Seymour."

"What sort of issues does he have?"

"He's scared of trains. Or maybe loud sounds in general. He pulls out of his collar when he's frightened and his foster family is worried he'll run into the street."

Anya immediately releases a barrage of questions — is the foster family's apartment well lit? Is there a yard where she could shoot photos? Will Seymour have had a recent bath? Will he sit on command?

"I don't know," I tell her, my smile growing. "I'm not sure."

She bites her lip, thinking, then announces, "But it's safe to assume he likes bacon."

Her enthusiasm is exhilarating. She seems like a different person — curious, passionate, animated. I feel the happy buzz of having done something right. Photography is the key to Anya . . . to getting her to rediscover some hope, some joy in life even without Billy by her side. We chat excitedly for the length of the walk, united in a new cause. There's even a flush of color in her usually sallow cheeks by the time we turn onto her block.

"So you'll e-mail Anya to let her know when she can take the photos?" Henry asks. He's been so quiet since we left the park that I'd nearly forgotten he was with us.

"I'll have to check with the foster family to see when we can get access to Seymour, but I know they want us to move forward quickly. He hasn't exactly been an easy —"

Anya makes a small sound and I follow her gaze down the sidewalk to see Huan, her neighbor, running toward us.

"I told June I'd find you," he says. "I'm so glad you're back." He reaches out and takes hold of Anya's hand. "It's Rosie. She was having trouble breathing and June called an ambulance."

"Where is she?" Henry asks. His voice has turned crisp, businesslike.

"They went to the emergency room at UCSF. I can drive you there."

Anya snatches her hand from Huan's and begins running toward the house.

Henry turns to say something to me, an unreadable look in his eyes. Before he can speak, I gesture for him to follow his sister. "Hurry!" I say. "Go."

When I knock on Lourdes's door to return Giselle, she invites me in for coffee. Leo is somewhere in the house — supposedly changing lightbulbs, but he's gone long enough that I wonder if he's fallen asleep in some clandestine corner of the house. I keep checking my phone, hoping that Anya will text to let me know how Rosie is doing. I'm having trouble focusing on anything else.

"Ow!" Portia howls. "Gabby bit me!"

"Gabby," Lourdes says, her voice calm but stern. "Did you bite your sister?"

Gabby shakes her head, her bowl-cut black hair swinging around her tiny ears. She gives an impish smile and points at Giselle, who is lying nearby on a plaid dog bed. Giselle lifts her head and cocks an eyebrow at her accuser.

"No," Portia says, rubbing her arm. "It wasn't Giselle. It was you, Gabby. You're an animal."

"No teeth," Lourdes says to Gabby. "Tell your sister you're sorry."

"Sorry!" Gabby chirps. She throws her arms around her sister's neck.

"No teeth," Portia sniffs. Despite their four-year age gap, Gabby wrestles Portia to the ground and sits on top of her. She bounces up and down on Portia's stomach until Portia shrieks with laughter. Giselle sprints over, barking. She rears up on her back legs and lands heavily on the pile of girls and they shriek louder.

"Monkeys," Lourdes says. She shakes her head and smiles. Lourdes has an arsenal of nicknames for her daughters. She calls Portia, her firstborn, "Lab Rat" or "Boss"; Gabby is "Monster" or "Animal" or "WMD." Collectively, they are monkeys, inmates, or nonsensical names like "shnoopidoops" and "boondaloos."

When I hear these names, I'm reminded of the many names I'd bestowed on Toby over the years. I called him "Turkey Smuggler" because he was so barrel-stomached he looked like he'd swallowed a large bird whole, and "Luigi" because his wild black mustache made me think of an Italian guy throwing pizza dough in the air. I called him "Daisy Clipper" because he pranced in a way that could have clipped the blooms off flowers, "Jasper" because it sounded like a name from the sixties and his coat flared around his paws like bell-bottoms, and "Motorboat" because when I scratched his rear end he released a happy, revving growl that sounded like a boat hitting a wake.

"I've been thinking," Lourdes says, studying me, "that maybe your whole descent into madness —"

"Thank you for that."

"— isn't just about Toby's death. I know how much you loved him. Believe me, I know. But maybe the way you responded was really a long-overdue reaction to all sorts of things. I mean, your mom, obviously. But more than that, too. You made your life so small and controlled for so many years — the same apartment, the same job, the same doomed relationships . . . maybe you were bound to blow up. And you're always helping other people, shifting the focus off yourself." She shakes her head. "You need to deal with your shit. You can only avoid your own issues for so long before they're forced to bite you in the ass for a little attention."

She's right, of course. I'm devastated by Toby's death, but I also know that losing him has made a host of other anxieties that I've been downplaying for years suddenly swell large, like a long-dry sponge dropped into water.

"I always tell my patients that grief is cumulative," I say to Lourdes. "But maybe what I should really say is 'Deal with your shit or it's gonna bite you in the ass.' "

Lourdes shrugs. "That's why I prefer to work with plants. They don't mind a few well-placed curse words."

CHAPTER 10

Two days later, after my last session of the day, I walk Giselle over to a three-story apartment building on the stretch of Carl Street that runs west out of Cole Valley. Once I realized that Seymour's foster family lived within walking distance, I'd told Anya that I would go with her to photograph him.

"I'm so glad to hear Rosie is doing okay," I tell Anya when she meets us in front of the building. "She came home from the hospital this morning?"

Anya swallows, nodding. The strap of her bag presses a harsh line into the shoulder of her filthy, ill-fitting coat.

I look up at the overcast sky. "Not great photo-taking weather, is it?"

Anya shrugs. She still looks as though she hasn't showered in days, but she seems to be maintaining a fixed level of grease, so I figure this means she must be bathing on occasion. "Fog isn't so bad," she tells me.

"It's actually better than bright sun." She reaches down to pet Giselle. "Hello, Giselle. Didn't know if I'd see you today."

"I thought she might help relieve some of Seymour's anxiety."

"And because you're still training her," Anya says, looking up at me. "To be a therapy dog, right?"

"Yes," I say. "Right."

When we're buzzed into the building, Giselle leads the way upstairs, lowering her head to inhale the scent of each step. I hear a few muffled barks coming from somewhere in the building, but by the time we reach the apartment, they've stopped. A tall man with a kind, but tired expression answers the door.

"Maggie?" he asks.

"Hi," I say. "Grant, right? This is my friend, Anya. She's the photographer I was telling you about. And this is Giselle."

"Ah," Grant says, smiling down at Giselle, "glad to see you've brought in a professional dog model to teach Seymour some moves." He steps back into his living room and gestures for us to follow. The room is a direct contrast to the cold, dull day outside — warm and bright and inviting, with lemon-yellow walls and soft-looking pillows in shades of orange lining a low white couch.

"Can I get you guys anything? Some coffee, maybe?" Grant asks.

Anya and I shake our heads. "We're fine, thanks," I say. "Everyone at SuperMutt is so appreciative of how patient you and Chip have been about this whole Seymour situation. I understand he hasn't made it easy for you."

Grant smiles sadly. "It just about kills us to have to send Seymour packing before he finds his forever home. I know he's bounced around between a lot of foster families, and we really thought we'd be the ones to keep him until he was adopted. This has never happened to us before." He shakes his head. "We're both consultants, and when we're staffed we work pretty horrendous hours — we decided a few years ago that it wouldn't be fair to have a dog of our own at this point in our careers. That's why we work with SuperMutt to foster dogs in between cases." He lowers his voice, presumably so that Seymour — *Where is Seymour anyway?* — doesn't hear him. "Seymour has been with us a lot longer than we anticipated — a lot longer than any other dog we've fostered. Chip and I are both staffed on cases again now, and we aren't around for him as much as we should be."

"I understand completely —" I say, but

Grant is looking more apologetic than ever.

"I hope it doesn't seem like I'm quitting on him," he says. "I really believe Seymour would be better off with someone who can be home more and keep a closer eye on him. Maybe devote a little more time to his training, building his confidence. He's a sweet dog . . ." Grant finally trails off, giving a small, resigned shrug. "I'm just really sorry it's come to this."

"There's absolutely no need to apologize." Sybil has told me that Grant and his husband have fostered five dogs for Super-Mutt so far, always paying for the dogs' veterinary appointments and various immunizations out of their own pockets instead of billing the rescue organization like most foster families. They're good, responsible people who have simply reached their wits' end. "Sybil and I are so grateful for everything you and Chip have done. You're both practically saints in my book. It must be incredibly difficult fostering dog after dog, getting accustomed to each new personality. It's a ton of work. And sometimes it's just a bad match — or life gets in the way. Really, we understand. You guys have gone above and beyond for Seymour — for all the dogs you've helped."

Grant looks relieved. "Yes, well. We're

happy to do it. We love dogs. I said that already, didn't I?" He laughs nervously.

"This is for the best," Anya says. "We're going to get Seymour out of here as soon as we can, and then you can move on to your next foster when you're ready."

I'm surprised by Anya's words and shoot her a grateful smile. "Besides," I add, "what are you going to do, sell your apartment and move because your foster dog doesn't like trains? It makes a lot more sense to move the dog than the people." I look around the room. "Where is Seymour, anyway?"

Grant gestures toward the couch. "His hiding spot."

And then I see his sweet, anxious face peering around a corner of the couch. I feel like I know him already — it's like seeing an old friend. A warm feeling blooms in my chest. I chalk this up to having stared so often at his photo on the website.

Giselle has caught sight of Seymour, too. She releases an excited whimper and tugs at the leash.

"Oh, hello, Seymour," I say softly. I hand Giselle's leash to Anya and pull a couple of biscuits from my pocket. I give one to Giselle and then walk toward Seymour. When I'm still a few feet away from him, I kneel on the floor and hold out the biscuit. I find I'm holding my breath, unsure how he'll respond, and I'm relieved when he folds his huge, drooping ears back against his head and pads over to me, tail wagging, head hanging low. He looks up at me from the tops of his big, brown, uncertain eyes. "Go ahead," I tell him, moving the biscuit closer. "It's for you."

Without breaking eye contact with me, Seymour takes the biscuit and holds it between his teeth on one side of his mouth so that half of the treat sticks out limply from between his lips. He looks like he belongs in that painting of dogs playing poker, a cigar hanging from his mouth.

"Aren't you going to eat it?" I ask, smiling.

But he just holds the biscuit there and wags his tail some more. He makes a sort of low sound, like a friendly growl. Really, more like a purr. Grant, Anya, and I all laugh.

"He does that," Grant says. "Chip thinks he's part golden, part basset, and part cat."

"Are you part cat?" I ask Seymour. His eyebrows rise and shift together, giving him a perturbed look. I stroke his head and then hold his huge ears back with both of my hands. Without his ears, his face looks just like a golden retriever's, all devotion and loyalty and trust. He practically oozes dignity. *How do dogs do that?* I look into his big brown eyes and feel that soft, melted-butter feeling spread through my chest again.

What happened to you to make you so scared? Seymour is still holding the biscuit, but now he rests his velvety muzzle on my wrist. Had someone hurt him? Who could do that to a dog? The thought turns my stomach. Seymour's steady breath is warm on my forearm. It's as much of an answer as I'll ever get.

"Oh," I say, "you are sweet, aren't you?" I turn back toward Anya and Grant, reluctantly taking my eyes off Seymour, and try to focus my thoughts. "We really just have to get people out here to see him. How could you resist this face? That photo of him doesn't do him any justice at all."

"Well, we're going to change that," Anya says decisively.

Giselle is straining against her leash now, eager to get a closer inspection of Seymour under way. "Let's see how they do," I say.

Anya walks Giselle over. Seymour tolerates her invasive sniffing with quiet poise, holding his head rigid, his tail wagging slowly, stiffly, and his big ears pressed back against his head in submission. He's half Giselle's height and she has to lie down on her elbows to sniff under him. When she stands, satisfied, she snorts into one of his ears.

"Don't make fun of him, Giselle," I say, laughing. Seymour shakes out his fur and his ears flop loudly against his head. "Even if it's tough," I add. I scratch under Seymour's chin and he gazes at me contentedly, the anxiety ebbing from his eyes.

I rock back on my heels and stand. As I do, a train rumbles by outside. Seymour immediately spins around and scrambles back behind the couch, his nails scratching against the dark wood floor.

"It's okay, Seymour," Grant calls softly. "It's just a train."

I don't say anything.

A moment later, once the train has passed, Seymour peeks out at us. He is trembling. He looks up at me as if he's waiting for an explanation for the monstrous noise that keeps torturing him.

"It's all right," I say. "Come here. It's gone now."

When Seymour takes a few cautious steps toward me I see he's left a little puddle on the floor behind him. Grant is already walking over with a roll of paper towels and a bottle of disinfectant spray. He clearly keeps both close-at-hand.

"Let me do that," I offer.

He waves me away, crouching down to wipe up the puddle. "We tried to push the couch back so he didn't have a hiding place anymore, but then he started running into our bedroom and peeing on the carpet every time a train passed. This seemed the lesser of two evils. Besides, he's attached to this little hiding spot. It seemed cruel to take it away from him."

"Where do you think he'll be more comfortable while we take the pictures?" I ask. "Here or outside?"

"Probably here. You could try outside, but I have to warn you he's pretty tough to walk. Skittish as a spooked horse."

"I think we should try," Anya says. "Natural light is always best for photos."

My vote would have been to stay inside, but since the only reason we're here is to try to get a good photo of Seymour to use on the website, and since this whole situation seems to have brought out some glint of Anya's more personable, outgoing self, I nod my agreement.

While Grant digs a leash out of a drawer, Seymour sits close beside me, leaning against my leg. "Better watch out," Anya says. "He looks smitten."

You've got the wrong girl, buddy, I think, and stand so that Seymour has to shift his weight away from me. I'm more determined than ever to get Seymour to bond with Anya. Giselle's leash is loose on the ground, so I pick it up and wrap it tightly around my hand. When Grant returns with Seymour's, he holds it out to me but I gesture for him to give it to Anya.

"Keep a close eye on him," Grant says. "He's faster than he looks. We've tried all sorts of collars and harnesses on him, but because of his, er, unique shape and wiggliness, he's managed to get out of all of them." He reaches down to lift Seymour's chin so that they look right at each other. "Keep your chin up, little man." I can see that Grant is attached to the dog and I have a brief flicker of hope that perhaps this will turn out to be Seymour's forever home after all. But then Grant straightens and I can hear the relief in his voice when he says, "Actually, I'm glad you're taking him out. Maybe a walk with an expert will do him good. The faster he gets over his leash issues, the faster he'll find a family willing to take him in, right?"

"Oh, I'm no expert," I say quickly. Grant looks disappointed. "But don't worry, we're going to find Seymour the right fit soon."

Sure enough, Seymour's whole body seems to wilt, becoming as droopy as his huge ears by the time we reach the bottom of the hall staircase. When I open the door at the bottom of the staircase, revealing cars whizzing by in the street, Seymour balks. He sits on his haunches, trembling. Anya tries to give him a tug, but he begins to swing his head from side to side, nearly pulling back out of his collar.

I swap leashes with Anya so that she's holding Giselle's and I'm holding Seymour's. Then I kneel down in front of him for a little pep talk. I smooth back his ears a few times. He looks deep into my eyes and then looks away. Into my eyes, then away. I put my hands on his shoulders.

"What are you going to do, stay inside for the rest of your life?" I ask him. It figures that I would somehow find the world's only agoraphobic dog. "Exposure therapy," I advise him softly, stroking his ears. "That's the ticket. *Desensitization.*"

Seymour cocks his head and whimpers.

"What are you telling him?" Anya asks.

"Psych talk," I say, straightening. "It's confidential." I pull another biscuit from my pocket and step backward through the door so that I'm standing on the sidewalk.

Seymour slinks toward me so reluctantly that I can practically hear him grumbling about his own damn canine impulses, his inability to reject food. He takes the biscuit from me. I pass his leash and a few biscuits to Anya and she hands me Giselle's leash.

Seymour isn't much better once we finally get him moving. He darts from one edge of the sidewalk to the other, his long fuzzy tail tucked between his legs. Each time a car passes, he rears back, terrified, whipping his head around to look at the offending vehicle, his body quivering, the whites of his eyes widening. I stick close to his side, worried he's going to yank his head right out of his collar and run away.

"Poor boy," Anya murmurs. "I'm tempted to pick him up."

I look from Seymour's chunky, solid body to Anya's rail-thin one. "I'm not sure you could. Besides, he has to learn to walk outside at some point, right?" The irony of my words does not elude me. I look away from Anya, feeling my face warm, and search the sky above the line of houses across the street until I see Sutro Tower high up on the hill in the distance.

Anya doesn't respond. After a couple of blocks of thrashing and near escapes, Seymour falls into an uncertain pace beside

Giselle. When Giselle stops to pee, Seymour hurries to do so, too, and then Giselle covers his puddle with another of her own. Seymour is oblivious to the offense, and pads quickly after her when she's done. His expression relaxes somewhat once he's plastered himself to her side.

"I think he has a crush on her," I say.

"Is there any chance Giselle's owners would take him in?"

I consider this possibility again, but still can't see a way to ask Lourdes without her pushing me to adopt him myself. "I don't think so."

Anya scans the streets in search of an inviting backdrop for a new photo. I focus my attention on the dogs, smiling at the way Seymour's short legs move twice as frequently as Giselle's long ones, and feel a hint of the peaceful happiness that always overtakes me when I see two dogs enjoying each other's company. I glance over at Anya and see that she, too, is smiling. Seeing Anya smile is practically equivalent to spotting a unicorn. *I defy anyone to tell me dogs aren't magic.*

"Do you think we could include Giselle in the photo?" Anya asks. "Seymour seems so much more relaxed with her."

I shrug. "I don't see why not. I'll just make

it clear in the description that he's up for adoption and she isn't. Who knows, maybe it will even trick a poodle fan into giving a mutt like Seymour a moment's consideration."

Anya pulls her camera from her bag and fiddles with it, swapping one lens for another. She shoots rapid-fire, a bunch of shots of the dogs walking together. Then we convince them to sit side by side in front of a large flower box full of bright pink geraniums by the entryway of a well-kept Craftsman home. I tie their leashes to the house's staircase railing.

Anya pulls a ziplock full of bacon from her bag, gives each dog a small piece, and then hands the bag to me. "I thought you could hold this above my head while I shoot. If a bag of bacon doesn't snag a dog's attention, nothing will."

"Good thinking." She crouches down to take the photos and I wave the bag over her head. "Very romantic," I say, admiring the scene. Seymour and Giselle both look up eagerly at the bacon, their tails trembling with anticipation. After a few minutes, Anya holds the camera toward me so I can see its screen. She clicks through a few of the photos she's just taken. Seymour and Giselle are so mismatched that the sight of them together is completely endearing, quirkily charming, and I'm relieved to see that Seymour's gaze is softer than it was in his earlier photo.

"These are great, Anya. I can't thank you enough."

Anya takes the camera back. "Get ready for your forever home, Seymour."

Giselle and Seymour jump up from their spot in front of the flower box to retrieve their bacon slices. I can't resist bending down to give Seymour a quick hug.

"What a good, brave boy you are!" I say.

Behind me, I hear the click of Anya's camera. I straighten, and as I do a train rumbles down Carl Street, a block and a half away. Suddenly Seymour's eyes go round and white with terror. He scrambles sideways away from us, and the leash, still tied to the house's banister, pulls taut. When he rears, whipping his head back and forth, I can see his collar slipping forward on his neck toward his ears.

"Seymour," I say, holding out my hands toward him. My pulse is thundering but I try to keep my voice soothing and low. "It's okay. You're okay, buddy."

I fumble in the bag for another piece of bacon, but it's too late, Seymour yanks his head right out of his collar. For one ever-so-brief second our eyes lock.

Don't run! The words don't have time to travel from my brain to my mouth before he has spun around and is racing down the sidewalk away from me.

The fear for Seymour's safety should send me running after him. It should be enough to push all of my own anxiety aside.

But it isn't.

I just stand there, my heart thrashing around like a wild animal trapped in a cage.

Giselle strains against her leash, whining, as Anya sprints after Seymour. A group of school kids rounds the corner at the end of the block, startling Seymour. He turns, scrambling, running toward the busy street. Anya springs off her feet, flies through the air, and grabs him, wrapping her skinny arms around his belly. He thrashes back and forth but she holds him tight. I take a deep breath. Anya murmurs to Seymour and after a moment he settles down and turns his head to lick her cheek.

I, for one, still haven't moved. Seymour's leash and collar are lying on the ground a few feet from me, but I can't take a step. Giselle is whimpering, her gaze darting back and forth from me to Anya and Seymour.

When Anya looks toward me, I can see the questioning look on her face even from a block away. After a beat of time, she stands, hoisting Seymour into her arms. Finally, as she's approaching, enough moisture returns to my throat that I'm able to hoarsely thank her. I can feel her eyes on me as I fumble to untie the dogs' leashes from the stair railing, my fingers trembling.

"We just have to teach you to walk, that's all," I hear Anya murmur behind me. "Oldest trick in the book."

I can only hope that she's talking to the dog.

CHAPTER 11

It's eight o'clock at night, and despite two glasses of wine and the hypnotic crackling of the fire, I still feel shaken by Seymour's near escape this afternoon — and my own reaction as I watched it unfold. I keep thinking of the pure, animal panic I'd seen in his eyes when he looked at me for a beat of time before spinning around and racing away, and how I'd done nothing to attempt to soothe him. What did he see in my eyes when he looked at me in that moment? Dogs are intuitive enough that he probably didn't even need to look at me to sense what I was feeling — an opaque sort of anxiety that only reinforced his own fears.

I've spent the last hour looking online for information on how to help an anxious dog, and even if I hadn't already made up my mind about not taking Seymour myself, everything I've read is further proof that we would not make a good match. I'm not surprised to learn that people and dogs are pretty similar when it comes to overcoming their phobias.

For fearful, anxious dogs, the ASPCA's website recommends "systematic desensitization and counterconditioning," a course of action that is, of course, familiar to me. Desensitization, for a dog who is afraid of city noises and walks like Seymour, would involve taking shorter, quieter walks in less busy areas, slowly building up to more populated streets, avoiding anxiety triggers, and making each walk as pleasant and uneventful as possible.

I think back to my first day of walks with Giselle nearly two weeks earlier, how I'd started with a blink-and-you'd-miss-it walk to the corner and back, taking progressively bolder "baby steps" on each outing. Of course, I haven't done a very good job of avoiding one of my anxiety triggers — heights — which might explain why I'm still not totally comfortable being outside even though I've made considerable headway. But I live in San Francisco now; heights aren't exactly avoidable. I hope I'm ripping off the Band-Aid — less systematic desensitization than shock exposure therapy.

The counterconditioning part of the ASPCA's recommendation is something

I've thought less about when it comes to my own treatment plan. The idea, according to the website, is to retrain, or recondition, the dog's mind so it associates a once-feared act with something good rather than something bad. With dogs, the best way to do this is using food — if every time a dog goes for a walk on a city street he gets a special treat, over time he will be reconditioned to associate the walk and the noises of the city with feelings of satisfaction and joy.

Maybe I should start hiding wine at the top of these parks Anya keeps taking us to.

Unfortunately, I'm pretty sure alcohol isn't the healthiest counterconditioning incentive for humans.

As I consider my own walks more, I realize that I do have something that is serving a similar purpose as a special treat would for a dog — helping Anya. Even though she isn't a patient, experiencing our relationship grow, the way she is opening up to me, telling me more about herself than I ever would have guessed she would have been willing to share during our one and only disaster of a counseling session, watching her pick up a camera again, encourages me to keep pushing open that sidewalk gate. I'm learning to associate my walks with something positive because I'm able witness the way Anya is slowly, but undeniably, improving. Anya's improvement is my biscuit.

I wish I could ask Grant and Chip to give Seymour a special treat every time the train passes. I can't imagine it would take long before Seymour would start thinking train equals food (and bonus: positive attention!). But it doesn't seem fair to ask Grant and Chip to undertake an extensive desensitization program for a dog that has already caused them so much trouble. Considering their work schedules and the unfortunate fact that Seymour frequently relieves himself behind the couch, it's a wonder the dog gets any walks at all. Besides, I wouldn't want to put any more strain on them and possibly risk their deciding that fostering dogs just isn't their thing. SuperMutt needs foster families like them.

My own work schedule, on the other hand, is light enough that I could probably take Seymour out for daily walks myself. Anya's schedule is even less full than mine and I wonder if I could wrangle her into helping me spearhead Seymour's ASPCA-recommended systematic desensitization and counterconditioning program. It seems to me that she could easily look for Billy as she walks Seymour — and maybe along the way she'll decide Seymour is irresistible and would be better off living with her and Rosie away from the rumble of the train.

I'm still clicking through various animal behaviorism and training websites, researching and plotting, when I'm startled by a knock on my door. I flick on the outdoor light and peer through the eyehole. Henry Ravenhurst is standing on my doorstep.

I glance over my shoulder at the state of my apartment and am glad to see that it looks innocuously neat — there's nothing, for example, that yells "Crazy Lady Who Only Goes Outside with a Dog" or, maybe worse, "Crazy Lady Who Only Goes Outside to Visit Your Sister." And luckily I haven't changed into my pajamas yet; I'm still wearing the jeans and blue sweater I'd worn during my outing with Anya earlier in the day. I walk my wineglass to the kitchen, take a quick, final swig for courage, and place it in the sink. Then I open the front door.

"Hey, Maggie," Henry says. "I'm sorry to drop by so late, and unannounced."

"It's fine. Is everything okay?"

"Yes," Henry says, playing with the strap of the messenger bag that cuts across his chest. "Yes," he says again.

"Would you like to come in?"

He hesitates, his eyes dropping down to my bare feet. My toenails, I realize, are each painted a different color — the result of a recent bout of insomnia.

"Well, you better decide one way or the other," I say. "It appears some of my toes are turning blue."

Henry smiles. "I won't take up too much of your time."

I wave him inside and shut the door behind him. "Have a seat. Can I get you something to drink?"

Henry sits in the yellow armchair. "Actually," he says, sounding a bit sheepish, "I brought this." He unzips his bag and pulls out a bottle of wine.

"Well, that's terribly selfish. Did you bring anything for me?"

Henry looks confused. Then he laughs. "I suppose I could share," he says. "If you're thirsty."

I take a few moments longer than necessary rifling through a kitchen drawer for the wine opener, trying to gather my thoughts. Other than Lourdes, Leo, and my patients, Henry is the only person I've invited into my apartment since I moved in. My pulse quickens. I'm not anxious, though; I'm nervous. It's an important distinction. I take a deep breath and head back into the living room with the opener and two glasses.

"So," I say, setting the glasses in front of him on the coffee table and handing him the opener, "to what do I owe this pleasure?"

Henry's sheepish look returns as I settle into the couch across from him. "The wine is an apology," he says, maneuvering the cork out with the opener. He pours the dark red wine into the glasses and passes one to me. "And a thank-you. Now that I think of it, maybe I should have brought two bottles."

We clink our glasses together. The wine is rich and warming, perfect for a foggy night like this one, and I feel it in my head immediately. I remind myself that it's my third glass; I'll have to be careful.

"One bottle is plenty," I tell Henry. "A bottle of wine is like the word 'aloha,' it can mean several things at once. Hello, good-bye . . ." I trail off. The other thing "aloha" means, of course, is "I love you." *Shit,* I think. *I might already be drunk.*

"Slow down, Maggie," he says, his eyes full of good humor. "We barely know each other."

I take another sip of wine as I recover from my embarrassment. "So tell me more about this apology."

Henry nods. "It's overdue, really. I didn't get a chance to say anything after that walk to Kite Hill because we had to race off to the hospital —"

"I was so glad to hear from Anya that Rosie is doing better."

"Well, she's out of the hospital at least. I hope Anya doesn't think that means she's in the clear, though." He shakes his head. "But I'm not here to talk about Rosie. I just wanted you to know that I saw how Anya responded to you during that walk. She really does think of you as a friend. She didn't want to see a therapist, and you could have left it at that. You could have just written her off. But you didn't. You found another way to help her, and you won't even accept payment for it." He looks down, studying his hands. "I'm ashamed of the way I acted when we first met. So I want to apologize."

"You were only trying to protect Anya. She's lucky to have you in her life, looking out for her."

"Well, now I realize that she's lucky to have *you* in her life. I'm sorry I didn't see it sooner. Anya told me that she went with you to take photos of that dog. Apparently, after she left you, she spent the rest of the day working on her computer. Not wandering around the city looking for Billy, not lying in bed and staring at the ceiling — working on those photos. Rosie's nurse said Anya even came downstairs at one point to make a grilled cheese sandwich. When I went over there tonight to check on Rosie, I saw the empty plate in Anya's room. She'd eaten it. The whole sandwich."

"And she survived?"

Henry laughs. "Yes, she ate something that she cooked, and lived to tell about it." His voice softens. "Really though, I'm just so relieved that she's starting to take care of herself. And that she's using her camera again . . . Thank you."

"She's the one doing me a favor with the photos."

He gives me a look. *"Maggie."*

"Okay," I say, smiling. "You're welcome. And apology accepted. Now can I ask you something?"

"Of course."

"Did you buy her that camera?"

He nods. "For her fourteenth birthday. Did she tell you?"

"No, but I had a feeling. Billy, the camera . . . you seem to anticipate your sister's needs."

"Except in your case. I didn't realize she

needed a friend."

"You found me; you reached out to me. I wouldn't be in Anya's life if it weren't for you. I'd say you're three-for-three."

Henry smiles. He sits back in the armchair and turns his head from side to side, looking around the living room. "Where's Giselle?"

"Upstairs. She's not mine — I said that, didn't I? She belongs to my friend Lourdes, who lives upstairs. I rent this apartment from Lourdes and her husband, Leo."

"You mentioned it, but I thought maybe you were just saying it."

"Why would you think that?"

"I just figured you must love dogs and probably have one of your own. How else could you summon the empathy I imagine you need to do a job like yours? I figured Giselle was yours and maybe you worried that it was hard for your patients to see you with your very-much-alive dog. I thought maybe you just told patients she didn't belong to you so they wouldn't feel . . . envious."

"You've been thinking about this a lot."

"Four, five hours a day, tops."

"Ah. Well, no, Giselle really isn't mine. In fact, if we listen closely, we can probably hear her running around upstairs."

We're both silent, but no sounds drift down from upstairs. The fire cracks. Henry cocks an eyebrow. "Your story is full of holes."

I laugh. "I have a secret," I say, "but this isn't it." Flustered, I look down into my wineglass. *Why did I say that?*

Henry just smiles. He has a nice smile; it floods his serious face with light. "Interesting. I'll file that little tidbit away for further dissection later." He moves to top off my glass with more wine but I hold my hand over it.

"Thanks, but I think I've had enough. I have an early appointment with a patient in the morning."

"Oh." He looks embarrassed. "I should go."

"There's no rush," I tell him. I hold up my glass and the bit of wine left in it catches the light of the fire. "Let's at least finish our glasses."

He nods and shifts back in his seat again. "So, what brought you to San Francisco? When I spoke with your old boss at the hospital, he sounded like he was still disappointed that you left."

"Oh, I was overdue for a change. I'd been in Philadelphia my whole life, and had held that same counseling position at the hospital for years. I'd been toying with the idea of starting my own practice and really wanted to focus on pet bereavement. And my friend Lourdes was giving me the hard sell to move out here and rent this apartment . . . and . . ." I hesitate. "I was in a relationship with a guy who — well, a relationship that had run its course. It seemed like a good time for a fresh start."

"Job dissatisfaction, great apartment across the country becomes available, relationship crumbles . . . sounds like the perfect storm."

I smile. "The winds of change blew me all the way to San Francisco." I start to take a sip of wine, then realize that if I do, I'll be finishing off the last bit and Henry might take it as his cue to leave. I lower the glass without drinking. "Well, you've seen my résumé and interrogated my former bosses . . . is it too soon to ask what do *you* do?"

Henry laughs. "Seems a bit nosy, but I suppose I can oblige. I'm a physician by training but I haven't practiced medicine in a few years. I've been working with a partner — an engineer — to develop a new type of medical device for patients with heart disease. A group of investors is funding our work, and we're about to begin a trial at a cardiovascular center in Los Angeles."

"Hence the upcoming move." I realize we're treading into troubled waters here, and hope I don't sound judgmental again.

Henry seems unfazed — he's either forgotten or forgiven how I'd chided him for leaving his sister during such a difficult period. "The timing is terrible on a personal level, but I have to oversee the trial. Our ideas . . . we really do think they could revolutionize cardiac patient care."

Maybe it's the wine making my thoughts a bit soggy, but as I listen to Henry it occurs to me that he and I have the same professional impulse — we see a wounded heart and want to fix it. He looks down at his wineglass, empty now, and then at mine. I smile, lift my glass, and take the final sip.

"Well," Henry says, "I suppose I should get going." We stand and walk toward the door together. "How about I call first next time?"

I'm not exactly clear on what he means, but I smile and nod.

"Good." He steps outside, then turns back toward me. "Aloha, Maggie Brennan."

"Good night," I say. He heads up the path and I shut the door behind him.

Much later, as I'm closing the shades in my bedroom, I catch sight of myself in the

206

reflection of the dark window and realize
that I'm still smiling.

CHAPTER 12

The photos that Anya took of Seymour and Giselle turn out to be every bit as wonderful as I'd hoped. In the best of the bunch, his golden coat glows richly and his mouth is open, midpant, so that he looks like he's grinning up at the camera, revealing his pink tongue and a neat row of bright white teeth. His big, black nose, wet with good health, nearly balances out his long ears. He looks playful and happy. There's still a hint of anxiety lingering in his honey-brown eyes, but it gives him a depth of personality that I hope is more endearing than worrying. Giselle, even in her pristine breed-standard glory, actually seems a bit overshadowed by Seymour, which serves our purposes well. Seymour is the star.

I upload the new photo to the SuperMutt website and tweak Seymour's bio for the umpteenth time. I don't want to misrepresent him; it would be completely beside the point and probably harmful to the poor guy if he ended up in a new home only to be moved once again because I had not been forthright about his issues with loud noises and leashes. But I decide there are ways to reveal Seymour's flaws while focusing on his many positives — his sweet nature, the trust in his eyes, how well he gets along with other dogs.

I do some research on basset hounds and golden retrievers and incorporate bits of each breed's temperament in Seymour's description. I even learn that his particular crossbreed — basset retrievers — is highly sought by those looking for the temperament of a golden in a smaller, potentially lower-energy package.

Well, what do you know, I think as I click through pictures of basset retrievers on my laptop, *goofy-looking Seymour is actually a "designer" dog in the vein of Labradoodles and cockapoos.* I stick that surprise bit of information in his description, too, and also add a little note to make it clear that Seymour is up for adoption, but the poodle in the photo is not.

I e-mail Sybil to let her know that I've updated Seymour's photo and description on the website. I think Saints Grant and Chip are willing to foster him a bit longer, I write, and I really think we'll get some new interest in him soon. I let her know about a few final auction items I've secured for the Super-Mutt fund-raiser. The gala is three weeks away, and I know she's busy pulling together all of the final details for the event.

As usual, Sybil replies immediately. That photo is perfect! What a stroke of luck to find a photographer who is not only talented but also clearly "gets" dogs — and is willing to work for free! Do you think your friend Anya would be willing to photograph the dogs that we'll have up for auction at the event? I'm thinking we could blow them up (maybe black-and-white?) and hang them around the cocktail party space. We would of course give Anya credit for the photos and include her contact information or anything about her business that she'd like to share — I bet she'll get a ton of interest. It's not in the budget to pay her at the moment, but maybe she'd be willing to do the work in exchange for the fantastic publicity? Maybe she'd even want to auction off a photo shoot? Or am I pushing my luck? You know me, Maggie . . . I get greedy when it comes to the dogs!

It's a great idea on many levels — great for SuperMutt, and great for Anya, too. I e-mail Sybil right back to let her know that I'll ask Anya about the additional work.

The sooner the better, Sybil responds. The

clock is ticking. It won't be long before we're toasting ourselves to a job well done. Couldn't do this without you, Maggie, and I can't wait to finally meet in person!

"Why wouldn't you go?" Lourdes asks when I tell her about the SuperMutt fund-raiser. "I thought the curtain fell on *The Agoraphobic Therapist.*"

I picture myself trapped below the heavy velvet folds of a stage curtain. "It did," I say. "Or it's in the process of falling. But this is different. You know I've never liked parties."

Lourdes rolls her eyes. "Yeah, but whenever I dragged you to one in college, you had fun. Admit it. You should go to the fund-raiser. Maybe you'll meet someone."

"How am I supposed to start dating again when I still can't walk outside without your poodle glued to my hip?" Giselle, smart girl, trots over to where we're sitting at the kitchen table and puts her head in my lap.

"Where there's a will there's a way."

Leo is out with some friends from work, so I'd had dinner with Lourdes and the kids and then helped her put them to bed. Now we're sitting at the kitchen table doing what we do best: working our way through a bottle of red wine and a bowl of spicy garlic-

and-Parmesan popcorn. I'd invented the popcorn recipe when we were in college, and over the years it had become our happy place in food form.

Lourdes brightens. "If you don't want to go to the party, will you at least let me set you up with one of Leo's friends? We could have him over for dinner — a double date! You wouldn't even have to leave home. Problem solved. Now that you're doing better, I really think you should start dating. But you should meet a lot of guys. Don't get serious until you find one you're sure you actually like this time. Don't jump into anything."

"What do you mean, 'one I actually like this time'? I liked John."

"Sure, you *liked* John. And you liked Rich and Simon and . . . who was the guy before him?"

"Another Rich. Rich the First."

"Right. Rich the First. He was likable, too."

I throw a piece of popcorn into the air and catch it in my mouth. "This is a problem because . . ."

Lourdes pulls a face. "You *know* why this is a problem. I've been telling you this since college. Just because you like a guy doesn't mean you should date him for years on end.

Like isn't love."

"I loved all of them, too. I liked them *and* I loved them."

"Rich? You loved Rich?"

"Which one?" I shake my head. "It doesn't matter. I loved both Riches."

"Okay, but even love isn't always *love*. You need to start cutting your losses earlier. These relationships you find yourself in drag on and on. It's like watching some boring French movie that you know is never going to actually go anywhere — it's all talking, talking, talking and jokes you feel obligated to laugh at just so you can be sure you're still alive."

I grin. "Tell me how you really feel." As usual, Lourdes's assessment of my love life is pretty accurate; I have a history of sticking with relationships that aren't likely to go anywhere. Lourdes thinks dating is like driving, that if you're alert and conscientious you can see the "Dead End" sign in plenty of time to turn off the road and take another route. Unfortunately, I seem to be one of those daters who get caught up in the motions of a relationship, rocked into complacency by pleasant scenery and a warm seat. *Asleep at the wheel,* Lourdes calls it. And I'll give her this — my relationships with men do all seem to end with a crash.

"I mean, take John, for example," Lourdes continues, on a roll now. "You told me a month into dating him that you knew you weren't going to be with him long term. And then you stayed with him eight more months! You're not a dog. You don't have to be loyal to someone just because he buys you dinner."

"I know, I know," I say. "You're right."

Lourdes does an exaggerated mouth drop. "I'm sorry, what did you say? I think this wine is affecting my hearing."

"You're right!" I repeat in a sort of stage whisper, cupping my hands around my mouth as though I'm yelling. I don't want to wake the kids.

Lourdes takes a satisfied sip of wine, watching me over the rim of her glass. She sets the glass down, her eyes narrowing. "Wait a minute . . ." She presses her elbows onto the table, leaning toward me. "Holy shit! Have you *already* met someone?"

For some reason I think of the way Henry's shirts fit him — close but not tight. I think of the line of his chin, how sometimes there is stubble there, and sometimes it is clean. How I can't decide which I like better. He looks like someone who cares about his looks but doesn't obsess over them. I'd never realized it before, but it turns out that I find the absence of vanity very sexy.

"You caught me, Lourdes," I say. "Vern and I have finally succumbed to an attraction that's been building for months."

Giselle, fed up with my lack of focus and languid pets, sighs and heads for her dog bed.

Lourdes looks at me from the corner of her eye. "Who is Vern?"

"Vern! Vern. Our mailman. He prefers 'mail carrier,' actually. He's quite evolved. And you know I'm a sucker for a man in uniform."

Lourdes snorts. "Maggie. You are not allowed to hook up with our mailman. He's sixty years old!"

"He has the calves of a twenty-year-old triathlete."

"And a comb-over."

"Love's a funny thing."

"Okay," Lourdes says, "but when you're running your hands through Vern's two hairs, who are you *really* thinking about?"

I give up. There's no point in trying to keep anything from Lourdes, anyway. She always gets it out of me eventually. "It's nothing. It's silly. He's the brother of the woman I'm helping. Anya's brother Henry. It probably isn't even ethical. Nothing's going to happen."

Lourdes lofts her eyebrows. "Not ethical? I thought you said she isn't your patient."

"Well, she isn't. Technically. But we met in a patient-therapist context. It's complicated." I give a little shrug. I really don't think of Anya as a patient, not a *patient* patient, anyway, though admittedly she's not a *friend* friend either. "It would just be weird."

Lourdes takes a large gulp of wine, finishing it off, and then begins gesticulating with her empty glass. "Life is fucking weird, Maggie! If you like someone, date him! Chuck the fucking vitamins already! Get your hands dirty! Go outside! Fuck the fear! Wear a sundress in the rain! Catch the flu! Feel it all! Fuck the rules!"

"That's it," I say, reaching for her wineglass. "I'm cutting you off. I feel like I just walked into Andrew Dice Clay's fortune-cookie factory."

Later that night, I e-mail Grant and Sybil letting them know that I'd like to help Seymour work on his leash skills and anxiety issues with the hope that it will aid in getting him adopted. Grant e-mails back right away to let me know that he'll make me a spare key first thing in the morning and that I should feel free to pick Seymour up for walks anytime. His relief is practically palpable.

Next, I e-mail Anya and ask if she minds if I bring Seymour along on our daily walks. The walks I take with Anya won't be baby steps for Seymour either — they're often pretty long — but we usually wind up in a park, and I suspect Seymour will enjoy the open space and be considerably more comfortable with heights than I am.

If Seymour proves to be too much of a distraction, I write, I'll work with him another time.

I don't mind, Anya responds. That ball of nerves needs all the help he can get.

CHAPTER 13

I arrive at Grant and Chip's apartment with Giselle in tow and my pockets bulging with counterconditioning incentives. Giselle had eaten the last of Toby's biscuits, and I only had a few scoops of his boring old kibble left in my apartment, so I'd scoured Lourdes's kitchen for special treats. I have a bag of Giselle's organic peanut-butter-and-molasses cookies, some cold cuts sliced into strips, diced chicken nuggets that Lourdes keeps in her freezer for Portia and Gabby, and even a few bites of leftover salmon from a salad. I've brought double the amount I think I'll need so that I can give Giselle a treat each time I give Seymour one — it doesn't seem fair to only reward Seymour. Besides, Giselle has earned every goody I can offer her and then some.

Grant is clearly in a hurry to get to work and runs Seymour downstairs when I ring the doorbell. I immediately drop down to

218

Seymour's level and tell him what a good dog he is and ply him with a few of the fancy peanut butter treats. He's shaking a little, but wags his tail slowly. The whites of his eyes are only slightly visible, which I take as a good sign.

"Seriously," Grant says, handing me the extra key he has made. "Come by anytime for Seymour." It's amazing that after one meeting he's willing to give me a key to his apartment, but I know it's an indication of how hopeful he is that our walks will eventually deliver Seymour into the arms of a more suitable family. Plus, I suppose he can see that I'm a dog person, and in my experience dog people tend to give other dog people the benefit of the doubt.

I'm relieved when Giselle and Seymour and I turn off the block before a train passes. I steer us down some of the quieter Cole Valley streets on our way to Anya's house, and continually ply the dogs with meat and fish and peanut butter snacks. I can only hope that Seymour's stomach can handle the smorgasbord of snacks and he doesn't end up leaving a nasty surprise behind Grant's couch after I return him to their apartment. Both dogs are plastered to my sides, gazing up at me with such unwavering intensity that they occasionally trip over their own paws. They're not exactly demonstrating impressive leash skills, but at least Seymour is so focused on the food that he hardly seems to be aware of what else is happening around him. His ears give a little twitch, his eyes widening slightly, each time a car passes, but if I hand him a treat in the exact same moment, he keeps pace with me. And he doesn't once try to back out of his leash.

When we arrive at Anya's house, she's sitting out on the front steps and her face looks drawn. Giselle runs to her, tail wagging, and Seymour, I'm pleased to see, follows suit, but Anya only pets them for a moment before standing.

"What's the matter?" I ask.

"Rosie's sleeping in the living room. I didn't want the doorbell to wake her, so I thought I'd just wait outside."

"How's she doing?"

Anya blinks and looks away. "She hasn't really been the same since she got home from the hospital. She sleeps a lot."

"Her doctor says it's okay for her to be home?"

"As long as we have a nurse here full-time. June's been sleeping on a mat on the floor next to Rosie's bed."

A full-time nurse must be expensive. It's

no wonder that Henry is adamant about going to Los Angeles. "And how are you doing?" I ask. "How are you holding up?"

Now Anya's eyes brim with tears. She swipes at them with the back of her hand. "Like crap," she says, staring at the ground. "I feel like I'm losing everyone at once."

It's the kind of genuine, forthright, self-aware admission that she would never have made to me when we first met. Giselle nudges her thin snout below Anya's hand and Anya begins petting her again.

"I'm so sorry," I say. "Even though it might feel like you're alone, you're not. Henry is moving away, but he's not leaving your life. He'll always be here for you. You can count on him. And I'm sure your other brothers will support you as well. And I'm here for you, Anya. I'm not going anywhere. Unless you want me to."

"You're okay," Anya mumbles. Giselle starts wagging her tail faster, encouraged. "And we're going to find Billy soon. That will help."

I smile, but don't say anything.

Anya looks up, scanning the sidewalk behind me. "Henry is coming again today," she says. "He called yesterday to ask if he could join us." On the word "us" her eyes move to meet mine, and I immediately

221

wonder if he told her about visiting me at my apartment.

"That's nice of him. Maybe you two should go on your own." I don't want to intrude if Henry is trying to spend some quality time with his sister before he leaves for Los Angeles, but even as I suggest the idea I realize I'm hoping Anya will shoot it down.

"Nah," she says. "Here he is now."

We meet Henry halfway up the path. "Morning," he says, smiling at me. "Is it just me, or do you have an extra dog today?"

I tell him that Seymour is the dog that Anya photographed for SuperMutt. "I'm hoping if he gets more accustomed to city walks, it will increase his odds of being adopted."

"But," Henry says, kneeling down in front of Seymour and smoothing back his large ears, "who could say no to you? Just as you are?" Seymour's long pink tongue laps him on the side of his face and he stumbles backward, laughing.

I'm afraid I might be beaming at Henry now. I know I'm struggling to restrain myself from pulling him to his feet and kissing him. Instead, I ask, "Any chance your apartment in L.A. is dog-friendly?"

Henry stands and shakes his head, smiling sadly.

We've just turned onto the sidewalk when the door of the neighboring house opens and Huan steps outside. "Good morning!" he calls. "Can I come?"

Anya shrugs.

Henry nods, waving him over.

Huan's face breaks into a grin and he jogs toward us. He stops beside Anya, flicking his hair out of his eyes. He's wearing a black T-shirt with a logo of a skateboard on the chest, but the overall impression isn't that different than if he were wearing an oxford. There's something so polite and earnest and good-natured about the kid that it's hard to resist the impulse to reach out and ruffle his shaggy black hair.

"Let's go find Billy," he says in a determined voice. "I love that dog." He turns to me. "My parents never let me have any pets. My dad says he's allergic, but I don't believe him. I think he just thought a dog would distract me from school."

"Your dad's a jerk," Anya says.

Henry gives her a look. "Anya!"

Huan laughs. "It's okay. It's kind of true." Then his face flushes. "He's a *well-meaning* jerk."

Anya rolls her eyes. "I've been looking for

Billy for weeks. Why are you jumping on the bandwagon now, Huan?"

"Filter, Anya," Henry says quietly.

"What?"

"You don't need to say every single thought in your head."

"Are you advocating self-censorship?"

"Yes," Henry says. "But I'm calling it human decency."

Anya shrugs, but I can see she feels bad. Actually, when she glances toward Huan, she seems almost shy. "Fine. I would be positively delighted if you would join us, Huan. We're going to Tank Hill." She turns to me and holds out her palm. I try to give her Seymour's leash, hoping they'll do a little bonding, but she snatches Giselle's instead and strides off.

"Sweet," Huan says, hurrying after her. "I love Tank Hill." He falls into step at her side and Henry and I trail a few steps behind.

I realize it's the first time I've been outside without Giselle at my side. *Recondition!* I think, and begin plying Seymour with bite after bite of salmon in the hope that it will distract both of us from the fact that Giselle is getting farther ahead.

"I wanted to help you from the beginning," I hear Huan telling Anya. "But I didn't know you were letting people come with you."

Poor kid. He's probably been watching her set off on these walks for weeks, gathering his courage to ask if he can help her. The crush he has on her is as touching as it is painfully obvious.

"Kite Hill, Tank Hill . . . How many hills are there in this city?" I ask Henry, glad to have him nearby as another distraction.

"Technically seven, but those are the really big ones that don't even include Kite Hill and Tank Hill. All together, there has to be close to fifty."

I hurry to open the bag of cold cuts now that Seymour has made his way through the salmon. It's hard to believe that I used to enjoy the meditative aspect of walking. *Did you get lost?* John used to joke when Toby and I returned from a particularly long walk. *Nope,* I'd answer. *Just untangling the knots.* That's how walking with Toby always felt — like I was working loose the kinks of the day.

I miss that sense of freedom, and peace. *When I'm better,* I think, *I'm going to walk these hills every day — with or without a dog by my side.* I'm surprised by the sudden intensity of my desire to do this, to be myself again.

"He'll be happy when he sees where we're

going," Anya says, looking back toward Seymour, who, despite a belly full of food, still has tucked his tail securely between his legs. "Dogs love this park."

Tank Hill is only a couple of blocks from my apartment, but I'd never made it up there with Toby because Lourdes had warned me that he might not be up for the climb. We head up a series of steeply twisting streets, making our way out of Cole Valley, and eventually the street ends and a dirt path begins, winding up through the bare, grassy park. The air feels damp and heavy with fog. If I were in Philadelphia, I would have said it was about to rain; but in San Francisco, I've learned, you just never knew. By the time we reach the top of the hill, we'll probably have entered another microclimate entirely.

I have to admit that these strange, wild little parks that dot the city are sort of magical. One minute you're on a street lined with tight rows of homes, and the next minute you're on an open, exposed patch of grass and rock with views in one direction or another or sometimes, to my dismay, every direction at once. Tank Hill is a particularly hidden one, tucked into the slope that leads up to Twin Peaks, skirted by roads that seem to protect rather than reveal the secret park around which they curve.

"There used to be a water tank up here," Henry tells me when we reach the flat area at the top of the hill. "According to Rosie, it was dismantled in the fifties."

We're all huffing and puffing from the climb — even Seymour seems momentarily winded, plopping himself down at my feet and panting as the cool breeze ruffles his ears. He lifts his nose and sniffs the air, catching some scent.

"Look," Henry says, pointing over my shoulder.

The direction he points, out toward the city, is exactly where I've been trying not to look. I take a deep breath and turn slowly. We're standing on a huge, craggy, reddish boulder, the edge of which hangs over a hill so steep it isn't even visible from where we stand. I can see the wooded silhouette of Buena Vista Park to the east, the long, verdant expanse of Golden Gate Park to the northwest. A hard wind blows toward us from the coast, which has been devoured by the fog. The fog hides most of the Golden Gate Bridge, too, though pieces of the bridge suddenly appear and disappear as the silvery clouds race and tumble through the sky. The land on the other side of the bay is completely hidden behind a dreary expanse of sky.

Just as the vertigo threatens to knock out my knees and send me tumbling off the rock, I hear Henry's voice near my ear. "Do you see it?" He points toward the stretch of Cole Valley just below us. I peer down, but the city is growing blurry — partly from my own vision, and partly from the thickening stream of fog. My throat tightens, something in my chest twisting, pinching. I feel as though I might be sick.

One.

Two.

Henry is close behind me; he puts one hand on my upper arm and levels his other arm over my shoulder, still pointing down toward the city. "Right there," he says. "The white house four up from that intersection, across from the big palm tree."

I manage to gaze blearily along the line of his arm to his finger and beyond, down toward the streets of Cole Valley, which suddenly, miraculously, come into focus.

"Oh," I say, surprised.

It's Lourdes's house. My blue door is hidden, but there is the fence at the sidewalk, the small plot of green that surrounds the house, the garden boxes in the rear yard, the thread of gray that is the stone path. My little oasis. The house feels so snug, so private, from inside, but from up here I see that it's packed in with the neighboring houses, the crowded city of streets and sidewalks and houses and people and life pressing right up against it.

Way up here on Tank Hill, exposed to the elements, I realize, looking down, *is probably more of an oasis than my apartment.*

Still, one long look is plenty. I'd like to turn back around, but Henry has his hand on my arm and the pleasant feeling of its pressure and warmth is enough to keep me there a moment or two longer. Seymour lies at my feet, gazing out at the horizon. He doesn't look worried.

Henry and I both hear a muffled noise and turn at the same time. Anya and Huan are walking along a far edge of the scrubby hilltop. Anya cups her hands around her mouth and yells out over the city. Her words are lost in the wind, but I know she's calling for Billy. Huan stares at her. Anya yells a few more times, and then they head back to where we stand on the boulder.

"See anything?" I ask.

Anya shakes her head. She seems to have fallen into a dark mood, her eyes still roaming over the streets below. I decide it's as good a time as any to tell her about Sybil's idea for the fund-raiser; maybe it will cheer her up — or at least distract her.

"The woman who runs SuperMutt was really impressed with your photo of Seymour," I tell her, explaining that Sybil hopes she'll be willing to take photos of the dogs that will be auctioned off at the fund-raiser. "She wants to blow up all of the photos and decorate the event space with them. It should be good publicity."

"Publicity for what?"

"Welllll." I flash her a quick, guilty smile, feeling Henry and Huan's eyes on me, too. "I *might* have let Sybil believe that you were a professional photographer . . . but only because there's no reason you shouldn't be. I saw you in action myself — you were fantastic. Totally in control. You took an anxious, tough-to-photograph dog and made him look happy and confident. As Sybil says, you made Seymour look like a real SuperMutt.

"So, I've been thinking," I continue, "that you should consider starting your own business. And if you were interested in doing that, the gala would be a great way to get your name out there. Maybe you could even donate a pet photography session as an auction item — it would be good publicity, and I bet the referrals would roll in once people saw your work."

Henry and Huan are both smiling encouragingly at Anya, but the look on her face is harder to read, so I just keep talking. "If you'd like, I could help you set up a business website. That's really all you'd need to get started. You seem to have all the equipment already."

Anya kicks at the ground with one of her huge boots. "Yeah," she mumbles. "Maybe."

I decide to ignore her hesitation. "The only catch is that we'd need you to get started right away. The gala is three weeks away and there are six dogs that are being fostered around the city that need to be photographed."

Anya shrugs. "I have some time on my hands. It shouldn't be a problem."

"Anya, you're a lifesaver. Really. Sybil is going to be thrilled, and more importantly, you're going to make a huge impact in getting these dogs into their forever homes as quickly as possible." I glance at Huan, who is giving Anya one of his not-so-subtle looks of adoration. "It seemed like you were lugging a lot of equipment when you photographed Seymour, so if you have a friend who could help you carry stuff when you take the dogs' photos, you definitely should bring him along."

"I'll be fine," Anya says. "It's not that much."

"Well, also, it might be helpful to have someone who can assist in wrangling the dogs — some of them might be more energetic than Seymour. You know, someone who could squeeze a squeaky toy over your head so the dog actually looks toward the camera, that sort of thing . . ." I trail off, looking pointedly at Huan, willing him to speak up. *Come on! Here's your shot, lover boy!*

Huan catches my look and his eyes widen. "Oh! I, um . . . I could do that. I could help you, Anya."

"I really don't need any help."

Huan glances at me and I give him a little nod of encouragement. "Oh, I know you don't. But it sounds fun. And my school schedule is kind of light the next few weeks."

Anya snorts. "Yeah, double majoring in computer science and economics sounds really light." She shrugs. "But, whatever. You can help if you want. Maybe you'll wind up adopting a dog. Give your old dad a conniption. Fight the power."

Huan laughs. For some reason, Giselle barks, startling all of us, and then we're all smiling, even Anya. Even without looking over, I can feel Henry's eyes on me.

Then it begins to rain.

"Crap," Anya says.

None of us move. My eyes blur, my eyelashes growing damp. I lift my palms and watch the raindrops bounce off of them. When was the last time I stood outside in the rain, just stood there and let it wash over me? Maybe when I was a kid. Maybe never; my mom was always worried I'd get sick. Anya and Huan and Henry jog toward the path but I stand there at the top of Tank Hill a moment longer. Henry stops and looks back at me.

"Maggie, are you coming?"

I shrug, grinning, and point my face up to the sky. Henry laughs. I shake the water from my hair like a dog and jog toward him.

The path is already turning slick with mud. Ahead of Anya, Giselle seems distraught, hopping from one side of the path to the other, trying to keep her paws out of the mud. Seymour lopes obliviously through the puddles, his fat paws spattering mud with each step. There's something carefree about his gait; his grin, tongue lolling from the side of his mouth, verges on ecstatic. My eyes blur again, watching him. Toby would have loved this, too, running down a grassy hill in the rain. I feel happy and sad and happy again. We're all slipping and jogging and wiping the rain from our eyes. Henry stumbles and I catch his elbow and then we're just sort of holding each other, shuffling and sliding and hurrying down the path. My heart races, but not in an unpleasant way. Below us, the city is a watercolor, all of its sharp edges softened.

We jog all the way down to Cole Street, and fall into seats at a table under the awning of the French bakery on the corner. Henry ducks inside and returns a few minutes later with a tray of hot chocolates and a stack of napkins. We pat our faces dry and watch the rain pour off the awning and the steam rise from our drinks. Giselle curls into a ball under the table and Seymour follows suit. As he wedges himself between my feet and Giselle, he releases an old-man groan that makes me laugh.

When Huan and Anya head back inside to pick out some pastries to bring home for Rosie, the atmosphere — our little table, sheltered from the rain by the orange awning, the car tires whispering over the wet street as they pass, the soft, blurred lights of nearby shops — turns irrepressibly romantic. Henry and I exchange smiles. My shirt is still damp, clinging to me. I should be cold, but I'm not.

"So, I was wondering," Henry says, "if

maybe I could take you out to dinner sometime."

I bite the inside of my mouth, trying to summon a response that won't make me seem like a crazy person, which rules out explaining to him that if we went to dinner there's a very good chance that I would start shaking, stop breathing, or feel the overpowering, irresistible urge to sprint home.

"Or the movies," he adds when I don't respond right away. "Or . . . just a drink?"

"Maybe we shouldn't make this any more complicated," I say. "Because of my relationship with Anya."

"But you aren't her therapist."

"Yes, but —"

Henry gives me a tight smile. "No, no, it's fine. Let's forget I said anything." He looks into the street, away from me.

He's leaving, I remind myself. Even *I* can't ignore that ticking clock. I can see it already: I fall for Henry and we date for a year, trying to make the long-distance thing work until eventually we acknowledge the "Dead End" sign that has been looming right in front of us the whole time.

What is taking Anya and Huan so long in there? I shift in my seat, pulling my feet away from Seymour. He peers up at me, knotting his brows together, concerned.

What's wrong? he seems to ask. His huge ears flick back and forth and his big black nose twitches and his eyes widen, picking up all of my signals.

I look away. Rain continues to pour, forming narrow, black slurries that hug the curb. I feel Seymour's body shift at my feet, hear his old-man sigh as he lays his head back down, but I keep looking out at the rain, and begin to count my breath.

CHAPTER 14

Despite Seymour's new picture and upgrade to "designer" dog status, there hasn't been any interest in him over the past few days. Sybil and I decide that we'll include him in the small group of dogs that we'll showcase for adoption at the SuperMutt fund-raiser. At previous fund-raisers, Sybil tells me, all of the dogs up for adoption had new homes by the end of the night, so it's as close to a sure thing as you get in the world of dog rescue. If Seymour doesn't find a forever home in the next few weeks, he'll find one that night.

Anya has invited me to another Sunday breakfast at her house. No burned eggs this time, she'd written in her e-mail. Apparently it was Henry's turn to cook. At the bottom of the e-mail, Anya wrote: Please bring Seymour and Giselle. I'd like to piss off Clive as much as possible.

When Grant opens the door for me on

Sunday morning, Seymour immediately comes out from behind the couch and trots over to me. His head is so low that the bottoms of his ears drag on the ground, but his body is doing a sort of submissive wagging thing and he's looking up at me with what is unmistakably happiness in his eyes.

"Good morning, little man," I say to him, handing him the first of many counterconditioning treats he's certain to receive that day. Giselle snorts into his ear and his tail wags faster.

"Seymour! You're willingly out of your cave!" Grant says, surprised. "He's really taken a shine to you, Maggie."

I hold up the bag of treats. "Food," I say. "The way to every dog's heart." I tell Grant about our plan to include Seymour in the SuperMutt auction.

Grant's face falls. "So he'll be here until then?"

"Does it soften the blow if I tell you that Sybil is sure he'll be adopted the night of the event?"

Grant sighs. "Sure. We can hang in there a few more weeks, can't we, Seymour? That's only one more run to the market for those behind-the-couch piddle pads we've all grown so fond of." Despite his sarcasm, I can see that Grant is relieved to know that

238

his record of keeping foster dogs until they find their forever homes will remain intact.

We manage to speed-walk off Carl Street without seeing or hearing a train. I ply the dogs with treats the entire way to Anya's house, and I'm happy to see that Seymour's tail is no longer tucked between his legs. He's not walking with the same happy-go-lucky confidence as Giselle, but frankly, that makes two of us. At least we're all outside, trying, and there have been no negative incidents to derail our progress.

"For some reason," Anya says when she opens the door, "Henry isn't making his usual waffles. He's making some complicated quiche thing and a salad with strawberries. You know someone's trying to be fancy when they put fruit on lettuce." She gives me a meaningful look that I pretend not to notice. "It's like he thinks the queen is coming."

From the direction of the dining room, someone bellows, "Breakfast!"

Anya rolls her eyes. "Clive." She looks down at the dogs. "Okay, team. I'm counting on you to be as annoying as possible."

In the dining room, Rosie lies on a hospital bed that is angled into a seated position, and Clive and Terrence sit on either side of her. Rosie looks smaller than she had when we first met, but she seems to recognize me and a faint smile passes over her lips. Her hair is wrapped in a beautiful red turban embroidered with shimmering gold thread.

"Do you like it?" she asks me, touching the turban. "If I'm going to be confined to a bed, I thought I ought to at least wear something snazzy. I don't want anyone to accuse me of fading away."

"Impossible," I tell her. "And I love it."

"Hello," Terrence says, nodding to me. He, too, looks different than he had the last time I was here — he seems paler and his eyes are red-rimmed and bloodshot. I wonder if he stayed over at the hospital with Rosie earlier in the week.

"Morning," Clive says.

"Good morning," I say.

Henry pushes open the door from the kitchen and flashes a small, uncertain smile when he sees me. "Hi, Maggie," he says, and sets a golden-brown quiche on the table.

"This looks delicious," I say. Anya waves for me to sit in the same seat I did last time. Giselle and Seymour settle down into the tight space between my chair and Anya and I give them a couple of peanut butter treats.

"I hope it is," Henry answers. "I'm trying something new. But I think I made too much." He looks over at Terrence. "No Laura or the kids? It's been ages since I've seen them."

"They have the flu. They haven't left the couch all weekend. I'm trying to keep my distance from them so I don't pass anything on to Rosie."

Rosie doesn't turn toward Terrence, so I'm not sure she's heard him until she says, "How much distance can you keep from your own family? If I get the flu, I get the flu."

"We want to keep you healthy," Terrence says, sounding plaintive. I can't help but feel sorry for him. It seems like he's continually trying, and failing, to win his grandmother's good favor.

"Well, you look like shit," Clive says, cutting into the quiche. "You probably have the flu despite your valiant efforts. Thanks for spreading disease."

Terrence runs a hand over his face and sighs. "I'm just tired. Long hours at the stores."

"I suppose that's what it takes to have a great big house in St. Francis Wood. The house that mattresses built! Who knew? And here I went to law school like a chump."

"You're not exactly starving, Clive," Terrence says.

"But from the looks of things, I'm not eating quite as well as you, Terrence." Clive barks out a laugh and Terrence's round face reddens.

Rosie says, "Are you four going to keep squabbling like this when I'm gone or is it just for my benefit?"

Everyone falls quiet, looking at her, and then Clive says, "Of course it's for your benefit. There's nothing we love more than your attention."

This makes Rosie smile. She attempts to lift a hand to Clive's cheek, but it falls back to her lap. Clive reaches out and grasps it and it seems to me that for a split second his bottom lip quivers ever so slightly.

Terrence turns toward me, the red blotches spreading on his cheeks. "Forgive me, Ms. Brennan," he says, "but I'm confused. Are you here in a professional capacity?"

"No," Henry says quickly. He clears his throat. "Maggie and Anya are friends."

I nod. "If anything, Anya is the one helping *me* in a professional capacity. She's been taking wonderful photographs of the foster dogs that are up for adoption through an organization that I —"

242

"You have time for that, Anya?" Terrence interrupts. "Volunteering? On top of looking for Billy and working at the frame shop and your classes?"

Anya, I'm pleased to see, has already polished off half of a slice of quiche. The dark smudges below her eyes seem to be fading, and a pink rosiness blossoming below her pale skin. "I stopped going to class. And I'm not working at the frame shop right now," she says calmly. "You know that."

"No, I don't think so." Terrence's voice seems to be getting louder. "Were you fired? What happened?"

"She's taking a short break," Henry says.

"A break from working part-time at a frame shop?" Terrence shakes his head. "Must be nice."

"Maybe *you* could use a break, Terrence," says Anya.

"I sure could. But I have bills to pay. Responsibilities." It doesn't sound to me like Terrence is trying to be cruel; it's more like he is so tired he doesn't know what he is saying. His shoulders are slumped, his large forearms as motionless as felled trees on either side of his plate. He looks around the table, blinking slowly.

"Is it just me," Anya asks, "or does it seem

like Terrence is in a particularly bad mood this morning?"

"He seems stressed," Henry agrees.

"Oh, Terrence is always stressed," Clive says, waving his fork dismissively. "He just usually hides it better. Under that mustache, I think."

Rosie releases a wheezing laugh. "Clive," she says, coughing and smiling. "You're a terrible person."

Clive waves his fork in the air again, does a little bow, and grins.

"Forgive me," Terrence says, turning toward me again. "I'm just trying to wrap my head around what exactly is going on here. You're a pet bereavement counselor, and Anya has lost a pet, but you're not her therapist, you're just her new friend? And you're going on all these walks with her out of some devotion to this brand-new, sprung-from-nothing friendship?" He looks around the table. "Am I the only one who finds this odd?"

"Terrence," Henry says. "What's gotten into you? You're being rude."

"It's fine," I tell Henry. I smile at him, grateful, but I don't need anyone to protect me. Well, except, you know, a dog. I reach down to pet Giselle, but Seymour's nose moves below my hand first, probably angling for another treat. "I know he's just looking out for Anya."

"Maggie believes me," Anya says. "She believes someone stole Billy. It's nice to finally have someone on my side."

I look at Anya, swallowing.

"Is that right?" Terrence asks me. "You believe that someone stole Billy? You believe he is alive?"

"Yes," Anya says. "She does."

"I'm asking your new friend Maggie."

Everyone looks at me. "Well, I . . ." My voice trails off. I feel Seymour lick my hand, and I reach down to pet him, hoping everyone will just move on.

"Maggie?" Anya says. "Tell him."

"Oh, just tell her the truth, Maggie," Clive says. "Put the poor girl out of her misery. You know as well as anyone that no one stole that dog. He ran away and he's not coming back."

Anya drops her fork and it clatters against her plate. "Shut up, Clive!"

I take a breath. "Anya," I say softly. "I told you from the beginning that I have no idea if Billy is alive or not, but that I'd like to help you."

Anya stares at me. "But I thought you believed me. I thought you were helping me look for Billy. You said if you were in my shoes, you'd do the same thing."

"I would. If I were in your shoes, I'd probably do the same thing. That's completely true."

"But — but you don't think I'm actually going to find Billy! You think he's dead."

"I don't know what I think, honestly," I tell her. "How could I claim to be sure of something that I have no way of knowing?"

"You could trust that *I* know," Anya says, locking eyes with me. She shakes her head, and her dark hair falls into her face. She doesn't bother to move it away. "I fucking hate that you've just been humoring me. I'm not a child. I'm not some fucking crazy person."

"But why does it matter whether Maggie thinks Billy was stolen?" Henry interjects. "You can't fault her for not being able to ignore the facts, can you? She's been nothing but honest and supportive since the moment she met you."

Anya stands abruptly from the table. Giselle and Seymour swing their heads to look up at her, tensing. I feel my chest constrict.

"Honest?" she spits. "You think Maggie's being honest with me, Henry? With *you*? You think she's training that poodle to be a therapy dog?" Her hard, empty laughter cuts through the room's thick silence.

No. No. No.

"Anya, please . . ." I say quietly, but I can't seem to get any more words out. I try to breathe in deeply, but come up short on air.

"Anya, sweetheart," Rosie says, her face twisted with concern. Terrence takes his grandmother's hand and whispers something to her.

"Stop looking at me like that!" Anya cries. "All of you! You all look at me like I'm crazy! You think I don't see it? I don't feel it? I know what you're thinking. But *she's* the crazy one." She swings her gaze to me, pointing her finger at my head. "This therapist you hired, Henry, to try to make *me* better? You think *she's* being honest? Here's the truth: Maggie can't leave her house without a dog. Even with a dog, she hyperventilates. She gets all panicky and pale and falls to the ground. You should see her!"

I can feel her eyes burning into my scalp, but I just stare at Giselle and Seymour, frantically trying to arrange my thoughts within the fog of shame and embarrassment and panic that swirls darkly through me.

"It would actually be funny if it weren't so fucking sad," Anya says. "She's supposed to be helping people? Helping me? *She's* the nutcase! You think I'm obsessed with Billy? She can barely even *talk* about her dead dog. That's what a mess she is. Right, Maggie? Apparently it's honesty hour. Time to come clean. You don't believe Billy was stolen, you don't believe he's still alive somewhere, and, oh yeah, you're *fucking crazy*!"

I stand and hear my chair screech against the floor behind me. I grip the dogs' leashes in my shaking hand. My mouth is dry. I want to stay and defend myself. I want to admit to my flaws, my irrational fears, my storms of panic — and to explain what I know is true: despite my shortcomings, and perhaps even, in some way, because of them, I can help people. My fear makes me weak, but it also makes me strong. But I look around the table and all I see are faces twisted in confusion and anger and concern, and I can't say any of it. I can hardly breathe.

I look at Anya and see that she is crying — sobbing, really. Henry rushes to her side, wrapping his arms around her.

"I'm sorry," I whisper.

The dogs trot along beside me as I make my way to the front door. We step outside, and then we run.

■ ■ ■ ■

"Maggie!" Lourdes cries when she opens her door. "Are you okay?" She moves to hug me but I hold out Giselle's leash.

"Stomach bug," I croak. "Better keep your distance."

"That came on suddenly . . ." she says, but I'm already hurrying down the path toward my apartment.

I stand in the bathroom, scrubbing my hands in the sink, tears running down my cheeks. I try not to think of how Seymour's tail had been tucked between his legs our entire run back to his apartment, how I hadn't given him a single treat or comforted him in any way, how lucky it was that he had not tried to run away. Who am I to say I can help him? Or Anya? I choke down a fistful of vitamins, feeling the scrape of each one in my throat, and then drag myself to the living room and collapse in an armchair, exhausted.

I miss Toby. He would have shoved his snout under my hand again and again until I petted him. He would have clambered up into my lap because even though he was big he believed he was a lapdog and I would have laughed under the weight of his love. I would have felt his beating heart and taken comfort in feeling sure it was steady, unchanged and unchangeable.

But I would have been wrong about his heart. It was not unchanged. It was not unchangeable.

It was his heart that brought us to the veterinarian. We needed a new supply of heartworm pills. What would have happened if I hadn't been in such a hurry to leave Philadelphia? I would have picked up a year's supply of pills from the vet he'd always seen, probably just purchasing them at the reception desk, never questioning whether it made sense to buy a full year's worth of medication ahead of time, despite Toby's age. Of course he'd live the year. He'd live far longer than that. I'd have purchased the pills without seeing the veterinarian and I would have had, what? Another month with him? Another few weeks? Or would I have noticed sooner than that what I had been too busy to notice in that first month in San Francisco? Would I have seen that Toby had slowed down, and that he was in pain?

The new veterinarian in San Francisco seemed like a nice man. He was handsome, even, something I noted in the moments before he pressed his stethoscope to Toby's chest and frowned. He peered into Toby's mouth, inspecting his gums. He moved his hands down the length of Toby's body, all the while chatting sweetly to him, telling him what a good-looking fellow he was, what a gentleman. When his hands reached Toby's hips, he fell silent. Toby licked his muzzle — a sign, I knew, that he was experiencing pain. The vet's brow furrowed and suddenly my heart was racing.

How was his appetite? the vet asked. Had he had any trouble with incontinence? Did he seem lethargic? No, no, no, I replied, my certainty shrinking with each answer.

"What is it?" I asked finally. "Is something wrong?"

He couldn't answer . . . yet. There would need to be tests. The clinic had an X-ray machine. Could I leave Toby for the afternoon?

I sat in the waiting room for three hours. I didn't take out my phone, or read a magazine, or chat with the receptionist, or walk out for coffee or something to eat. I sat there. The hours felt like days. I knew I would hear bad news — that afternoon, or in a month, or in a year. But I knew it was coming. That's the rub with dogs. We pack a lifetime of love into a too-short span of time. We have to watch them die. We have to let them go.

When the vet finally called me back into the exam room, Toby greeted me with his usual bright-eyed grin. He had cancer, the veterinarian told me, a bone tumor, and in all likelihood was in a considerable amount of pain. Worse still, the X-ray showed that the cancer had already spread to his lungs.

My hands stilled on Toby's back. I began to sob. "But he's been fine! He can't be in pain."

"Some dogs are like this," I heard the vet say from far away. "They don't show their pain. They just keep going, as long as they can." He paused. "But Toby's pain, I'm very sorry to tell you, must be significant."

I shook my head. This man didn't understand. I *knew* Toby. I would have known if he were in pain. Even as I protested, I thought of the way he ran now: a slow lope, his hind legs stiff. I thought of the way he groaned when he lay down and how rising back up took twice as long as it used to. How I had to lift him onto my bed at night. But these were signs of age, maybe a touch of arthritis — not pain. Not cancer. Toby's tail was always wagging; his eyes were always eager; his spirit was as bright as it had been the day we met thirteen years earlier.

"It's hard for us to know what's going on until we see something like this," the vet continued. I knew he was pointing at the X-ray, but I couldn't look at it again. The vet paused. "Once we see this, there isn't room for doubt. The pain is evident and it will only worsen — quickly." His tone was definitive, but it somehow held a question, too. I knew what he was telling me in his kind, certain, heavy way. I knew what he was asking.

I couldn't take my hands off Toby. I petted him over and over. *I'm so sorry,* I told him with my mind. *I didn't know. Why didn't I know?* I didn't ask him why he hadn't told me that he was in pain, because I was sure he *had* told me, in his manner, and I had missed it. I had failed him. I had let my friend suffer because I was distracted and hopeful and focusing on moving forward, and I needed his help.

Toby looked at me with his familiar gaze, full of dignity and trust and cheer, even now, and his tail beat slowly against the bench I sat on. It struck me that he was trying to reassure me, but there are so many things he might have been communicating in those moments.

Despite being in decent touch with reality, despite my profession, despite knowing the average life-span of a dog of Toby's size, it turned out that some part of me had believed that Toby would live forever. I knew, because my patients told me, that I wasn't alone. We think that because our dogs are by our side every day, because they are our best friends, because the love we feel for them is so pure, so funny and beautiful and profound, that *our* dog will be the dog that beats the odds. Should it have been a shock that my Toby had reached the end of his life? No. But it was. It was.

I knew what I would have told a friend if she were going through this. It was what I would tell my patients when I opened my practice the very next week. *This is our responsibility. This is the burden of loving and caring for a dog. We have to know when it is time to say good-bye.*

I kept my arms around Toby as the veterinarian inserted the needle. I felt my beloved dog grow heavy in my arms, the weight that I'd felt so many times before, leaning up against me on the couch, pressing into my leg on our walks, tripping excitedly over my feet whenever I came home, the weight I was feeling for the last time. I tried to memorize the way his long, soft, black fur felt below my palms. The shape of his muzzle, the wet warmth of his gray beard, the lovely golden brown of his eyes, happy and devoted even now, as we parted.

We had met when I was nineteen years old and now I was thirty-two. What would my life have been without him? I hoped he knew how much he meant to me, and how much I loved him.

I felt his breathing slow. Thirteen years we'd been together, and now, suddenly, our time was over. I wasn't ready to live without him, but I couldn't let him feel my fear. He'd taught me how to be brave, how to keep moving, how to see the beauty of the world glimmering even through darkness.

"You are such a good boy," I whispered to him over and over again, holding him close in my arms. "And you have given me so much joy."

I felt his last exhale, a final breath that warmed my forearm and then was gone.

CHAPTER 15

I'm staring into the fire in a sort of hollowed-out, post-cry haze when the doorbell rings.

"I'm still not feeling well, Lourdes," I call. "I'll talk to you tomorrow."

The doorbell rings again. I groan, standing. My legs ache from running home from Anya's house and my chest has a scorched feeling. At some point in the evening, I'd poured myself a glass of wine but it's still on the coffee table, untouched. I take three deep breaths.

"Lourdes, honestly —" I start to say, opening the door.

It's Henry. He looks the way I feel — sad and exhausted. "Maggie, I'm so sorry. I wanted to follow you right away after you left this morning, but Rosie was really upset and had a coughing fit. I couldn't leave."

"Oh no! Is she okay?"

"Health-wise, she's stable. But she's wor-

256

ried about Anya. She knows she's not going to be around too much longer, and I think she'd do anything to be sure that Anya is going to recover from all of this."

I open the door for him to pass through. "Do you want to come in?"

He nods and walks past me, dropping down onto the couch. I sit across from him, not wanting to be too close. I'm afraid he's there to admonish me for hiding my mental instability all this time, for the charade I've been acting out. I wonder if he plans to call my old boss in Philadelphia to tell him about my behavior, to warn him that he should think twice before recommending me again. I know how protective Henry is of his sister, how angry he must be with me.

So far, though, he's just looking at me sadly. "Anya lashes out when she's hurt," he says. "She shouldn't have said what she said this morning."

"She had every right to say it. Everything she said was true."

Henry doesn't seem surprised by my admission. "That's not the point. She shouldn't have announced it like that. You've been trying to help her."

I look down at my hands. "I haven't done a very good job."

"You've done more than anyone else." He

sighs. "Listen, Maggie. I'm not going to lie. If I'd known what you were dealing with when we first met, I don't know that I would have felt comfortable enlisting you to help my sister. But everything is different now. I *know* you. I've seen you with Anya; I've seen how you've helped her. You listened to her and understood how important photography is to her. You convinced her to pick up her camera again. She's been talking about SuperMutt and the idea of starting her own photography business for days. Do you understand what a big deal it is that she's even thinking about something other than Billy? We were all at our wits' end, but you found a way to get through to her. You *did* help her, Maggie. You *are* helping her. It's such a relief."

I give him a halfhearted smile. He's leaving for Los Angeles soon, and I guess now he'll be able to go without feeling quite so worried about his sister.

"Do you think I could have one of those?" he asks, looking at the wineglass on the table.

I nod. "I would have offered you a glass earlier, but I thought you were here to tell me what a horrible person I am. I didn't want to fuel a tirade."

When I stand and walk by him on my way

to the kitchen, Henry reaches out and touches my wrist, stopping me. "You know I don't think that you're a horrible person, right? That couldn't be further from the truth."

I look down at his hand on my wrist. The reflection of the fire moves in his eyes. *He's leaving,* I remind myself. *He's just another dead end.* I step away from his grasp and walk toward the kitchen. When I return, I hand him the glass of wine, careful not to allow my fingers to touch his.

"Thanks," he says. He shifts in his seat, his expression hesitant. "So, I'd like to ask you about the stuff Anya said, but we don't have to talk about it if you'd rather not. We can just drink our wine, enjoy the fire. I don't have anything against companionable silence. It's my favorite kind of silence, actually."

Maybe it's the kindness in his eyes. Or maybe it's the fact that he's leaving, that I'll probably never see him again, and there's nothing to lose. I take a deep breath and tell him everything.

"My mother is agoraphobic," I begin. "She hasn't left the house in over twenty-five years without being heavily medicated. So I guess you could say she taught me everything I know." I smile to let Henry know that I'm joking, but his steady gaze doesn't waver. I shrug. "Note to self: Never lead with a mental health joke."

Now he returns my smile. "At least not a bad one."

"Ouch! In matters of psychology, humor is relative. And by 'relative,' I mean 'mother.' "

Henry's smile turns sly. "I'm just surprised you're willing to joke about the situation. Don't jokes about agoraphobia hit a little too close to home?"

I burst out laughing. "That's the spirit."

"Anyway," he says, growing serious again, "I really do want to hear everything. Please go on."

"You sound like me. Am I being shrinked?"

He strokes his chin with one hand and pretends to write in a notebook with the other. "Patient uses humor to deflect attention . . ." he murmurs.

So I tell him how my mother had packed my childhood schedule in an attempt to ensure that I didn't inherit her phobias, and how I now suspect this was even the motivation behind the acquisition of our family dogs. I tell him about my fear of heights, and how I've hidden it from my parents for years because I didn't want to worry or disappoint them. I tell him that in graduate school I learned that the fear of heights isn't all that dissimilar from other phobias like the one my mother has — they're panic disorders rooted in anxiety. So even though I only became agoraphobic recently, I realize now that low currents of anxiety have coursed through much of my life.

Then I tell him about adopting Toby, and how much I had loved him. I tell him what a comfort he'd been to me throughout my twenties, how his exuberance and gregarious spirit had changed the way I viewed the world and pushed me to be more outgoing, even inspiring me to finally make the decision to leave my job and move across the country.

All the while, Henry listens, his gaze never losing that sheen of kindness and warmth.

I tell him about Toby's death, and how when I walked home from the veterinarian's office I'd been struck by a panic so terrifying that I'd been sure I was either dying or going crazy, and the fear of experiencing that sensation again had kept me home for one hundred days.

"For a while, I told myself that I was shocked by Toby's sudden death, and I was grieving. I tell my patients not to be too hard on themselves in the painful period of time following the loss of a loved one, that it's okay to give in to the grief, to allow yourself to really feel it. I made excuses for my own behavior in the name of grief. But, really, it's always been more than grief — it's been fear, too. Irrational, but debilitating fear." I sigh, looking down into my wineglass. I still haven't taken a sip. "It's hard to explain."

"You're doing well," Henry says. "I'm sure it's difficult to talk about."

"It was meeting Anya, and wanting to help her, that finally motivated me to find a way to get better. It turns out that dogs can be very effective at helping agoraphobes leave their homes, so I started borrowing Lourdes's dog and taking her on walks. Giselle isn't a therapy dog — and I'm not training her to be one in the literal sense — but she has helped me."

"I've always had this feeling," Henry says, "that all dogs are really therapy dogs."

I've probably circled this thought a thousand times, but have never formulated it so concisely before. It seems to me that it's the sort of thing only someone who loves dogs could say. "Yes, I think you're right."

"So, what does it feel like? When the panic hits?"

I close my eyes, thinking. "It's like being

trapped somewhere where there isn't enough air. It's like being completely disoriented and dizzy. It's like walls closing in on you, but it isn't walls, it's your own skin tightening — around your neck, your chest, your heart, your veins."

"Jesus. And you feel that way every time you walk outside?"

I open my eyes, shaking away the sensation. "No, not anymore. I'm much better — though I still haven't tried to go outside without Giselle. It's worse around heights, or when I'm not sure how to get back home. So San Francisco isn't exactly the easiest place for me right now. But . . . you know Sutro Tower? Up on Twin Peaks?"

Henry nods. "When I was a kid I thought it looked like Poseidon's staff — his trident. I had all sorts of elaborate fantasies about how San Francisco used to be Poseidon's underwater kingdom and that he left his trident behind when the ocean receded. Even now, every time we have an earthquake, a part of me still thinks maybe it's Poseidon's doing — somewhere out there in the ocean he's sending a signal to his trident, making it shake."

I smile. "We should really give back that old guy's cane before someone gets hurt."

"Hell hath no fury like a doddering Greek god."

"Well, with all due respect to the pantheon, I hope Poseidon never gets Sutro Tower back. I feel better when I see it up there. It orients me. I always look for it when I'm out on a walk. The hardest days are the ones when the fog hides it. Anyway, now you know my two secret weapons in the fight against panic: Giselle and Sutro Tower."

"Makes perfect sense," Henry says, shrugging. "But your secrets are safe with me."

And I actually believe that what I've said *does* make sense to him, and that his opinion of me hasn't changed. I lean back into the armchair, feeling a weight lift off me.

"Since the company of a dog is so calming for you, have you thought about getting another one?" he asks. "Or does it feel too soon?"

"I'm sure I will someday, but I'm just not ready yet. I think I'll know when the time is right. In the meantime, I have Giselle. She's my Band-Aid dog."

"She seems like a happy, solid sort."

"She's a good dog," I agree. "Why don't you have one of your own? You clearly like them."

"To tell the truth, I always sort of thought of Billy as my dog, too. Anya did all the heavy lifting in terms of caring for him, obviously. But I was a doting uncle."

"You miss him. I guess I didn't realize. I'm sorry."

Henry gives a "what can you do?" shrug. "He deserves a happy ending. He was so good for Anya. He was there for her every single day, through thick and thin. For a girl who lost her parents, that means everything." His eyes shift away from mine for a moment, and I can almost feel the heaviness of his thoughts.

"It's interesting," he says. "I think that losing our parents made us all become slightly different versions of the people we used to be — or the people we would have become. Clive has become more cynical, more sarcastic. He's left a steady stream of ex-girlfriends in his wake for the last decade. I think he's still too terrified of loss to let himself fall in love. Terrence went the opposite direction — he got married, had children, and now he's intensely devoted to his family. He'd do anything for them. And Anya has become this very independent, thorny sort of person. When I first saw that happening, I gave her Billy. I thought a dog might help draw her out."

"And you?" I ask.

Henry gives me a questioning look.

"Who have you become?"

"Ah." He rakes his fingers through his dark air, and when he pulls them out, his hair sticks out in all directions. He makes a stressed-out face. "The worrier?"

I laugh and shake my head. "You're the caretaker," I say. "The glue."

"Anya would probably accuse me of being *super* glue. I'm a bit overprotective for her taste."

"Yes, I do recall an irate maniac jumping out of the bushes to yell at me during my first visit to her house."

Henry cringes, laughing. "Sorry about that."

"It's okay. You've kept me on my toes."

His smile fades. "It's not just Anya. I feel responsible for Billy, too. I wish things could have been different. It's hard to not know what happened to him. It's hard to keep yourself from thinking the worst."

Opening up to each other in this way feels inevitable, like something Henry and I were meant to do. It's getting harder and harder to remind myself that he's leaving, that I should curb my growing feelings for him.

"It's been difficult to keep Toby's death from overshadowing his life," I say. "I'm

266

sure that's an even bigger challenge when you don't know what happened to your dog, when there's a question mark hovering over the death."

Henry sits back. He studies me, smiling. "You're very easy to talk to, Maggie. It must be nice to know you're able to bring comfort to so many people."

"Am I comforting you? I thought I was just commiserating."

"Maybe it's the same thing."

"Sometimes," I agree.

"Whatever it is, I feel better when I'm with you. I'd like to think I'm special, but I suspect a lot of people feel better when they're with you."

"Flattery will get you everywhere." I smile, but my heart is beating fast. *People,* I remind myself, *are full of flattery before they say good-bye.*

Eventually, I walk Henry to the door, but he seems reluctant to leave. I guess I'm just as reluctant to say good night as he is, because we both stand there facing each other, neither of us reaching for the door handle. Without moving his eyes from mine, Henry puts his hand on the curve of my shoulder, then runs it down the length of my arm, takes hold of my hand, and lifts it to his mouth. His gaze is full of desire, but there is something questioning there, too, ready to stop if I ask him to. He presses a gentle kiss against the base of my thumb, all the while watching me. He turns my hand in his and kisses my palm, and then the inside of my wrist. He slides the sleeve of my shirt up, his fingertips warm against my skin, and kisses my forearm.

He's leaving, I warn myself with every kiss. *He's leaving. He's leaving. He's leaving.*

But I can't stop him. I can't look away. I can barely breathe, can barely even blink until he slides his hands into my hair and I close my eyes and we kiss.

I have no idea how much time has passed when Henry pulls back slightly and says, as though he is picking up some thread of conversation that we dropped only a moment earlier, "You know, there are a lot of dog-friendly restaurants in San Francisco. There are all sorts of places we could go together. It doesn't have to be the movies."

I smile. He runs his thumb lightly over my lips, his fingers resting under my jaw.

"You have the most beautiful smile," he says.

And so we kiss some more.

CHAPTER 16

Anya doesn't text or call all week, and she doesn't respond to my e-mails. I force myself to continue taking Giselle over to pick up Seymour for walks around the neighborhood. I know how easy it would be, without the mission of helping Anya, to slip back into days followed by weeks of not leaving the apartment, so I make myself think of Seymour, and how I'm helping him.

In the late afternoon on Thursday, after my last appointment of the day and long after I've returned Seymour and Giselle to their homes, Sybil calls. She almost never calls, preferring e-mail, and so when I see her name on my phone's caller ID I pick up right away. She is frantic.

"Oh, Maggie, thank God you're there! I'm all the way up in Tahoe — long story — and I just got a call about a dog tied up outside of the Whole Foods near you. One of the parking attendants says the dog was there

269

when he arrived early this morning and she's been there all day. She's a pit bull and I guess no one wants to get too close to her. She's probably a total sweetie, but you know how people get with their raging pit-bull profiling. The attendant was going to call the police, but then someone else who works at the store told him to try us first."

Sybil pauses, out of breath. "I can't get back to the city for hours. Do you think there's any way you could swing by and check out the situation? If you can't keep the dog overnight, that's fine. I already know of a foster home for her, this couple that loves pit bulls, and I can have them pick the dog up from your place tonight. I just want her off the street and out of the System."

"The System" is Sybil's term for the San Francisco SPCA. The System isn't a bad place for a dog — it's certainly better than the streets and it's a no-kill shelter, so as long as a dog is considered "adoptable" he'll remain there until someone takes him home. But the quieter, more hands-on care of a foster family is a gentler pit stop for a dog on her way to finding her forever home.

"And is it raining there?" Sybil continues breathlessly. "The guy from Whole Foods said it's raining. That poor dog."

I glance out the window. The rain looks light — the dog is likely cold and wet, but at least the driving rain I'd heard pounding the house the night before has stopped. Or has the dog been tied up outside all night? I listen upstairs for Giselle and hear her nails clacking lazily across the hardwood floor.

"It's drizzling a little," I tell Sybil. "But don't worry, I can walk over right now and pick up the dog."

"Oh, Maggie, thank you. I'm so relieved. I'll call Ty — that's the parking attendant — right now and let him know you're on your way. How quickly can you be there?"

"Fifteen minutes or so. It's not far from my apartment."

"Do you want me to arrange for her foster family to pick her up from your place tonight?"

"Yes," I say. "I think that would be best."

I knock again on Lourdes's door, harder this time, my heart sinking. It's the third time I've knocked. I pull out my phone and try calling both her cell and home phone again, but she doesn't answer. Mentally, I'm kicking myself. *Why did I just assume that someone would be home with Giselle?* It was a stupid, stupid mistake. Lourdes had been talking for months about giving me a key to her house for use in case of emergencies, but we'd somehow never gotten around to it. I cup my hand above my eyes and peer through the window beside the door. Giselle sits in the darkened hallway, gazing up at me, her tail swishing slowly behind her. Her brow is furrowed in confusion. I don't want to knock again and agitate her; she's clearly the only one home, and as clever as she is, she's not going to unlock the door for me.

My heart sinks another notch when I call Sybil back and her voice mail picks up. I decide not to leave a message. What would I tell her? *So sorry, Sybil, but that abandoned, soaking-wet dog will just have to go into the System because I can't walk the fifteen blocks to the supermarket by myself.*

No. I'm not going to let a forsaken dog sit out in the rain any more than I could have let Anya walk out of my life without at least trying to help her all those weeks ago. Some things are bigger than my own problems, and people and dogs in desperate need are among them. I pull the hood of my coat over my head and step off Lourdes's front stairs and into the rain.

If only it could be so easy. If only I could just summon up the necessary determination, and do it. Instead, when I open the gate and step onto the sidewalk, the pavement tilts below my feet. I feel my throat tighten, the terrible squeezing sensation in my chest. I grab hold of the gatepost, gasping for breath, holding on so tight that splinters cut into my skin.

One.

Two.

I try to fool myself into believing that Giselle is right there beside me, steadying me, urging me to walk forward, but it's no use. I'm going to pass out right there on the sidewalk. It doesn't seem possible that my heart can go on beating so quickly. I manage to stumble back through the gate, slamming it shut behind me. Lourdes's house is a blur in the gray afternoon mist. I hurry toward it, slipping on the wet stones of the path, thumping my feet hard against the front steps until I hit the dry landing below the underhang. I sink down and pull my knees into my chest and breathe, breathe, breathe, but my whole body seethes with panic and shame.

Inside the house, Giselle barks. I shake my head, trying to clear it.

Who can I call? *Henry.* Maybe he'll agree to pick up the dog for me. But when I try his number, he doesn't answer. I try Lourdes again, but she doesn't answer either.

"Where is everyone?" I say aloud, slapping the phone against my palm.

Who else can I call? Not a patient, obviously. I scroll through the contacts in my phone, realizing that nearly all of them live in Philadelphia. My world here in San Francisco is pitifully small.

In the end, I'm left with only one name: Anya Ravenhurst.

I'm sure that if I dial her number, she won't pick up. Henry promised that he would try to get her to call me so we could talk about everything that happened, but my expectations remain low. She thinks I betrayed her, that I lied to her about believing her. She isn't going to forgive me anytime soon, if ever. I'd e-mailed her to explain that she was right about me, that I was agoraphobic and couldn't go outside my apartment without Giselle, and that I didn't blame her for feeling the way she did about me. I told her that I still hoped she would be reunited with Billy, and that I would love to help her keep looking for him if she'd let me come along again. She never responded.

And now she is my last hope. I text her, hoping the message will pop up on her phone screen and she'll read it before she has a chance to stop herself.

Urgent. Abandoned dog in front of Whole Foods in the Haight. Can't pick up dog myself. Foster family lined up if we get dog to my apartment. Can you help? Please call ASAP.

A moment later, my phone rings. I stare at it, frozen with shock and relief, but when I pick up, Anya's voice is brisk. "I'll help," she says, "but you're coming with me. I'm going to walk to your apartment and then we can pick up the dog together."

"Oh, Anya," I say quickly. "Thank you for helping, but . . . I can't go with you. Did you get my e-mail? You were right. Everything you said. I have this disorder that makes it impossible for me to go anywhere. I panic. Giselle is locked inside her house, and I'm not ready to go outside by myself. I can't do it."

Anya is impatient, dismissive. "You won't be by yourself. You can put a leash on *me* if you need to. I'll be there soon."

"No! No, Anya, you don't understand —" I look down at my phone and realize she has hung up.

I sit there, leaning against the door, shivering. I'd like to go down to my apartment, put on some dry clothes, turn on the fire, and swallow a bucket of vitamin C. But I'm too tired. When I release a series of sneezes, Giselle smashes her nose into the window

275

beside the door, angling for a better look at me, her expression curious and questioning. Even though I'm pretty sure I now have a cold, maybe even a full-blown case of the flu, even though I know Anya is going to burst through the gate any minute and attempt to drag me out into the city, I can't help smiling a bit when I see Giselle's peachy cotton-candy pouf of fur flattened against the window.

Dogs.

Ten minutes later, Anya strides through the gate at her usual freight-train speed. Her face is flushed and underneath an Indiana Jones–type hat, a thick swath of her dark auburn hair is stuck, either by sweat or rain or grease, to her forehead. A leash and a collar hang from one of her hands. I rise to my feet as she bounds up the stairs toward me.

"Here," she says, holding out the leash. "Let's go."

I stare at her. "Anya, I'm not going to put a leash on you."

"It's for the dog, Maggie. The one we're going to rescue?"

Even to my ears, my laugh sounds a little hysterical. "Oh. Right. Good thinking."

"You really thought I was going to let you put a leash on me?"

"No! I . . . I don't know. Maybe. I'm not thinking clearly. What you're asking of me, I can't —"

Anya folds her arms across her chest. "You're coming with me."

"Please just listen to me. I know I'm not your favorite person right now, but please find another way to punish me. I can't walk out there. I . . . I'll have a panic attack. I lose my breath and my heart rate goes crazy and I get dizzy. I might pass out, hit my head. I don't know. I never know what's going to happen."

Anya's expression remains hard.

"You're angry with me," I say, trying again, "but it's that dog we need to think about right now. Can't you just get her and be mad at me later? There's no one else I can call. I really need your help."

"I'm here, aren't I? I *am* helping you. It may not be exactly how you *want* to be helped, but we don't always get to choose, do we?"

Behind me, I hear Giselle's breath as she snorts in our scents through the crack below the door. I look beyond Anya, toward the gate. A wave of the usual pre-panic symptoms washes over me. The throbbing flutter in my chest. The shaking fingers. The tightening throat. I squeeze my hands into fists and release them.

Anya watches me. "Listen, I've made up my mind. I'm not going without you. We'll rescue that dog together or not at all." When I don't answer, her tone shifts, softening ever so slightly.

"I really don't care," she says, "if you cry or you shake or you faint or you crap your pants or you look like a fucking crazy person. You've seen me scream Billy's name from the top of practically every peak in the city, and did I care that you were watching me? Did it stop me from doing what I needed to do? No. So, whatever, Maggie. Do what *you* need to do. If you fall on the ground convulsing, I'm going to pick you up. I'm stronger that anyone gives me credit for. I'll be with you the whole time. We'll walk to the supermarket and we'll walk back, and before you know it we're going to be in your apartment and you're going to have rescued a dog who needs your help and that will make all of the shit you're going to go through in the next thirty minutes worth it. That's what I tell myself when I'm up there screaming for Billy. I'm going to find him and it's all going to be worth it."

The whole time she speaks, I stare at the gate. How will I live with myself if I don't help that dog? If I can't push my irrational

278

fears aside and walk fifteen blocks? I nod. "Okay," I say.

Anya immediately grasps my elbow and steers me down the stairs, along the path, and through the gate.

"Slow down," I gasp, but already we're on the sidewalk.

"Nope," she says. "Let's just do this. One foot in front of the other. Forward, forward, forward. That dog's been out in this rain long enough."

I wish I could walk with my eyes closed. Instead, I stare at my feet. We make it past a couple of houses before I trip. The sudden stumble makes my throat feel so tight that I'm sure I'm suffocating. I yank my hood from my head, sucking in long, wheezing breaths. The rain is falling harder now, and cold. It snakes its way under my shirt and runs down the length of my back.

"Okay," comes Anya's clipped, purposeful voice beside me. "What do you usually do when this happens?"

"I . . . count . . . my . . . breath."

"You count your breath?"

I shoot her a look.

"Fine. You count your breath. Are you doing it? You don't seem like you're doing it. Do it."

I close my eyes and try to ignore the

impulse to hightail it back to my apartment. The ground shifts below my feet. I could be through my door in less than a minute. *Someone else will rescue the dog, won't they? The rain isn't that cold. She'll be fine in the System. She'll survive. She'll be okay.*

I press back these thoughts, disgusted.

One.

Two.

Three.

Four.

My vision clears. The ground solidifies. I straighten. Anya takes my elbow again and we hurry forward, moving ever farther from my apartment. Sutro Tower is behind us. When I glance back, it's immersed in rain clouds, gone.

Anya drags me along. She seems to decide that talking will distract me. Not talking, actually — listening. Anya does all the talking. She tells me that she has photographed two other dogs for the SuperMutt fundraiser since we last saw each other. Huan went with her. He wasn't much help, but she thinks there is a chance he might end up adopting one of the dogs they shot — a "funny little brindle hot dog" that had taken a shine to him (*Richard Nixon,* I think, remembering the dog from the website) — if he could ever get himself to move out of his parents' home. Not that she should throw stones, she realizes, though she does think there is a significant difference between living with your elderly, ailing grandmother and living with your parents who cook dinner for you every night and leave your laundry folded on your bed on Tuesdays. Still, she sounds impressed that he's considering this small act of rebellion — adopting a dog.

Anya tells me that Rosie seems weaker now than she had even last weekend. Henry and Clive and Terrence have started talking about putting her into hospice care. Anya hates the idea, but she isn't blind. She knows her grandmother is not getting better. And Rosie probably won't even care that much about leaving home — she's never been attached to that house.

"It seems like everything is changing at once," Anya says. She thinks that whenever they finally talk to Rosie about the hospice plan, her grandmother will probably laugh at her for being so resistant to the idea. Rosie has always embraced change. "She's a real rolling stone," Anya says. " 'This house is just a *thing*,' she used to tell me all the time. 'It's not like it can love you back. On your love list, always put the beating hearts at the top.' "

This phrase — "the beating hearts" — pierces through the dull jumble of my thoughts as I hurry along, eyes pinned to my feet.

"Oh, and," Anya continues, jumping from subject to subject like they are rocks that lead the way across a river, "I e-mailed with Sybil about putting together a photography session packet for the SuperMutt auction. She's really cool, by the way, just like you said. She wants me to bring a bunch of business cards and hand them out to people. I think I'm going to do it. The whole photography-business thing. Anya Ravenhurst Photography. I'm going to sign up for a small-business class at City College next semester. I'll have to go back to working at the frame shop, too, because I know it'll take a while before I make any money with photography. Maybe I'll never make any money with it. But it'll keep the framing job from sucking the life out of me. We're here."

I glance up from the sidewalk, blinking. "What?"

"We're here. We're at the store."

I look around and laugh. I actually laugh. I can't believe it. I must have fallen into a kind of trance listening to Anya talk. I made it the whole way to the market without having a full-blown panic attack.

Anya releases my elbow and we hurry through the parking lot side by side. Lying on the wet sidewalk, her white-and-brown fur slick with rain, is a thin pit-bull mix. A red, prickly-looking rope runs the short distance from her neck to a bike rack. Someone has placed a bowl of water just within her reach; it's overflowing with rainwater. The dog watches our progress across the parking lot as though she knows we're there for her. Every few seconds, she shivers, her bony ribs moving below her fur, her dark eyes never leaving mine. I see her wide jaw tighten as we approach. Her white, slightly folded ears stick straight out on either side of her head, negating some of her intimidation factor. She looks a little like the Flying Nun.

Suddenly the dog leaps to her feet and begins barking, straining against the red rope, but when I stop a few feet away from her she immediately quiets and begins furiously wagging her tail. Her winglike ears press back against her head and she sticks out her tongue a few times as though trying to lick me even from three feet away.

"Hey there, sweetheart," I say softly. I start walking again, murmuring gently. When I reach her, I hold out the back of my hand. She sniffs it and then licks it, her whole

283

body shimmying in greeting. "You're not so tough, are you?" I say, petting her cold, wet head. I turn to Anya. "I should have brought a towel. She's soaked."

"We'll have her home and dry soon enough," Anya answers. "I did remember these." She squats down beside me and pulls a few dog biscuits from her pocket. The dog devours them so quickly it's hard to believe they were ever there. Meanwhile, Anya fastens the new collar around her neck and clips on the leash. She fingers the knot in the prickly rope. "This is too tight. We're going to need scissors."

One of the parking-lot attendants catches sight of us and hurries over. "Is this your dog?"

"No," I say, standing, "but we're taking her with us. I'm Maggie. Are you Ty? Sybil from SuperMutt sent us."

"Oh, good timing. She's been barking at customers and my boss was about to call the police."

"Can we borrow some scissors for this rope?" Anya asks.

Ty jogs into the market and returns with scissors. We cut the dog free, thank Ty for his help, and start off across the parking lot. Anya holds the leash out to me.

"Want to do the honors? I think you've

earned it."

I look at the leash. A huge part of me wants to wrap it around my hand, to feel the downward pull of the dog, grounding me, distracting me, propelling me forward. But I'd made it the whole way there without that feeling, and I'd survived. "Nah," I say. "You take her."

Anya nods. The rain is driving sideways now and we have to bend our bodies into it, breaking into a near jog on the sidewalk that runs across the street from Golden Gate Park. I can see the dark opening of the tunnel that leads to the path where I'd had the panic attack the day Toby died. Within moments, we've passed the tunnel; it's behind us, and even though it's raining, a warm feeling brims within me, like the mild glow of sunrise lightening the sky.

The dog doesn't seem to mind the leash and walks easily between us, her tail wagging. Every few steps she looks up at one or the other of us with what I would swear is a look of relief. She's energetic but doesn't have the boundless, quivering enthusiasm of a puppy; if I had to guess, I'd say she's probably three or four years old. It's a nice age for a dog of her size; it's the age when a dog really settles into herself but doesn't yet show physical signs of aging. It's probably how old Seymour is, too.

"What should we call her?" Anya asks.

The dog's white ears flap with every step, and if you squint at the brown patch of fur between them, it looks a bit like bangs. "How about Sally? After Sally Field. You know, *The Flying Nun?*"

Anya gives me a blank look.

I laugh. "It's this show from the sixties. My mom has a weird attachment to it."

Anya shrugs, slipping the dog another treat. "Here you go, Sally."

In my apartment, we peel off our wet jackets and I run a towel over Sally. She loves the massage, flicking her rump from side to side and leaning into me, woofing happily as I dry her. She's one of those dogs that grin when they're excited, her lips curling up at the ends and her eyes shining. I take out Toby's bowls and food and hand them to Anya. She doesn't ask why I still have them; I'm sure she knows I simply have not been able to throw them away. She pours food for Sally and I turn on the fire in the living room and put a kettle on the stove for tea. While I wait for the water to boil, I text Sybil to let her know that we have the dog. She texts back immediately — *Oh,* now *she answers her phone,* I think — with her usual effusive gratitude and confirms that the foster family will pick up the dog in a couple of hours.

BTW, she adds, *I passed on your contact info to someone this week — a woman named Linda who adopted a dog from us 7 years ago. The dog just passed away. She's devastated.*

When I return to the living room, Anya is sitting on the floor in front of the fire. Sally is stretched out beside her, her head resting peacefully on Anya's thin thigh, her eyes half closed. Her tail thumps against the floor as I approach, but she doesn't lift her head. Nearby, the food bowl has been licked clean. I hand Anya a mug of tea and sink into the yellow armchair with the other. I sip the hot tea, feeling it travel down my throat, warming my chest. The sound of the rain outside is steady and calming. The windows grow cozily steamy. Anya absently strokes Sally's head, her hand resting for a few moments and then starting again. The dog twitches one of her ears, stretches, and sighs deeply.

"Any chance you'd consider keeping her?" I ask.

"I couldn't. It would feel like I was giving up on Billy."

"You wouldn't have to stop looking for him. And if you found him, you could still keep Sally, couldn't you? Your house is big enough for two dogs."

Anya shakes her head. "I'm just a one-dog person. Maybe someday I'll want another, but for now one feels right."

At the moment, of course, she doesn't have *any* dogs, but I'm not about to point this out. "I know what you mean," I say. "I was the same way with Toby. You become each other's pack when it's just the two of you." I look into the fire, debating how to proceed. "I want you to know that I always felt it was fine for you to have hope that you'll find Billy. I never misled you about that." I take a deep breath. "At the same time, he's been gone six weeks now. I know this isn't what you want to hear, and I'm not saying you should stop looking if you're not ready to stop, but a dog out there in the city, on his own —"

"He's not on his own."

"But —"

"He's *not,*" she says again. Sally's eyes are open now, and though she doesn't lift her head, she manages to shoot me a look that says, *Must we talk about this now? I've had a rough day.* "I told you," Anya continues. "Billy's not out there on his own. He didn't run away. Someone stole him."

She sounds certain, and the lack of anger or defensiveness in her voice stops me from responding right away. How can she possibly be so sure? "Is there something you haven't told me?" I ask.

She shakes her head, looking puzzled. "No. I've told you everything."

I believe her, but now, for the first time, I begin to wonder if there might be something — some critical, missing fact — that she has filed away on a subconscious level, something that makes her certain she'll be reunited with Billy. What if all of this — her obsession with finding Billy, her anger — is tied not to grief, but to some hidden knowledge that she can't access? In the end, isn't that what intuition usually amounts to? Some part of the brain assembling the facts, drawing conclusions that may seem unfounded, but are actually based on a series of subtle clues that are often all too easy to ignore?

I decide to let the subject drop for now, but resolve to raise the question with Henry. I realize that I've been so focused on offering Anya support through friendship, and in so doing, trying to help myself get better, too, that I haven't ever truly considered the possibility that she might just be right. But who would want to steal Billy?

"Sally *is* sweet," Anya says, stroking the dog's ear. "She seems like a good dog. Why don't *you* keep her? Or, if not her, why not Seymour? I see the way you are with him. Is it because of Toby?"

I nod. "I'm just not ready. I think it would be a mistake to rush into adopting a new dog."

Anya looks at me. "I know you know a ton about grief and how to deal with it and what the proper steps are and all of that, but maybe, sometimes, that stuff misses the mark. Maybe the love of a dog is exactly what you need to pull you through this. I'm not saying Toby is replaceable — in fact, I'm sure he's not. I'm sure you'll never have another dog like him."

"No," I say quietly. There is something heartbreakingly bittersweet about the fact that there will never be another dog like Toby. It's a testament to what a uniquely wonderful dog he was, and a reminder that I will never stop missing him.

"Seymour won't be at all like Toby. He won't replace him, but he could still be . . ." Anya trails off, thinking. "He could still be your life jacket. He could keep you afloat."

"I could say the same to you about Sally."

"But Billy isn't dead. Toby is." When I don't answer, Anya says, "You'll probably never get over him." She says this matter-of-factly, like she's holding out medicine

290

that I have no choice but to take.

Even though my eyes fill with tears, I don't feel overwhelmed by sadness. Maybe it's that I just walked all the way to Whole Foods without having a full-blown panic attack. Or maybe it's simply that time is marching on, and the understanding that I will never stop missing Toby doesn't strike me as harshly as it once had.

"You're right."

I feel a release as I say these words, a sense of acceptance. We carry our loves and our losses with us, and even though we can't know what is ahead, along the way we learn — it really doesn't matter from whom, dog or human — how to keep moving.

CHAPTER 17

A few days later, Linda Giovanni is crying before she even reaches the couch. I hand her a box of tissues, smiling at her sadly. She's very beautiful, even as she's crying. Her caramel hair is swept expertly over one shoulder and her pronounced cheekbones curve elegantly toward her sapphire stud earrings. She's not the sort of person I would have pegged as an adopter of rescue dogs, which just goes to show that you never do know until you ask.

So I do. "Will you tell me about Morty?"

She presses the tissue to her eyes, smudging her mascara. "I adopted him seven years ago from SuperMutt. We think he was about three then." She fumbles through her purse, pulls out her phone, and passes it to me. On the screen is a photograph of a saggy-faced bulldog with heavily lidded black eyes, a pre–face-lift Sylvester Stallone. It's hard not to grin at the sight of him. They must

have turned a lot of heads together —
Morty with his slobbery jowls and fantastic
underbite waddling along beside chic, sleek
Linda.

"What a love," I say.

Linda's lip trembles. "He was a good boy."
She takes the phone into her hands again,
gazing at it for a moment before dropping it
back into her purse. "He was like my child.
Or my best friend. Both, I guess." She plays
with the tissue in her hand. "When I
adopted him, I was thirty-six and single. I'd
sort of given up on meeting my forever man.
I just didn't think he was out there. And I
didn't think I was going to have kids.
Honestly, I wasn't sure I *wanted* kids. I
thought, instead, I'd get a dog. And then I
— well, I fell head over heels in love with
Morty." She looks down. "I know that
sounds silly."

"Not to me."

Linda sighs. "Some people need yoga, or
a long run, or a big cup of chamomile tea
with honey. I just need to hear my dog softly
breathing while he sleeps nearby. I need to
see his chest rising and falling, sweet and
steadfast." Her face, smooth just a moment
earlier, falls into a topography of folds and
shadows, like a bedsheet dropped to the
floor. "I loved taking care of him," she

continues shakily. "I loved how he loved me. I work in fund-raising at the De Young Museum, and for a brief time, before my friends convinced me I was going more than a little overboard, I considered finding another job that allowed me to bring Morty to work with me." She shakes her head. "It was a strange time for me, but having Morty made everything seem a little brighter. He was very funny."

"Was he? In what way?"

Linda looks up at the ceiling, remembering. "He was so expressive! I swear, I could tell exactly what he was thinking just by looking at him. He couldn't speak, of course, but he could really communicate — better than some people I know!" She laughs, sniffling.

"Anyway, the amazing thing was that a couple of months after adopting him, I met Mario, my husband. And then a year later, we had a baby boy. We have a little girl now, too. I couldn't possibly love my children more, but the truth is I don't know if I would have had them if it hadn't been for Morty. Loving him changed me. It made me more open to all of it — love, life, family." Her face crumples again. "I just miss him so much. I feel . . . shattered." Her words are half swallowed by a sob. "I don't feel like anyone really understands."

I nod. "That's one of the things that makes losing a dog so difficult. Some people don't understand what an important relationship it is. It's hard to feel like it's okay to mourn the way you need to mourn when you're afraid people might judge you. But love is love," I tell her. "Loss is loss."

Linda blots at her eyes again, sniffling.

"Morty was a true member of your family," I say. "He changed your life in the best possible way. You're devastated. Of course you are."

She lowers her voice. "Sometimes I think I can still hear him. There's this phantom dog-collar-jingle thing happening all the time."

"Perfectly normal." How many times had I heard a dog barking in my neighborhood and thought, for one split second, that it was Toby?

She smiles sadly, gratefully. "Sybil said you would understand." She looks away, swallowing. "I worry that I should have had a second opinion. The veterinarian said it was time to let him go, and so I did, but now I wonder if I did the right thing. Did I do everything I could for him? I keep asking myself that. Did I fail to give him the best care? After all he did for me . . ." Linda presses her hand against her mouth.

I look her straight in the eye and say, "I'm sure you took excellent care of Morty. The fact that you're so worried about him, even now, shows that. But the best way to wring that guilt out of your system is to talk about it. We'll talk and talk until we've wrung out the guilt and all that remains is the love, the love that you felt for Morty, that you'll always feel — the love and the gratitude."

Linda nods.

I ask her to tell me more about him. "Did he get along with your children?"

"Oh, yes," she says. Her spirits seem to lift as she considers the question. "I'm afraid he thought he was one of them."

I smile, settling back into my chair, and listen.

When Anya texts me the next morning to see if I'll join her to look for Billy, I decide not to bring Giselle or Seymour. I haven't tried walking completely alone yet, but with my newfound confidence from the Sally rescue mission, I feel hopeful. This seems like the next logical step, and I know I should give it a try now while I have some momentum. I push through the sidewalk gate, breathing deeply each time the pre-panic fluttering and clenching begins in my chest. I remind myself to think positively, to relax my arms at my sides, to drop my shoulders when they grow tense.

It rained overnight, and now the whole city has that electric glow that sometimes happens when the sun emerges after a rainstorm. I breathe in the warm, wet pavement scent, letting it fill my lungs.

When I arrive at the house, Anya, Henry, and Huan are gathered outside. I feel my heart swell a little at the sight of them and quicken my step. Henry smiles. It's a private smile, one that hints at everything that passed between us in my apartment a week ago, and I return it, blushing. Anya's glance carries a glint of amusement, confirming my suspicion that on my pale cheeks a blush looks like a five-alarm fire.

"Where's Giselle?" she asks.

"I decided to make this trip on my own." Anya and Henry both lift their dark eyebrows, looking undeniably like siblings. I laugh. "I made it in one piece. Impressed?"

"Yes," says Henry. "That's great, Maggie."

"Too bad, though," says Huan, sounding disappointed. "We're headed to Corona Heights Park. Giselle would have loved it."

Anya smacks him on the shoulder. "Maggie's going to love it, too. People without dogs can appreciate parks, you know."

Huan rubs his shoulder, looking confused.

"Yet another place I've never been," I say cheerfully. My newly reclaimed freedom makes me feel buoyant.

We head off along the sidewalk, quickly forming pairs with Anya and Huan taking the lead. After a couple of blocks, Anya and Huan are far enough ahead that they're out of earshot.

I nod my head toward them, looking at Henry.

"What? Anya and Huan?" Henry shakes his head. "He's had a thing for her since they were kids. She doesn't give him the time of day, never has. I think poor Huan is stuck in the 'friend zone.' "

"I don't know. Looks to me like there's something going on there. Something's clicking."

Henry watches them again. They are about the same height and their steps are perfectly in sync, Huan's purposeful march a match for Anya's long stride. Their heads lean slightly toward each other. Anya's sharp laugh floats back toward us.

"Maybe you're right." Henry sounds surprised and pleased. "Speaking of clicking, I brought you . . ." He looks at me and his smile changes, his voice trailing off.

"A gift?" I ask. I bat my eyes to make him

laugh. "For *moi*?"

"Well, yes. But now I'm a little embarrassed — I don't think you need it anymore."

"If it happens to be another bottle of wine, I can tell you right now that I'll always be in need."

Henry grins, relaxing again. "It's not wine this time." He reaches into his coat pocket and pulls out a tiny metal replica of Sutro Tower. It's about three inches high, the kind of thing you might find in a touristy souvenir shop. "I couldn't figure out how to wrap it."

I take the tower from him, turning it in my hand.

"You said you felt better when you saw Sutro Tower," Henry says quickly. "That it kept you from feeling lost. So I thought you could carry this one in your bag, and then you could see it even on the foggy days. I mean, it obviously isn't going to guide you home, but maybe it will still make you feel better. Except now you're doing so well on your own. You don't even need it." He shakes his head. "It a ridiculous gift, anyway," he says, reaching to retrieve the tower.

"No," I say, wrapping my fingers around it. I end up holding his outstretched hand, too. "I might not need it, but I love it. You can't just give a girl a tiny replica of a transmission antenna and then take it back."

Henry laughs. We both glance up the street at the same time, just as Anya and Huan turn the corner, falling out of view. Our hands are still clasped together between us, holding the tower, and now he wraps his other arm around me, pressing his palm into the small of my back, pulling me close, and we kiss.

When we separate, he nods toward his gift, smiling. "I know it's silly."

"It isn't," I tell him. "It will make me think of you." *Even once you're gone.*

Anya and Huan are waiting for us at the base of Corona Heights Park. We walk across a small stretch of grass to a fenced-in dog park where there is, unsurprisingly, no sign of Billy. What *is* surprising here is the view; this place must have the most panoramic vista of any dog run in the country. Beyond the far line of fence, all of downtown San Francisco is on display, the gray-blue span of bay and the silver curves of the Bay Bridge, too. Out of habit, I start to drop my eyes to the ground, but then I stop myself. I take a few deep breaths, swallow, and look straight out. I feel only the tiniest tremor of anxiety, a mild uptick in my heart rate.

In the run, a large, lumbering Bernese mountain dog gallops around with a bouncy, agile boxer. A cocker spaniel chases them, barking.

And then I see him, my good-luck charm: a puppy. He's an absolutely gorgeous black Labrador retriever, straight out of a dog-food commercial, with a round tummy and glossy coat. He tries to catch up with the other dogs, but keeps tripping over his own outsized paws. I watch him, laughing, and when I look over at Henry, he's smiling at me.

We turn and follow Anya and Huan up a winding dirt path that rises along a short, steep trek to an outcropping of red rocks that carve an impressive silhouette against the blue sky. The hills and valleys of the city — crowded, undulating stretches of houses and apartment buildings and offices — glimmer in the sun. To the west, at the top of Twin Peaks, the red-and-white spokes of Sutro Tower jut high into the sky. I run my fingers over the tiny version that I now have in the pocket of my coat.

Anya walks the perimeter of the peak, shielding her eyes from the sun with her hand and peering down into the city.

"Billy!" she yells. Her voice is steeped with

familiar, heartbreaking anguish.

Huan hangs back a few steps, studying her. Then he walks up right beside her and cups his hands on either side of his mouth.

"Billy!" he yells. His voice booms down the hill, scaring a few black crows into the sky in a flap of wings and a single piercing caw. Anya's head jerks toward Huan, her expression running quickly from sorrow to surprise to confusion to something softer — gratitude, maybe. Or acceptance.

I cup my hands on either side of my mouth. "Billy!" I scream out over the city. "Billy!"

Anya stares at me.

"You're right," I tell her. "That does feel good."

I feel Henry step up beside me. "Billy!" he yells. "Billy!"

Anya is shaking her head, trying not to smile. "You know," she calls over to us, "you don't have to hide it. You guys are a . . . thing. Why would I care? I like both of you."

"We like both of you, too," Henry calls back, nodding toward Huan.

Anya glances at Huan and rolls her eyes. "Whatever," she mumbles. She strides toward the path, her cheeks blazing.

Huan kicks at the dirt, grinning to himself for a moment before hurrying after her.

■ ■ ■ ■

On our way back to the house, with Anya and Huan once again out of earshot, I ask Henry whether he thinks there is any chance that Billy might actually have been stolen. He seems surprised.

"No, of course not. Who would want to steal him? Has Anya convinced you that's what happened?"

"Not exactly. It clearly makes way more sense that he just got out of the house somehow and wandered away . . ."

"But?"

"Well, Anya is just so sure that someone stole him. She's *certain* that he's alive somewhere. I keep wondering if maybe she knows something she doesn't even realize she knows, and that's why she came up with this theory about Billy being stolen."

"I'm not sure I understand."

I sigh. "I don't really understand either. I guess I just wanted to know if you thought there was anyone in Anya's life who might want to . . . I don't even know. Punish her? Hurt her?"

Henry's eyes widen. "I sure hope not." He thinks for a moment. "Frankly, I don't know that she even has enough friends to have enemies, if that makes sense. She doesn't know that many people. She's always kept to herself. I don't think she keeps in touch with anyone from her high school. There are the people she works with at the frame shop, Huan, Rosie, Clive, Terrence, me . . ."

"She and Clive seem to have a fairly antagonistic relationship."

"Oh, but they've always been that way. It's harmless. Clive can be a bully, but he'd never do anything as bad as steal her dog."

"And Terrence?"

He shakes his head. "Terrence wouldn't hurt a fly."

"How about the nurse? What's her name? June?"

Henry looks skeptical. "Really? Why on earth would my grandmother's nurse steal Billy?"

"I don't know. I don't know! I just feel like we're missing something here. Anya is *so* sure. It's hard not to believe someone with that much conviction. And she knows Billy the best, right? If she says he wouldn't run away, wouldn't even wander out of the house if someone accidentally left the door open, shouldn't we at least consider believing her?" I run my hands through my hair. "Will you just talk to Clive and Terrence about it? I don't even know what I want

304

you to ask them, but maybe something will come out of it. And then we'll know we've exhausted all the possibilities before you leave for . . ." Anya and Huan are waiting ahead on the sidewalk in front of the house, and I let my words trail off.

Henry grows serious. "About that. I've been wanting to talk to you —"

"Hey, Henry," Anya calls, interrupting him. "For someone so focused on work, you sure take your sweet time getting to the office when Maggie is around."

Henry pulls out his phone and checks the time. He grimaces. "I do have to go. I'll talk to you later, okay? And I'll . . ." He hesitates, glancing at Anya. "I'll think more about what you said."

"Thanks."

After Henry drives away, I ask Anya and Huan if they are photographing any more dogs that week.

Huan nods. "We have two more dogs to shoot before the auction next Saturday." He looks embarrassed. "I mean, not that I'm doing the photographing. I'm just pressing the squeaky toys and carrying the equipment and dog treats. Anya's doing all the real work. The art."

"You're helping," Anya says matter-of-factly.

Huan beams. "I should get back to my schoolwork," he says. "Big exam tomorrow. See you at the fund-raiser? Anya invited me."

"Oh, good. I'll see you," I say vaguely.

Huan ducks his head to his chest and hurries off toward his house. When he reaches his front door, he turns and waves. Anya lifts her hand to wave back, and then drops it to her side when she catches me watching her.

"What?"

"Nothing." I smile.

Anya crosses her arms in front of her chest. "You *are* going to the fund-raiser, aren't you? Sybil is expecting you. You basically planned the whole event, didn't you?"

"No, no. I just solicited a few donations."

"Whatever. Stop evading the question. Are you going?"

I sigh. "No, Anya, I'm not going. I haven't told Sybil yet. But parties and I . . . don't mix."

"Leaving your apartment didn't seem up your alley last week either, and look at you now."

"This is different. I've always had this thing with parties. But it's going to go off without a hitch — Sybil is a fund-raising machine. You'll have a great time."

"Me? Oh, no. If you're not going, I'm not going either."

"But you have to go! It's going to be great for your new business. Don't miss out on my account."

"I've already decided. I don't like parties either."

"Anya, come on. You can't pull this every time you want me to do something. You're not in charge of fixing me."

Anya laughs. "No shit. But I really *don't* like parties. You're the only one I'll even know there other than Huan. What the hell are the two of us going to talk about for hours on end if you don't come? I'll probably get drunk and do something stupid and then no one will want to hire me and my photography business will go up in flames even before it really *is* a business and it will all be your fault."

I let out a low whistle. "You are really good at this guilt thing, aren't you?"

Anya's lip twitches.

"Is it enough if I tell you I'll think about it?" I ask. "That's all I can honestly say right now."

Anya smiles. Not her little half smile, but a full, broad smile that makes her look young and, though she would probably hate me for thinking it, sweet.

"I guess it's enough," she says. "For now."

CHAPTER 18

The week leading up to the fund-raiser goes by quickly. Sybil included my name and professional title on the list of sponsors on the SuperMutt gala invitation, and each day I receive a few e-mails and calls from prospective patients interested in learning about my counseling services. I'm relieved to find that my appointment schedule for the month ahead is slowly filling.

Maybe this little practice has legs after all, I think.

Every morning before my first appointment of the day, I walk over to Grant and Chip's apartment to take Seymour out for some reconditioning. Sometimes I take Giselle along, but sometimes I don't. I have even begun to stop at the café on Cole Street for a latte and croissant. These outings aren't devoid of the usual symptoms, but I survive and, mostly, I enjoy them. I'm finally feeling like myself again, though even this feeling is strange — like awakening to find that you are who you've always been, but your entire life is different than you remember. I'm living alone, without Toby, in San Francisco, a city I still feel I hardly know. It's time to make friends, to build a life here. Henry is leaving and who will remain? Lourdes, Anya, Sybil. Considering this, I decide I owe it to Sybil and Anya — and myself — to attend the SuperMutt fund-raiser. If anything happens — if it feels like too big of a step — I'll just go home. Simple.

A few days before the event, I call Henry to ask if he'd like to come with me. I know he's leaving for Los Angeles soon afterward, and figure we might as well enjoy one official date together before he goes.

"I'd love to," he says. "But I have a few work calls that evening that might make me a little late. Is it okay if we plan to meet there?"

"Of course," I say, though I can't help feeling disappointed. I'd hoped that Henry's presence would help distract me on the journey across the city to Sea Cliff — the farthest I've been from my apartment since Toby died. But I decide making my way there alone will be good for me, one final test of my progress. And knowing that I'll see Henry soon after I arrive at the gala should be an excellent reconditioning incentive.

The afternoon of the SuperMutt event, I head upstairs to raid Lourdes's closet. The girls are sitting on the inside staircase, waiting for me; apparently Lourdes has promised them that I'm going to do a fashion show. When I bend down to hug them, Lourdes cries out:

"Wait! No!"

I look at her sharply.

"Portia has some kind of bug," she warns.

Portia blinks up at me. She does look sort of wan. My stomach flip-flops. *When was the last time I took my vitamins?* It's been days. Maybe weeks. I force myself to reach down and hug her. Lourdes watches me, amazed.

I look at her and shrug. "I can handle it."

Upstairs, Lourdes hands me a few dress options to try on in the bathroom. "I wish I could come with you tonight," she calls from the bedroom as I change. "This sick kid is really cramping my style."

"It's okay," I call back. "I have a date, anyway." I step out of the bathroom in a silver cocktail dress with cap sleeves and a thin black belt.

Portia and Gabby's eyes grow wide. "Love it," Portia breathes. Gabby nods in agreement. They're sitting on the floor, eating crackers from a bowl. Giselle is having a field day, scarfing up the crumbs that fall to the carpet, her tail whipping around at a mile a minute.

Lourdes looks down at her children and rolls her eyes, then strokes Giselle's back. "How I love you, Giselle," she says. "I would have to vacuum so much more if you weren't around." She cocks her head, evaluating the silver dress. "Maybe. Try another."

"Oh!" Gabby says. "I have something *beautiful.*" She races out of the room.

When I come back out in a knee-length black dress that's a bit too slinky for my taste, Gabby dumps a yellow tutu and a puffy pink cat costume and a pair of sparkly purple fairy wings at my feet.

"Well," Lourdes says, grinning wickedly, "aren't you going to try them on?"

"Oh, Gabby, these *are* beautiful," I say. I pick up the dress and hold it against my chest. "I'm just worried they might not fit me."

Gabby's forehead wrinkles. She looks down at the glittery assortment of costumes, then back up at me. She plants her hands on her hips. "Mags," she says, her little pixie voice turning stern. "You get what you get and you don't get upset."

That evening, as dusk paints the sky a beautiful shade of slate blue, I settle into the back of a cab in a comfortable navy sheath with a scalloped neckline. The car rises and falls over the city's hills, speeding away from my apartment, toward the party. I finger the replica of Sutro Tower in my purse, but I don't look at it. I want to look through the window; I want to see my new home. It's incredibly beautiful. I'd forgotten how the city at night could look like an upside-down sky, each light twinkling like a star, like something eternal, something you could have faith in, maybe even wish upon.

The house is large and contemporary, all glass and steel and pale stucco with oversize globe lights hanging on either side of the entryway. I knock on the enormous red-lacquered door and moments later a petite woman with a wide, sparkling smile opens it.

"Please tell me you're Maggie!"

I nod, immediately recognizing her enthusiastic voice. Still, it's hard to believe that this is Sybil Gainsbury; the woman I'd envisioned for months as an earthy Joan Didion turns out to be a black Dolly Parton.

"Sybil?" I ask, but she's already grasping my hands in hers. Her shiny dark hair is piled high — and I mean *high* — on her head and her curvy figure is hugged by a long tangerine-colored dress with a rainbow rhinestone border along the low-cut neckline. Even with the mountain of hair and the high heels (also rhinestone encrusted), she can't be more than five feet tall. Just the sight of her makes me glad that I forced myself to come. Looking at Sybil is like looking at a puppy — there's a wonderful effervescence about her, a heartwarming, happy glow that immediately cheers me.

She hooks her arm through mine, guiding me out of the entryway. The house has gleaming hardwood floors and stark white walls; savory smells mingle with the faintly sweet scent of fresh flowers. Before Sybil steers me in another direction, I catch a glimpse of a large living room swarming with servers and caterers in party preparation mode. The house, I realize now, is set high on the coastline overlooking the ocean. The sun is in its final moments of setting and the distant sky over the ocean holds ribbons of color — salmon and gold and robin's-egg blue.

Perfect, I think. *It's a panic-inducing twofer: a party on a cliff.*

"Isn't this house unbelievable?" Sybil asks, angling her head toward mine. "They don't call this neighborhood Sea Cliff for nothing!"

I laugh uneasily.

"Anyway, the Jacobsens, our hosts, are amazing. So generous year after year. And wait until you meet their dogs, Angie and Max — *gorgeous* shepherd mixes with the sweetest temperaments. Former Super-Mutts, naturally." She waves her hand upward as we pass one of those modern staircases that look like they're floating. "The dogs are up there, somewhere," she says, then pauses for effect, "with their nanny!" She laughs, but it's a delighted sound, not a mocking one. *To each their own,* her shrug seems to say. Something, maybe the rhinestones on her dress, makes a little tinkling noise with the gesture.

When we step into the bustling kitchen, Sybil calls to a tuxedoed man standing in front of a counter crowded with bottles of alcohol. "Hey, handsome! Do you think you could pour us a couple of champagnes? I owe this lady a drink . . . or ten!" She looks up at me and winks. "A wee bit of party lubrication is in order, don't you think?"

"Absolutely." I might agree with anything Sybil suggests at this point, that's how charming she is. It's no wonder she has managed to place homeless dogs in hundreds of Bay Area homes. Who could say no to this woman? Champagne in hand, we clink our glasses together and drink.

Sybil links her arm through mine again and steers me toward the living room. "Maggie, Maggie, Maggie," she says. "I'm so glad to finally meet you in person. I don't know why, but I had this nagging concern that you might not show up. That maybe I had dreamed up this organized and competent and proactive dog lady who swooped into my life five months ago and helped relieve some of the burden of this passion project of mine." She smiles. "My imagination can get the better of me."

"You've been a big help to me, too, Sybil. More than you'll ever know."

Her perfectly arched brows rise in protest.

"No, really. I only knew two people in San Francisco when I moved here. And you welcomed me wholeheartedly. You made me feel part of a community right from the first day I reached out to you. You helped me get my practice off the ground. Honestly, I should be the one thanking you."

Sybil clinks her glass against mine. "What can I say? The one thing that tugs on my heartstrings as much as a stray dog is a stray person."

I laugh. "Well, I think I'm here to stay. Turns out San Francisco is my forever home." My own words surprise me. I look around, admiring everything but the view. The living room spans the width of the house and is bookended by huge twin fireplaces that are filled with candles. Large, artfully wild looking arrangements of flowers in shades of red and maroon bloom above skirted cocktail tables. In a corner of the room, a jazz trio warms up their instruments. There is a small stage in front of the windows with a podium from which I assume Sybil plans to conduct the auction.

Sybil watches me take in the room. "And the pièce de résistance . . ." she says, waving her hand with a graceful flourish. I turn and see that the wall behind us holds the seven three-by-five-foot black-and-white photographs of the dogs that we picked for the silent adoption auction. "Didn't Anya do an amazing job? I don't know where you found that girl, but I'm sure glad you did."

I'm overwhelmed by the power and beauty and wit of the photographs. Each one fairly hums with the spirit of the dog it portrays;

joy, devotion, sweetness, mischief, trust, dignity, and humor radiate from the dogs' eyes. Below each photograph, Sybil has printed and enlarged the descriptions that I wrote. The dog's name and, in parentheses, the name of their famous doppelgänger, are boldfaced in capital letters at the top of each bio. I walk along the row of photographs, my smile growing with every step. There's Vivien Leigh (the sassy little schipperke mix with the lustrous black fur), Charlie Chaplin (the black-and-white Boston terrier with the tragicomic expression), and Marcia Gay Harden (the golden retriever who . . . honestly, just looks a hell of a lot like Marcia Gay Harden).

I slow in front of Seymour's photograph. In it, Giselle is in blurry motion, a fuzzy shape at his side, bringing the crisp outline of Seymour to shine in the spotlight. His big ears flop forward adorably on either side of his head; the little sprockets of blond hair around his nose stick straight into the air as if daring you not to smile. *He'll be adopted tonight,* I think, feeling a twinge in my chest. A long table beneath the photographs holds blank sheets of paper on which prospective dog adopters will place their bids.

Sybil puts her arm around my shoulders, squeezing me. "Powerful, aren't they?" She shakes her head, marveling at the wall of images.

I nod. "It's amazing to think that this time tomorrow each of these dogs will be settling into a new home, changing someone's life for the better."

"Yes, a lot of dogs — and people — are going to see their luck turn around tonight. Even poor, troubled Owen Wilson," Sybil says, nodding toward Seymour's photograph. She gives my shoulder one more squeeze, then releases me and claps her hands. "Let's get to work!"

Anya and Huan arrive with the first wave of guests. Anya is wearing what appears to be a boy's silver tuxedo over a white T-shirt. The tuxedo pants are tucked into her ever-present lace-up combat boots, but at least the boots have been polished. And for the first time since I met her, her hair looks freshly washed. It's pulled up in a high ponytail, a shiny auburn cascade of hair falling down her back. Somehow, the whole effect is remarkably fashionable. When she turns to inspect the installation of her photographs, I see what looks like a bundle of tiny white tea roses tied around the band of her ponytail. Anya catches me looking and lifts her hand, poking at the flowers self-consciously.

"It's a wrist corsage. I think Huan is pretending this is the prom," she whispers. "I didn't know what to do with them. I don't wear bracelets."

"They look lovely in your hair."

Anya rolls her eyes. Her nose piercing, a simple silver ball tonight, gleams.

"How's Rosie doing?" I ask.

"Better," Anya says, unable to contain a relieved smile. "We had lunch together today, just the two of us, and she was . . . *herself*. Funny and sharp. She told me I smelled like pickled onions and that I ought to take a shower before someone drops me into a Gibson." Anya laughs. "I don't know. Maybe I shouldn't jinx anything by saying this, but I think she's going to be around a while longer."

I smile. "I don't think hope can jinx anything."

The house is quickly filling with people. I pull at the neckline of my dress, trying to get some cooler air against my skin.

"Are you okay?" Anya asks. "Do you want to find a less crowded spot?"

Before I have a chance to fully probe my anxiety level and come up with an answer, Sybil appears at my side. She gives a little squeal when Anya introduces herself and

320

then launches into a stream of effusive thanks for all of Anya's hard work. I tune them out and take a few deep breaths, and am happy to find that I really am just overheated, nothing more.

"Do you think one speaker is going to be enough for this big room?" Sybil asks me, peering worriedly into the growing crowd. "The sound technician guy has another speaker in his truck, but he's adamant we don't need it. I swear we had two last year. If no one can hear what we're auctioning off, we won't get any bids!"

I'm fairly certain that Sybil could make her voice heard over a fire alarm, but I can see that she's anxious about the situation, so I tell her I'll find the sound technician and insist he bring in the other speaker. I spend the next twenty minutes helping him, and afterward there is a minor issue with the crudités that needs sorting out, and then a distinct smell drifts down the staircase that proves to be a digestive issue with one of the Jacobsens' shepherds (luckily, the dogs' nanny swiftly handles the cleanup). By the time I make it back into the living room, the party is in full swing. I wander through the crowd, searching for and not finding Henry, feeling warm but not uneasy.

I look around the room, glancing into the

faces of everyone I see. Some are smiling, some laughing, some regaling their tight little pack with a story, others listening. I see a woman frown into her drink, and a man staring toward the window in a daze. Music and snippets of conversation hang in the air. The whole room moves, arms gesturing and embracing, lips curling, eyes crinkling, throats swallowing, hands touching ties and tucking loose strands of hair back into place. I could be home in my apartment, cozy below a blanket of comfortable quiet, a book in one hand, a glass of wine in the other. Or I could be here, in the thick of life, living.

It's the beating hearts. That's what Rosie told Anya. *It's the beating hearts that matter.* There are a lot of beating hearts in this room.

At one of the bars, I spot Anya chatting with Huan. They look like they're having a good time, their cheeks pink, their heads bent toward each other. As I make my way to them, Huan leans forward and kisses Anya. I stop, surprised. I half expect her to pull back and slug him, but instead she places her hands on his shoulders and leans into the kiss. They both look giddy when they part. Anya glances around, blushing, and sees me. She covers her eyes with one of her hands and shakes her head, embarrassed but laughing, and waves toward me with her other hand.

"Maggie!" she calls. "Get over here."

Huan snags an extra glass of champagne from the bar. He holds it out for me.

"I'm interrupting," I say. "I'm sorry."

"What do you mean, interrupting?" Anya says. "We're here to protect each other from the awfulness of parties, remember? We're in this together."

"Exactly!" Huan says cheerfully. "Parties are terrible!" I'm pretty sure that Huan is having the best night of his life. He might even be a little drunk. When he slips his arm around Anya's waist, she doesn't shrug him off. In fact, she seems to lean into him.

I ask if she has booked any photography sessions yet.

"No," she says, "but I keep having to restock the business cards that Sybil told me to put out on all of the cocktail tables."

"That's a good sign."

"A *great* sign," Huan heartily agrees.

Anya looks at the floor and kicks one of her boots around. I sip my champagne, listening to the music. It seems to me that Huan and Anya inch a hair closer together.

I clear my throat. "Henry should be here any minute." I only say it to reassure them that I don't plan to be their third wheel for the rest of the night, but Anya's face darkens.

"Oh, Maggie."

"What?"

"I thought you knew. He didn't call you?"

I feel my heart begin to rattle around in my chest. "I don't know. I haven't checked my phone all night. Why?"

Anya and Huan exchange a glance. "Something happened with work," Anya says. "The schedule got moved around and they needed him in L.A. right away. I can't believe he didn't tell you."

My stomach twists. "He left already?"

"I think so. He said he was on the last flight of the day."

"Oh," I say. I gnaw on the inside of my cheek. "But he'll be back, right? In a few days? Next week?" I can't wrap my head around the idea that Henry would move without saying good-bye. *He wouldn't, would he?*

"I'm not sure, Maggie," Anya says, looking doubtful. She shakes her head and her ponytail swishes back and forth behind her head. "I'm so sorry."

CHAPTER 19

Thirty minutes later, when Sybil makes her way to the podium to open the bidding for the auction items, I'm still in a daze. I try not to think about the fact that Henry has left, but it's hard to think of anything else. After Anya told me the news, I checked my phone, but there were no messages. I remind myself that I always knew our relationship wasn't going anywhere. Still, I never expected him to leave without saying goodbye. I guess a part of me had thought we would work around the obstacles in our way, hightail it off the road before we ran into that dead end. I'd hoped we'd make our own map.

At the podium, Sybil is thanking the Jacobsens for hosting the gala. "Thank you also to everyone in this room for your continued support of SuperMutt Rescue," she continues. Her voice is every bit as clear and engaging as I'd known it would be, with or without the extra speaker. "Because of you, we have found forever homes for sixteen dogs already this year, and over three hundred dogs since I founded the organization seven years ago. Over *three hundred dogs!*" Even from where I stand toward the back of the crowd, I can see that Sybil's eyes are shining. Her usually big laugh sounds shaky. "Looks like we've already reached the part of the evening's program when I get emotional. Whew! How long did that take me? Twenty, thirty seconds? It's a new record!"

The room fills with the cozy sound of two hundred people who are united in a cause laughing together. "We love you, Sybil!" someone calls, prompting someone else to cry out, "Hear, hear!" A woman near the podium passes a tissue forward and Sybil accepts it with a self-deprecating shrug. She wipes away her tears and then pretends to wring out the tissue. The room fills with laughter again.

"Anyway," she says, "it's easy to throw around numbers without much thought, but I just hope you all stop and consider this one from every angle. *Three hundred dogs.* Three hundred *families,* adults and children whose lives have expanded with love because they welcomed a rescue dog into their homes. All of it thanks to *you.*

"The money that we raise here tonight and throughout the year goes toward the food that our foster families provide for the dogs in their temporary care, preventative care for all dogs including our critical spaying and neutering program, veterinarian bills for sick and senior dogs, and of course vaccinations for each and every adorable puppy I can get my hands on. Anyone who has ever witnessed a rescue dog meet his forever human for the first time — or who has looked into the eyes of a rescue dog and felt that click of love lock into place, that knowledge that you're about to embark on a wonderful stretch of time with a new best friend — knows the truly profound meaning of this work.

"Now, I'll easily admit that these dogs aren't perfect. Some have a taste for couch legs. Some spot the mail carrier coming two blocks away and don't stop barking until the poor guy or gal is two blocks in the other direction. Some hog the bed and snore so loudly you wake up thinking there's an earthquake." Sybil pauses, cocks an eyebrow. "Okay, that last one might have been my ex-husband."

We're all right there in the palm of her hand, laughing.

"These dogs aren't perfect, but here's the kicker, folks." Now she leans into the microphone and says, quietly, as though revealing a secret, "*We aren't perfect either.* And these dogs love us anyway, flaws and all. They look at us like we're the most amazing beings on earth, don't they? So sure, we're helping them, but anyone who has ever rescued a dog knows that what we do for these animals is a drop in the bucket compared to what they do for us.

"That said, I am so grateful that you all open your hearts and your homes and — you knew this was coming, didn't you? — your wallets to the deserving dogs of Super-Mutt Rescue. Let's see . . ." She pretends to study a piece of paper on the podium, checking things off a list. "I've laughed, I've cried, I've talked about dogs. Looks like it's time for the auction!"

She scans the room, holding her hand above her eyes. "Maggie Brennan! Maggie, where are you? Wave your hand!"

I reluctantly raise my hand.

"There she is! Okay, folks, this next portion of the evening is possible thanks to Maggie's hard work. Maggie is a pet bereavement counselor — she runs her own practice, you can Google her — and yet she still has found the time over the past few months to wrangle all of the donations for this year's auction. Without a doubt, this is the most impressive lineup of donations we have ever received. Thank you, dear Maggie!"

There is polite applause, and a few smiling faces turn toward me. I give a little wave, feeling my face warm.

Sybil's auctioneer skills are remarkable to witness; she points and shouts and rattles off numbers at a speed that makes the crowd titter with amusement and excitement. A little glimmer seems to spark in her eye each time a bid is topped, though it might just be the light reflecting off her rhinestone-encrusted ensemble.

"And now," she says, "we have up for auction a wonderful photography session with the talented pet photographer Anya Ravenhurst. As some of you know, Anya was kind enough to donate her services more than once to benefit this event. Over the last couple of weeks, she has been traipsing all over our city to photograph the dogs that are up for auction. The result is this glorious series of photos that decorate our space tonight." She gestures toward the wall across the room from where she stands, and it seems to me that every head in the room turns to admire the photographs, an appreciative murmur rising from the crowd. "Don't worry, I'm going to open the silent bidding for those adorable pups just as soon as this portion of the auction is complete — but for now, don't you think we should all put our hands together for Anya? What a great job she has done!"

The room erupts into applause. Beside me, Anya crosses her arms and shuffles her boots against the floor, but I can see she is pleased.

Sybil launches into the bidding for Anya's photography session and the bids quickly rise from one hundred to five hundred dollars, to seven hundred, to nine hundred, landing at last on one thousand dollars. Sybil slams her (rhinestone-encrusted) gavel and Huan and I each give a little cheer. Anya still has her arms crossed in front of her chest, but she seems to hold herself a little taller as Sybil moves on to the next auction item. Huan gazes at her with admiration and then, suddenly, as though unable to contain himself any longer, he grabs her hand and kisses it. She smiles and shrugs, her cheeks reddening.

Something hard tightens around my throat and I feel my heart begin to pound. I whip my head around, looking to see if the path to the door is clear should I need to run out of the room. But my breathing, I realize, is even. I don't feel like I'm dying or going crazy or in danger of passing out. I just miss Henry. I wish he were here, too. I wish I could have seen his handsome, serious face break into a proud grin as he witnessed Anya's accomplishment. I wish things didn't have to end. That's all. My heart is pounding because I miss Henry.

"This next item," Sybil is saying, "is a stunning diamond tennis bracelet —"

Behind me, I think I hear a man's voice call my name, but when I turn I see only the same people who have been standing behind me since the auction began. I face Sybil again.

"— conflict-free diamonds in a platinum setting —"

"Maggie."

I spin around and there is Henry. Before I even know what I'm doing, I throw my arms around him. "Anya said that you left!"

He shakes his head. "Without saying good-bye to you? I would never do that. There was a schedule change, and I thought I was going to leave today, but . . ." He trails off, holding my hands, his smile almost shy. "You look beautiful, Maggie."

Anya catches sight of her brother. "Henry! What are you doing here?"

331

When Henry sees Anya, his expression changes into one I can't read. "Anya, I need you to come outside with me. All of you, actually." Without saying anything more, he turns and heads for the door. Anya, Huan, and I look at one another, confused, then follow him through the crowd.

"What's going on?" I ask in a low voice when I catch up with him.

"This afternoon, when I was on my way to your apartment to let you know that I needed to leave for Los Angeles tonight, I decided to stop and talk with Clive and Terrence about Billy. I promised you that I would, and it didn't feel right to leave without doing it." As we step outside, Henry's voice falls away.

On the sidewalk in front of the house stand Clive and Terrence. Clive has a broad smile on his face. Terrence, on the other hand, looks as though he might pass out. His eyes are bloodshot and his skin has a yellow cast.

At Terrence's side, a white, scrappy-looking, fairly chunky dog strains at the end of a leash.

"Billy!" Anya cries. The dog leaps forward. Terrence loses the end of the leash he'd been holding, but it doesn't matter, Anya and Billy are sprinting toward each other, colliding into an embrace when Anya drops to her knees. Billy wriggles happily in her arms, licking her neck and face. The dog looks fat and happy, more like he has spent the last two months eating his way through Italy than wandering the streets of San Francisco. He springs onto his back legs and presses his front paws against Anya's shoulders. She falls onto her back, laughing.

I watch their reunion with a mix of shock and delight — and, I'll admit, the tiniest, sharpest sliver of envy. My eyes brim with tears. Henry puts his arm around me and pulls me close to his chest.

"I don't understand," I whisper to Henry. "Did they have something to do with Billy disappearing?" Before he can answer, Anya rises to her feet.

Terrence's hands are wedged into the pockets of his pants. Tears roll down his heavy cheeks. "Anya," he says. His voice is strained, wavering.

Anya's eyes grow wide as she reads the look on his face. "*You* stole Billy?"

"I . . . I . . ." Terrence sputters, his lip trembling. He looks down at the ground and nods.

I see Anya's hands ball into fists. "What the fuck, Terrence! Why?"

He wrings his hands together, looking everywhere but at his sister. "It's — it's complicated. My business is failing. I'm going to have to close the East Bay stores. Maybe the San Francisco one, too. If something doesn't change, I'm going to have to declare bankruptcy. I'll lose the house. The kids' schools. Laura . . ." He trails off, half stifling a sob.

"You're going to have to do a better job than that," Henry says sternly. "Tell Anya everything."

Terrence nods. He wipes at his tears with the back of his hand and takes a deep breath. "You're Rosie's heir, Anya. The house will go to you after she dies." His voice drops. "It's worth millions."

Anya sinks back down to Billy's side and wraps her arm around him. "What does that have to do with Billy?"

"Well, you know that for a long time now, we — Henry, Clive, and I — have been taking care of you and Rosie. I mean . . . financially. And I've always been happy to do that. You're my sister! Rosie is my grandmother. But lately, my business . . . everything is falling apart. I started thinking, how is Anya going to take care of that house after Rosie is gone? You can't even afford to take care of yourself. And what do you need with that big house anyway?"

I'm surprised that Anya doesn't even attempt to disagree; it's almost as though she is only half listening. As she grows quieter, calmer, Terrence grows more agitated.

"But Rosie would never hear of changing her will! The house is going to you." A fat tear rolls down his cheek. He lumbers down to his knees, clearly uncomfortable, and takes hold of his sister's free hand. "I'm not proud of what I did, Anya. All I can say is that I was desperate. I was out of my mind worrying about what would happen to my family if we went bankrupt, and I just got angrier and angrier thinking of that big expensive house sitting there, falling apart around you, neglected, while my family lost *our* home." Terrence swallows. "So I took Billy. I knew he meant everything to you, and I did it anyway because I was desperate and scared and not thinking straight. I knew you'd go crazy looking for him. I thought it was the only way to make Rosie see that you aren't capable of managing her estate. I thought I could get her to change her will. If she left the house to me instead, I could sell it and dig myself out of this hole."

Anya pulls her hand from Terrence's, staring at him. "So it was a two-part plan? First, I go crazy and then Rosie dies?"

Terrence hangs his head and his shoulders begin to shake. "No," he mumbles, "not die . . . just go into hospice . . ."

"Oh, phew," Anya says, her voice thick with sarcasm, "for a second there I thought you were *majorly fucked up,* Terrence."

He moans. "I don't know what I was thinking! I mean I do I was thinking about myself, and Laura, and the kids. But I should have been thinking about you, too. I'm sorry. For what it's worth, I was going to give Billy back as soon as I convinced Rosie to change her will. I was going to say I found him."

"What a hero," Clive says.

"And what about you?" Anya asks, whipping her head around to look at Clive. "What was your role in all of this?"

"Ignorant innocent!" Clive says cheerfully. Then he glares down at Terrence. "And, now, enraged brother. I've already told Terrence he's going to be on family-breakfast cooking and cleanup duty for the next decade."

"So what are you doing here?" Anya asks.

Clive looks hurt. "I'm here for you, Anya." He shrugs. "I'll always be here for you."

Anya gives him a small, lightning-quick smile and he returns it with one of his own. Terrence's bloodshot gaze flicks back and forth between them and he releases another agonized moan. Anya looks at him and rolls her eyes. She digs through the pockets of her tuxedo coat, finally pulling out a threadbare handkerchief.

"It's Rosie's," she says, handing it to Terrence. "So I don't know if your conscience will allow you to use it."

Terrence takes the handkerchief but doesn't seem to know what to do with it. He stares at it, blinking his round eyes. A few tears cling, trembling, to his giant walrus mustache. Anya sighs and grabs the handkerchief and swipes it brutally below each of his eyes and once along his mustache. Terrence holds himself very still throughout as though he is waiting for a blow to fall. Anya stuffs the damp cloth back in her pocket.

"You're an idiot," she tells him. "You know that, right? Why didn't you just ask me?"

"Wh-what do you mean?"

"What the hell do I want with that huge house? I don't think I could live there after Rosie is gone anyway. And I'm going to be too busy working at the frame shop and getting my photography business off the ground and taking classes and volunteering with SuperMutt to take care of it. If you'd asked, I would have just given it to you."

Terrence pales, sinking back on his heels. "Really?"

Anya shrugs. "Rosie would have, too, I'm sure, if you ever asked her. You're always hemming and hawing around her. But you're her grandson. She would have helped you."

It's the beating hearts, I think.

Anya gives Billy a couple of soft thwacks along the side of his belly and he immediately drops down and rolls over, wriggling below her scratches. Anya grins. It's as though her brother's betrayal has slipped entirely from her thoughts; all she can really focus on is Billy. "How'd you get so fat?" she asks her dog.

"The kids," Terrence says sheepishly. He reaches out to pet Billy, but then seems to reconsider and pulls his hand back to his lap. "He sleeps on Mason's bed, and Sophie gives him treats every five minutes. They always wanted a dog. They've been in heaven, I'm ashamed to say. I kept telling them they were feeding him too much, but they love him. That's why I haven't brought the kids around the house lately — I was afraid they'd tell you Billy was with us. I told them — Laura, too — that you asked us to dog-sit for a while."

"What were you going to do when they finally saw Anya — or any of us?" Henry asks. "Weren't you afraid they'd tell us Billy had been with them the whole time?"

Terrence blinks. "I — I don't know," he admits, somehow reddening a shade deeper.

"Diabolical mastermind," Anya mutters. There is a trace of pity in her voice. She fingers Billy's collar. On a turquoise background, a chain of fluorescent-pink hearts catches the light that falls from the windows of the Jacobsens' house. "What's this atrocity?"

"A gift from Sophie. She spent all of her allowance money in the pet store around the corner from us. She'd been saving for a new doll but she said she'd rather get Billy a new collar."

Anya's lip twitches. "So she's not an ass-hole like her dad."

"I guess I've used up all the family ass-hole stock. There's none left."

"Even for Clive?" Anya asks, jerking her head toward her brother.

"Clive took his share at birth."

"Even I," Clive says, "draw the line at dognapping, dear brother."

Terrence's shoulders slump again, his eyes shining with shame. Anya stands. Beside her, Billy flips to his feet and shakes out his fur. Anya holds out her hand to Terrence and he takes it, lumbering to his feet.

"I'll talk to Rosie," Anya says. "Maybe we can sell the house and just keep enough of the money from the sale to cover a nurse's salary and her medical bills. We're rolling stones, Rosie and me. We don't need much."

Terrence shakes his head. "I — I don't know what to say, Anya. I'll make sure you're always taken care of."

Anya gives a sharp laugh. "Thanks, but no thanks, Terrence. I'd say your big-brother instincts are questionable at best these days. Anyway, I'm not worried. I'm a business owner now. My pet photography sessions go for a thousand dollars a pop." She gathers up Billy's leash even though it's clear he would remain plastered to her side with or without a restraint. Anya had been right, of course; it's hard to imagine a dog like Billy ever showing the slightest interest in running away. His black eyes gaze up at her with concentrated focus; I don't think he'll let her out of his sight again; nor her, him.

"Maggie, meet Billy," Anya says, turning toward me. There's only the slightest hint of "I told you so" underlying her tone.

I bend down to pet his head, feeling his bristly fur beneath my palm. With his keen, shining black eyes and shock of white fur, he really does look an awful lot like Albert Einstein. "Welcome back, Billy. At long last."

"I think we'll head out now," Anya says, "unless you think Sybil needs me for something else."

I shake my head. "I'm sure she'd want you to enjoy your reunion."

Anya glances at Huan and he immediately steps forward. "I'll go get the car," he says, but then doesn't move. I have the sense he wants to make sure Anya isn't planning on abandoning him now that Billy has returned.

"You're not my chauffeur, Huan. You don't need to pick me up. Billy and I will come with you."

Huan grins.

"So we're — we're okay, Anya?" Terrence asks.

She studies him, her eyes narrowing, and taps her pointer finger slowly against her lips. "Sophie and Mason really love dogs, huh?"

Terrence gives a very small nod, as though he worries a verbal answer might land him in a trap.

"Well, they can't have Billy, obviously. They're going to be heartbroken, aren't they?"

Again, Terrence gives a barely perceptible nod.

"And it would probably only add to their heartbreak if they knew their dad was a dog thief, huh? A scum-of-the-earth sociopath determined to prove to their great-grandmother that their aunt is a head case?"

Terrence winces. "Anya —"

"Let me finish," she says sharply. "Super-Mutt, the rescue organization that Maggie and I volunteer with, has a lot of really great dogs in foster care that could use a good, forever home with a couple of loving kids."

Terrence takes a deep breath, running his hand over his face. "Ah," he says. "Okay. Yes. We'll pick out a dog for the kids as soon as possible."

"By that," Anya says smoothly, "I assume you mean you'll pick out a dog tomorrow."

Terrence blinks. He glances at Henry, and Henry nods stonily.

"Yes," Terrence says quietly. "Of course. We'll adopt a dog tomorrow. The kids will be thrilled."

"Yeah, well, don't expect any public service awards," Anya says drily. "Besides, it's not just for the kids. You're clearly under a lot of stress. A dog of your own will be good for you." She glances toward me. "A very wise lady told me that for some people, maybe even for a nut job like you, Terrence, a dog can have the same effect as Prozac."

Clive barks out a laugh.

Anya turns to Henry. "Thanks for getting Billy back for me."

"You were right all along," Henry says. "Just like Mom. 'Hope for sun.' "

Anya's eyes swim. She holds up her left hand, the one without the camera tattoo. "Maybe I'll get it tattooed here." She draws her finger along the back of her hand. " 'Hope for sun.' "

When Henry stammers, clearly troubled by the idea, Clive chimes in. "I think it makes more sense to tattoo Mom's saying onto Terrence's hand."

Terrence pales, backing away.

Anya laughs. "Anyway, Henry, thanks. If you weren't moving to Los Angeles any second, I'd offer to make you breakfast. Some of those burned eggs I know you love."

Henry smiles. "Let's talk tomorrow, okay? There's a lot I need to tell you. But in the meantime, you should know that it was Maggie who insisted I talk to Terrence. She's the one who deserves your appreciation."

"Thanks, Maggie," Anya says. "Really. For everything."

"Thank *you*," I say.

She nods, then turns and starts heading down the block. She's a few steps away when she suddenly spins around and runs back to me, Billy bounding along at her side. Before I know it, her thin arms encircle me, squeezing with surprising intensity.

"Let's keep going on those walks, okay?" she says. "I'm going to need to work these extra pounds off Billy. He looks like an overstuffed sausage." Then she drops her voice to a whisper. "And don't forget what I said about having a dog be your life jacket."

I nod. She rejoins Huan, and the three of them — Anya, Huan, and Billy — set off down the street again. Henry puts his arm back around me, smiling. I wipe at my eyes, laughing a little.

"I'm going to call a cab," Terrence says wearily. "I guess I'll be spending the evening perusing the SuperMutt website."

"Check out Sally," I say, thinking of the sweet white dog with the lips that curled into a grin and the Flying Nun ears. "Her foster family says she's great with kids."

He nods, pulling out his phone.

"Are you sure you shouldn't take a bus?" Clive asks him. "Hell of a lot cheaper than a cab." Terrence's shoulders sink and Clive claps him on the back, laughing. "Oh, fine.

344

I'll drive you home, you sorry sack. My car's around the corner."

"Do you want to go back to the party?" Henry asks me.

I nod. "Things should be wrapping up soon and I promised Sybil I'd help clean up a bit." I turn toward the house, not trusting myself to look into Henry's face. "I guess you have a flight to catch."

"No. I changed my ticket so I fly out first thing tomorrow."

"Oh."

Henry seems puzzled by my reticence, but I'm not sure how much enthusiasm I can muster at this point. How excited could I really be that he is sticking around another, what? Nine, ten hours?

"Well," he says slowly. "Long day. I could use a drink."

I wave over my shoulder. "Open bar. Tickets are only one hundred dollars."

"A one-hundred-dollar cocktail?" Henry lifts his eyebrows, smiling. "Anything for the dogs, I suppose."

The moment we're through the door, Sybil catches my eye and waves, looking frantic.

"That's Sybil, the director of SuperMutt," I tell Henry. "I better see what's going on. You'll be okay on your own for a bit?"

"Take your time. You can find me at the bar when you have a free moment."

It seems that a few of the auction items are missing, and we need to locate them before the people who won them start asking for their coats and leaving for the night. I promise Sybil I'll find the missing items and set off to check in with the other volunteers working the event. It isn't long before I learn that one of them moved a box of donated items into a book-lined study tucked away in a corner of the first floor.

As I gather the box into my arms, I find myself replaying the turns of the night in my head — my solitary journey across the city, surviving the crowd of the party, the sweet reunion of Anya and Billy, Anya's parting words to me. I think of Seymour leaving Grant and Chip's apartment tomorrow, heading out in his tentative, worried way toward a new life. I might never see him again. My throat tightens.

I hurry back out to the party and find Sybil, dumping the box into her arms. "I'm going to bid on Seymour," I tell her. I can't seem to stop smiling.

Sybil's eyebrows shoot up. "Oh, Maggie! Why didn't you tell me earlier? I just closed the bids. All of the dogs were adopted!"

I race over to Seymour's photograph. Below it, running the length of the sheet of paper, there is a list of names and bids. I scan to the bottom of the list, where Sybil has circled the winning bid.

Henry Ravenhurst.

My thoughts run together in confusion. *Henry?*

He's beside me then, nervously clearing his throat.

"I don't understand," I say. "You want to adopt Seymour?"

He reaches into his suit jacket and pulls a photograph from the lining's pocket. It's one of Anya's photographs, the one of Seymour and me during our first walk together, taken just before Seymour managed to slip out of his collar. I remember feeling fraught with anxiety during that walk, but in the photograph I'm smiling. I look happy. Seymour gazes at me with love in his eyes.

I breathe out, surprised by the beauty of the photograph. It looks like a dog and his person, like two beings who have decided to spend as long a stretch of time together as they are allowed.

"Anya gave me the photo," Henry tells me. "She thinks the two of you belong together, and I have to say, especially looking at this photo, that I agree. I thought I could keep Seymour until you're ready for him." I open my mouth to speak, but Henry presses on. "You know, I understand that falling in love again is difficult — it's nearly impossible not to think of how it will end. Sometimes it feels like there's so much to lose that it's hard to remember how much there is to gain."

I look up at him, my eyes stinging. "But you're leaving."

"Yes and no. That's what I wanted to tell you. When I got the call about the schedule change, I realized that when push comes to shove, I just can't do it — I can't move to L.A. At least not full-time. I'm going to be there Monday through Friday, overseeing the trial, but I'll keep my apartment here and come up every weekend. It will be a lot of travel, but I'm determined to make it work. It's only temporary, anyway. The trial won't last more than a year."

He lifts his hand to my cheek. "I just found you, Maggie. The whole 'aloha' thing — I can't seem to do it. I can't say hello, good-bye, and I love you all at the same time. Hello and I love you — those I can handle. Good-bye . . . why would I want to say that?"

He kisses me, and then I kiss him, and

then we kiss some more, with no end in sight.

That night, for the first time since he died, I dream of Toby. He is a flash of soft fur beneath my hands, beside me for just a moment, and then, too quickly, he races away, springing forward in a black flash. It's the run he had for so many good years, free of pain, a buoyant gallop full of joy and wonder and beauty.

"Hello!" I call after him in my dream.

The word is still on my lips when I wake up, lift my head from Henry's warm chest, and see Seymour sleeping soundly at the foot of the bed. We'd picked him up right after the gala, knowing Grant and Chip wouldn't mind. He's breathing deeply now, his fat paws twitching against the blanket, so I lay my head back down and count his slow, contented breaths, matching mine to his, until I fall asleep.

One.

Two.

Three . . .

CHAPTER 20

"Is this it?" Henry asks, slowing the car.

"Yes."

We've been driving up the coast for over an hour. Henry has reached for my hand a few times, but each time he does, Seymour, who sits in the middle of the backseat with his head hovering between us, flicks his nose under our clasped hands until we have to release each other and pet him instead. We indulge him every time. Despite my assurances that we are heading somewhere fun, despite the back windows being cracked for his sniffing pleasure, Seymour has been panting anxiously the entire drive. We're still getting to know each other, so maybe it isn't fair to assume he's going to like our destination. If he doesn't like cars, maybe he won't like beaches either. Like humans, no dog is quirk-free.

I lean my head back against the seat, thinking of the call I'd made that morning to my mother. I heard the emotion in her breath when I told her that Toby was dead, and the smile in it when I told her about Seymour. In between the two, I told her everything — the one hundred days at home, the small anxieties that I'd allowed to build up over the years without telling anyone, and the way Giselle and Seymour and my friends helped me work my way through them.

"Oh, Maggie," she said. "Why didn't you tell me?"

"I just — I didn't want to worry you."

"That's supposed to be my line," she answered. "*I'm* the mother." I could hear her struggling not to reveal how hurt she was. "But you're doing better now? You're leaving your apartment? Every day?"

"Yes. Every day. I promise."

"Good." Her voice cracked on the word. She was silent a moment, then cleared her throat. "And work? How has it weathered this storm?"

"It's been slower than I'd hoped," I admitted. "But I'm starting to think of ways to expand the practice. I've been speaking with the director of SuperMutt about the possibility of training some of the rescue dogs to be therapy dogs. There are so many people out there with phobias and anxieties that could be helped by the companionship of a dog — and the dogs would benefit, too, getting a forever home and an important new job. I'd work with both of them — the people and the dogs. I'm looking into an Animal-Assisted Therapy certification course."

"It sounds like a good complement to your practice," my mom said. "The human-dog bond can be so healing."

"Why don't we get you a dog? After I finish the course, I could fly out to Philly for a visit and check to see if there are any suitable dogs at the SPCA. I could work with both of you."

She was quiet. I knew the dark bird of panic that was spreading its wings inside of her at that moment; I'd lived for too many months with one of my own.

"Mom," I said, "you don't have to give me an answer right now. Just tell me you'll think about it, okay?"

"Yes," she said finally. "I will."

And I believed her.

Henry pulls the car into a spot in the small parking lot. Stretching to the north and south are soaring cliffs that lead down to a chain of sandy coves. Even from the car, we can hear the roar of the ocean as it breaks against the beach. Despite the paved parking lot, these are wild beaches, with steep, crumbling paths and powerful waves. I take a long, deep breath, push open my door, and sling my bag onto my shoulder.

Seymour hops out of the backseat and sniffs the air. He's excited now, his tail wagging and his eyes bright. He spots the path that leads down to the beach and tugs against the leash and starts doing one of the full-body shimmy things I've learned he does when he's happy. The tip of his tail trembles.

Let's go! his eyes implore. *What are we waiting for?*

Pebbles skitter out from under my feet as we make our way down the path. Behind me, Henry slips, landing heavily. I turn and hold out my hand to him but instead of letting me pull him up, he pulls me down. He wraps his arms around me and kisses me for all of two seconds before Seymour is clambering on top of us, licking our faces and snuffling into our necks. Henry ruffles Seymour's fur, laughing.

Once we're down on the beach, Henry gives my hand a squeeze and heads off with Seymour to check out an area of boulders around the edge of the cove. I walk down to the frothy water, kick off my shoes, and sit, digging my feet into the wet sand. Then I pull the box of Toby's ashes from my bag. This is the exact spot where he rested on that day months earlier, staring out with such uncharacteristic calm at the sea. I hold the box, warm from the floor of the car, in my lap. The sun sparkles harshly against the water but I don't take out my sunglasses. I want to see it all, to feel it all — when you're too concerned with protecting yourself, I've realized, you risk missing the beauty of every day.

Each time the ocean retreats, I hear Henry chatting unself-consciously with Seymour, encouraging him to explore. I'm reminded of my theory that you get the right dog for the right period of your life. *Maybe,* I think, *if you're lucky, you get the right guy, too.*

I stare out at the water, missing Toby. He was a good dog, and he changed my life and helped shape the person I've become. Losing him feels like losing a piece of myself. But it's time to keep moving — moving is, after all, what Toby liked best. It's what he taught me to do.

I'm not going to release Toby's ashes into the waves like I once planned. I just can't. I came here to show Henry and Seymour the beach that Toby and I loved. And I came here to mark Toby's death in quiet ceremony, not because it is the last time I'll think of him, but simply because I love him.

I can so clearly remember the way Toby looked lying on the beach that day that it feels almost as though I can still see him beside me, gazing out at the ocean, thinking about . . . who knows what? The beauty and peace and power of the natural world? All of the years of his life that had led up to him finding himself on that breathtaking beach in California, including whatever pain or joy that first, mysterious year of his life held? The shortening stretch of time that lay before him? The fish he would eat if he could just get his paws on them?

I smile, lost in happy stories, remembering.

On the way back to San Francisco, the car hugs the turns of the coast. Henry and I open our windows and let in the cool, salty air. Seymour, tired at last, is curled in a tight ball in a corner of the backseat. Every once in a while, I stretch back to pet his soft, warm side.

We cross the Golden Gate Bridge and cut through the city. When we reach Cole Valley, Henry keeps driving.

"Where are we going?" I ask.

"You'll see."

We wind our way up Twin Peaks, the city below us expanding, its buildings and streets shrinking. With every turn, Sutro Tower looms larger. At the top of the hill, Henry parks the car. In the backseat, Seymour springs onto his paws, panting.

I peer out at the enormous tower. "I don't know, Henry," I tease, pulling the replica from my bag. "The real deal up close and personal kind of makes this one look a little . . . cheap."

Henry pretends to huff. "I'll have you know that is the finest Sutro Tower replica on the market."

Outside, my stomach does a little flip as we near the wall on the edge of the lookout. "Is this okay?" Henry asks. "It's normal to feel some vertigo up here. I think everyone does."

I nod.

Henry points out the line of Market Street that cuts through the city below, leading toward downtown. "And that's the Mission," he says, showing me where to look. "There's a great restaurant there that projects old movies on the wall of an inner courtyard." He moves his finger over toward a neighborhood called Nob Hill and tells me that when he needs to clear his head he walks through Grace Cathedral's outdoor labyrinth. He moves his finger again and says that a black speck out in the bay is actually a ferry headed to Tiburon, where we could go for dockside beers and fish and chips at a place called Sam's.

"It's usually sunny there," he tells me. "So we can escape the summer fog."

As I listen to him, the flip-flopping sensation in my stomach slows. I reach down and pet Seymour. *That's life,* I think, feeling my last bit of anxiety drain away. You just hope that your excitement for the life you could be living — the life you *can* live — will be enough to soften the needling pricks of your fears.

Back in the car, we drive slowly down the steep, curving road, edging our way back into the city.

"Where to next?" Henry asks.

It's exactly what I always thought Toby would say if he could speak — what most dogs would say, probably, if they could, their joy overflowing, infectious, wise. *Where to next?*

I look at Henry, thinking of all the places we could go.

"Home?" he asks.

"No, not home." Seymour presses his wet nose against my neck, making me laugh. "Not yet, anyway. Surprise me."

I open my window all the way and settle in for the ride.

ACKNOWLEDGMENTS

It is with enormous thanks that I acknowledge:

My editor, Emily Krump, for her generous and thoughtful partnership in this endeavor, and for pushing me to expand and ground the story in all the right places. Emily, this book is better for your hand in it, and I'm so grateful.

The tremendous team at William Morrow, including but not limited to Liate Stehlik, Jennifer Hart, Kaitlyn Kennedy, Molly Birckhead, Carolyn Bodkin, Serena Wang, Martin Karlow, Emin Mancheril, and Diahann Sturge.

My wonderful agent, Elisabeth Weed, for her astute guidance, and for laughing at my jokes.

My dear friend Jeanette Perez, who just can't seem to shake me, and whose suggestions always hit the mark. My heartfelt thanks also to Issabella Shields Grantham,

Alison Heller, Meg Kasdan, Carol Mager, and Phil Preuss, whose insights and support strengthened this book.

Tara Cronin for answering my questions about pet bereavement counseling and for introducing me to *The Grief Recovery Handbook* by John W. James and Russell Friedman, which proved to be a valuable resource. Thank you also to Caroline Schram for answering my various questions about veterinary medicine. Despite the wise counsel I have received, I've exercised dramatic license in the writing of this book.

My parents, my friends, and the many Donohue, Mager, and Preuss family members whose encouragement means the world to me.

Phil, for being my touchstone, day brightener, and best friend — in other words, my real-life forever love interest. And Finley, Avelyn, and Hayden, for bounding through our days with an inspiring amount of puppylike gusto.

My dogs! How I've loved each and every one. Cole, I could not ask for a sweeter fur companion during these busy years of raising a family and building a career. One version of happiness is writing with an undemanding dog snoring nearby.

King Oberon, my good boy, you remain perpetually underfoot. This one is for you.

P.S.
INSIGHTS, INTERVIEWS
& MORE . . .

■ ■ ■ ■

ABOUT THE AUTHOR

■ ■ ■ ■

MEET MEG DONOHUE

Meg Donohue is the *USA Today* bestselling author of *How to Eat a Cupcake* and *All the Summer Girls*. She has an MFA in creative writing from Columbia University and a BA in comparative literature from Dartmouth College. Born and raised in Philadelphia, she now lives in San Francisco with her husband, three young daughters, and dog.

■ ■ ■ ■

ABOUT THE BOOK

■ ■ ■ ■

A CONVERSATION WITH MEG DONOHUE

What inspired you to write this story? Maggie insists that the relationships we form with our dogs can be just as profound and emotional as our relationships with other humans. Were any of the relationships between your human characters and their dogs inspired by your personal experiences as a pet owner?

I've had the privilege of loving many dogs in my life, but this particular story was inspired by a Portuguese water dog named King Oberon — Oe (pronounced O-E) for short. Oe entered our family when he was a puppy and I was a senior in high school; he later moved with me to New Hampshire (where I went to college), New York City (where I worked and went to graduate school), Evanston, Illinois (during which time I married my husband), and finally to San Francisco. He was at my side through

371

every twist and turn of my young adult life. Oe died when he was thirteen years old, shortly before the birth of my first child. I can't help wondering if he let go at that moment in time because he sensed that the healing love of a new baby would help to mend my broken heart. He was one of my very best friends — my "dog soul mate," as Maggie says of her dog, Toby — and I continue to miss him every day. It's a loss I'll always carry with me, alongside the many life lessons I learned from him.

A couple of years ago, I began to think of a story told from the perspective of a therapist who specializes in helping people grieve the loss of their pets — a woman who, despite her expertise, finds herself in considerable emotional turmoil when her own dog dies. After a bit of Internet research revealed that pet bereavement counseling services exist, I contacted a local counselor with experience in this niche of grief therapy and she kindly allowed me to pick her brain on the subject. Our conversation fascinated me; I went home and immediately began writing this novel.

The gift to myself throughout this process was that I was able to write about Oe. While all of the other characters in *Dog Crazy* are fictional, Maggie's Toby is my Oe in nearly

every way except name and breed. And
though Toby's death propels Maggie down
a path I've never taken, the huge love that
she feels for her beloved dog is an experience I'm grateful to have had as well, and
to share in these pages.

Dog Crazy *shows how humor can still be*
found in times of sadness and struggle.
Do you think it's important for people to
hold on to their sense of humor when cop-
ing with something as difficult as losing a
loved one?

I don't want to generalize, but I do think
that laughter can be cathartic when dealing
with the death of a dog. Humor is a key
component of the dog-human bond; dogs'
enthusiasm for life is sweet and charming
and often — as anyone who has ever put a
dab of peanut butter on her dog's nose can
attest — hilarious. As we search for peace
after loss, reminiscing about the funny, joyful moments we've shared with our pets can
be both uplifting and insightful. Continuing
to find the humor in life is one way to honor
the spirit of a departed companion.

San Francisco is so vividly depicted in
Dog Crazy *that it really becomes a*

character in the book. Why did you decide to set the book there?

I live in San Francisco and am continually inspired by this city — its geography, architecture, culture, weather, and people. Setting the story here allowed me to funnel my observations of the city through the minds of my characters. But I didn't develop the story and then set it in San Francisco; those two actions were intertwined all along. The story developed the way it did because the characters live in this particular place, a

Oe on the beach in California — memories of the day this photograph was taken served as inspiration for an important scene in Dog Crazy. *Courtesy of the Author*

374

city of heights and vistas, uniquely beautiful, dog-friendly parks, and smart, quirky,
empathetic people. This was a San Francisco
story from day one.

**Who would you say is your dog's celebrity
doppelgänger?**

My husband and I adopted our dog, Cole,
through an organization that finds homes in
America for stray Taiwanese dogs. *How* we
came to be hooked up with this particular
organization is a story for another day, but
suffice it to say, hooked we were. Cole was
billed as a Taiwanese mountain dog (also
known as a Formosan mountain dog) but
it's pretty clear that there's a German
shepherd and probably a few other dog
breeds scattered throughout his family tree.

The point — I have one! — is that Cole is
quite debonair. At seven years old he's been
prematurely gray for years and his brow is
appealingly furrowed. I'm sure you'll glance
at the photo on the next page and wonder
why on earth I've included a film still of
George Clooney from the movie *The Descen-
dants*. The answer, you'll be shocked to
learn, is that *this is not a photograph of
George Clooney*! It is a photograph of our
dog, Cole. Wearing a Hawaiian shirt.

Courtesy of the Author

■ ■ ■ ■

READ ON

■ ■ ■ ■

MEG DONOHUE'S FAVORITE DOG BOOKS FOR ALL AGES

Sometimes we read to be transported into foreign emotional landscapes; other times we read for the pleasure and comfort of having the familiar illuminated. Dog books fall into the latter category for me. My favorite ones feel as though they were written by kindred spirits — dear friends with an enviable ability to articulate just how I feel. Each of the following books holds a special place in my heart, and has in one way or another inspired my own contribution to the genre.

WHERE THE RED FERN GROWS
by Wilson Rawls
This action-packed story of a boy and his faithful raccoon-hunting dogs, Dan and Ann, captured my imagination as a dog-crazy kid and has stayed with me ever since. In fact, thanks to this book I spent a chunk of my childhood pretending that our neighborhood park was the Ozarks and my

dog was a coonhound. My fondness for the breed was later cemented at summer camp in Vermont, when I fell head over heels for the camp cook's dog, a coonhound named Gypsy. If YouTube had existed back then, Gypsy would have been famous; when you told her that you loved her, she responded with two short barks and one long howl — a crystal clear bark version of *"I love youuuuuuuuu."*

THE ACCIDENTAL TOURIST
by Anne Tyler
Macon Leary, grieving the tragic death of his young son and his subsequently dissolving marriage, is already at his wit's end when his dog, Edward, shows new signs of aggression. Enter one of my all-time favorite fictional characters: quirky, optimistic dog trainer Muriel Pritchett, the bright light of this poignant, funny, and steadily uplifting novel. I continually marvel at Tyler's ability to make the characters in this book wonderfully eccentric, painfully real, and entirely sympathetic.

FANCY NANCY AND THE POSH PUPPY
by Jane O'Connor,
Illustrated by Robin Preiss Glasser

When you have three daughters under the age of six, you not only read a lot of Fancy Nancy books, you read them again and again . . . and again. Luckily, I'm always happy to dive into this sweet story of Nancy's quest for the perfect puppy. No matter how many times I read this book, I can't help but smile when Nancy, deciding that "unique" is even better than "fancy," welcomes her new mixed-breed shelter pup with open arms. This one will always hold a place of honor in our family's library.

YOU HAD ME AT WOOF
by Julie Klam

Do I adore this memoir or Julie Klam herself? It's a testament to Klam's irresistibly warm and funny voice that I honestly don't know the answer to that question. You'll laugh, you'll cry, and you'll hug your dogs a little tighter when you finish reading the exquisitely entertaining lessons the author has learned from rescuing Boston terriers. Julie Klam is a tremendous gift to dogs, dog lovers, and readers alike.

DOG SONGS
by Mary Oliver

Whether or not you typically read poetry, I can assure you that if you love dogs, you will love this remarkable book of autobiographical poems that — like all great dog books — is as much about living as it is about the dog-human bond. Oliver distills her wonderful observations into beautifully succinct turns of phrase that sink right into you, making this collection easy to read and yet impossible to forget. My copy is dog-eared, underlined, read and reread with great enjoyment, more than a few tears, and huge admiration for Oliver's heart and talent.

The employees of Thorndike Press hope you have enjoyed this Large Print book. All our Thorndike, Wheeler, and Kennebec Large Print titles are designed for easy reading, and all our books are made to last. Other Thorndike Press Large Print books are available at your library, through selected bookstores, or directly from us.

For information about titles, please call:
  (800) 223-1244

or visit our Web site at:
  http://gale.cengage.com/thorndike

To share your comments, please write:
  Publisher
  Thorndike Press
  10 Water St., Suite 310
  Waterville, ME 04901

B	E	HP	SS	A
11/18	11/21	3/19	12/17	5/21
10/19		1/20	7/19	
8/20		11/20	6/21	